END IT BY THE GUN

A NOVEL

KENECHUKWU OBI

Black Rose Writing | Texas

The final approval for this literary material is granted by the author.

First printing

This is a work of fiction. Names, characters, businesses, places, events and incidents
are either the products of the author's imagination or used in a fictitious manner.
Any resemblance to actual persons, living or dead, or actual events is purely
coincidental.

ISBN: 978-1-68433-073-7
PUBLISHED BY BLACK ROSE WRITING
www.blackrosewriting.com

Printed in the United States of America
Suggested Retail Price (SRP) $18.95

End It By The Gun is printed in EB Garamond

I dedicate this one to those who believed in my creative writing talent all through the past difficult days and years that followed immediately I became pregnant with the dream of giving something to the literary world. I also extend thanks to Aidan, Editor at PaperTrue Editing Service in San Francisco, California for her helpful editorial eyes.

END IT
BY THE
GUN

CHAPTER ONE

I have a problem. And, what would that be, you ask? Well, I am a writer, and I have come to realize that I should not have written my eleventh fiction story, whose success gave birth to the whole mess my life became. My decision to write that story was not an easy one. I was a man truly besieged with the urge to write. I was a man who had a war raging inside his head. Several voices in my head were fighting it out amongst themselves—There were those that urged me to focus on the reasons why I should not go ahead and write my eleventh story, these reasons kept exploding like fireworks, and in many directions, in my head at every hour of the day; there were also those that kept on pressing me that it was a *real* man that pushes forward in spite of facing numerous downfalls. These paradoxical thoughts argued, they jostled, they fought each other in a struggle to dominate my mind.

Give up on writing!

Keep on trying, and success will come!

You don't have what it takes to be a Shakespeare or Hemingway!

But you have the ability to touch the lives of others!

How many times will you fail to learn from your experiences which show you that you have no future as a writer, even if you decide not to give it up?

This is your purpose. You will shine!

You're only deluding yourself!

It's alright to fail!

My head ached, burning up with the battle that was neither being won, nor lost. I just had to get off the seat and take a walk. I very much had to. I needed to try and get a chance to think clearly, in spite of the rumblings in my disturbed mind.

"You *are* a writer, Beck," I said to myself, "And, writers *exist* to write...Not writing this story will amount to a denial of the love you have for writing."

And, there was no stopping me from then onwards. The small pep talk proved to be a stronger motivation than anything else since I started off on my eleventh fiction story just as I returned home from the walk.

I had no strand of doubt that I could write excellent stories, which would go on to become foundations for blockbuster movies, though it was a big shame for me that none of my first ten stories impressed the executives of any of the movie studios whom I previously approached. They all had different ways they said my stories were not right for them.

"Your story idea does not seem to go with our branded message."

"It doesn't just seem right for our studio."

"Sorry, this is not good enough." However, all those discouragements did not prove to be enough to dampen my spirits—I was determined to try again, press on, push ahead until I achieved my breakthrough. I could not be more fired up by rejections. "Come on," I said to myself, 'you're not going to take 'no' for an answer. Those studios *need* my talent! I can do it!"

"Beck! Are you still doing that?" I heard her say.

"Yes. I am, Julie," I replied. Julie was my wife. Julie's impatience could never be caged enough for me to speak more words than she wanted me to.

"Get realistic!" she screamed, and went on to say, "Do you need a palm reader now to let you know that you're not good enough? Do you need God to step down from heaven to tell you, or do you need uncle D to step out of majestic pandemonium to tell it to you?"

"Uncle D?" I asked, confused at who that might be.

"I was talking about the devil!" replied Julie angrily, "Do you need *him* to let you know that you're not good enough so that you come to your senses?"

"I think I'm a good writer," said I, trying to convince myself more than her.

"But not good enough! Those men want nothing but the best," came her reply.

"I know that, honey."

"But, which you can't produce!" she retorted sharply.

"I think I can," said I, sounding determined.

"Really?" It was her habit to doubt me and put me down.

"I know I can," I said, trying my best to convince her this time.

"Give it all up!" she shouted dismissively.

"I will...but only after I have tried the big boss at Paramount Pictures with my new story," I informed her.

"You are so crazy, Beck!" she shouted. "Stop building castles in the air."

Julie had these temper tantrums that sometimes belched forth like molten lava from an erupting volcano. She stood tall at just five feet six inches. She was a blonde from Houston, Texas, having a round face. Her smiles, that she would give often, were attractive, but her anger, which exploded once in a while, were terrifying. On a good day, her laughter would give any man, who found it hard to control his groin area, a huge erection. Overall, she was not that bad a personality to me—A woman, who could cook like a Michelin-starred chef, and, well, made by the almighty creator, she was indeed a good asset. Julie and I had more than liked each other right from our seventh grade. Our chemistry had been amazing. The attraction that we felt towards each other was strong, so intense it was that it had this overwhelmingly domineering urge to possess. It was this urge that led us to the thing that lots of people in this world love to call "relationship." I must say that Julie and I only had sex occasionally, and that was because we were not the kind of people who would identify themselves as a pair of promiscuous dogs that could think of nothing else.

"Oh...Great... That's so nice....," Julie had responded back in our high school days, when I first shared my dream to become a writer with her. "It would be nice to see you achieve it," she said, being quite excited to hear of the ambition that raged within my soul like a wild fire. This excitement surged into her with the tremendous force with which a very dry desert soil, which has not known wetness for years, can absorb water. A beaming smile stood on her face, exposing her fine set of white teeth, which had not yet been discolored by drinking coffee – a habit that she picked up after her marriage. I must confess that it felt quite nice to have someone so close to me appreciate my dream.

"Do you really believe I can go all the way and achieve it?" I was quick to ask.

"Yes, you can, Beck," she said with a smile, "It would be really nice to see movies based on your stories."

"Are you convinced?" I asked, trying to see whether she truly meant it.

"Sure! What are friends for? I will support you every step of the way. I believe in your dream, Beck." She did sound very convincing back then. I couldn't help but feel flattered and loved.

"Give me a kiss. A gentle one, right at the tip of my nose."

"No."

"You are just joking. You will not deny me, will you?"

"I will."

"You must be joking. Please tell me that you are."

"You're blind, Beck. Can't you see that I am?"

Julie and I always listened to each other. We were so supportive of each other that we shared our burdens, hopes, and dreams of a future which we thought would be flowing with milk and honey. What more could I have longed for? Our relationship was not perfect though. But, I can positively say that it was one of the best around...well, until I gathered the courage to let her realize that I would go on to write my eleventh fiction story. So, was everything perfectly normal after that? Oh God, no! My decision, very much like a stone thrown into a pond, created a lot of ripples. And, the foundation stone for the mess in my life was only about to be laid.

CHAPTER TWO

Julie had said that I had gone crazy because I had insisted on not giving up on my pursuit of the movie studios. I was in our living room, reading through the draft of my developing eleventh story, when she came to me with an early morning cup of coffee. It was only a day after I had begun writing my story—a Friday. She was absolutely furious to see what I was doing.

It was clear that she had had enough, as she nearly threw the hot coffee onto my face but managed to check her anger at the right time to prevent herself from doing so. I had been lucky. Julie angrily thumped the cup of coffee on the wooden table that I was sitting on, spilling some on it. I was, to her, the most disgusting thing around—like a thousand flies that kept buzzing around her eyes. I had filled her with an irritation that made every inch of her body itch with infuriation. She was so annoyed with me that she stormed away from my presence into the only bedroom we had and shared in our small rural Nebraska bungalow. It was a bungalow that had one kitchen, one lavatory, and a living room that lacked a rug on its floor and any sort of interior decoration. Our bedroom had a rough floor, two windows and one bed that was not the large type, but was okay for us. All we had in our living room was a wooden dining table with two wooden seats beside it and a green couch. Julie would not just stop there, that I knew very well about the woman I married. But, what I could never have guessed was what she was actually up to. I had always known her to be someone else whenever she got furious.

I vividly remember one day we had an argument—She lost her temper and threw a glass of water at me. We were taking a walk together, when a girl, whom I did not know, waved at me. I raised my right hand and waved back at her. Julie did not make any comment there. There was no way I could see that she had read any meaning into my seemingly harmless gesture. She succeeded in making me feel that there were no qualms. It was only when we got back home that she opened up.

"Who was that?" she queried. I did not understand whom she was talking about at that time. I was hungry and had my mind on grabbing an apple from the fridge.

"Who?" I asked, almost absent-mindedly.

"Beck, don't you get all slippery now!" Julie's tone had changed completely. In fact, she was almost growling. Anger had crept into her. "The girl you waved at! Who's she?" It was only then that I understood what she wanted to know.

"I don't know her," I began, "She waved at me, and I waved back. Just that. I've never seen her before. Please don't tell me that you're not thinking that I've been hitting on her."

"Don't lie to me!" she screamed.

"I'm not lying," I pleaded.

"You fucking liar!"

"I'm not lying! I've never seen her before. I swear!"

"Bloody liar!" she repeated.

"Wait a minute! You think I've been seeing her?"

"Go away from me, you bastard!"

"Stop calling me names, Julie! Believe me! I've never seen her before!"

"What's her name and size of her G-string panties?"

"What the hell's this? I don't know! I've got only your own G-string size in my long-term memory. Come on!"

"Bloody liar!"

That was it. The glass of water had left her right hand and was flying straight towards my face now. I was so lucky to have got out of the glass's path fast. It had nearly hit my face. I took it that perhaps God still wanted me to keep on having the face He had given me, otherwise the story of my face would have been different today. It was only when the glass had struck the wall and shattered on the floor that Julie realized how stupid she had been in allowing her anger to put her through what she had done.

Julie became misty-eyed and tear drops began to trickle down her eyes. It was almost as if a tap had been turned on at once. She covered her face quickly with her hands, in shame. Her mouth opened, and she cried. I found her more attractive when she cried like that. This ensured that I could not find a way to be angry at her despite her insane act. Believe me, I tried hard to be angry at Julie, but those tears coming from her eyes arrested me. Getting angry with her proved to be tougher than smashing a mountain with bare hands. Those tears just disarmed me. It was as if their cold long hands had extended to caress my whole body, calming me and putting me at ease.

"Beck, I'm sorry," Julie had said to me, her tone so very soft, so very seductive, "I don't know what got over me...Please, I'm sorry."

I had no choice but to take her in my arms like a loving mother. I am no woman, this I knew well. But, she felt so very tender and calm in my arms. She looked up at my face like a child that needed to suck her mother's breasts. I must confess that I would have offered her mine if only they had not been created to always be tiny, dry, and without the ability to yield even the smallest droplet of milk. One is to love and forgive his wife always, isn't it?

"That's okay," I said to her calmly, "I love you." Then, I began to wipe off the tears on her face which were beginning to roll down her face and drop on the green satin dress that she wore.

"I love you too," she said in between her teary-eyed sniveling.

I did forgive her, but I knew well that she was still a long way from knowing how to keep her anger in check.

But, that day, Julie had just stormed away! What was she really up to?

Chapter Three

My whole body tickled with fear when Julie stormed into our small-sized bedroom. This move left my mind very active as it tried to make sense of the scenario I would likely face. My instinct suggested lots of things, which I decided to ignore. *Julie will come back and hit my face hard with the long heel of one of her shoes! She will return with most of my clothes and burn them right in front of me!* I managed to stay calm, ignoring all these strange thoughts that crept into my mind. But, when my gut feeling suggested that Julie might come at me with a knife or a gun, I knew that there was no longer any time for me to just sit and watch. There had actually been a hand-gun somewhere in our bedroom, which I had bought.

It was pure and downright fright that dragged me from my seat and got me up on my feet as fast as it could, which took no more than three seconds. I dashed off to our small kitchen, with the intent of picking up something that I could use to defend myself with. Anything! My heart was pumping as fast as a deer, and it did not want to take it easy. It just kept thumping against my chest so hard that I thought its aim was to tear up my chest and fall off. I could not find anything that made sense to me as far as acquiring a good object that would help me defend myself was concerned.

I finally picked up a fork and a knife. My mind was totally made up: I would have to defend myself as necessary if Julie attacked me, love or no love. I then tiptoed out of the kitchen with my weapons. Upon reaching the kitchen door, I peeped through the door that led to our bedroom to see if Julie would step out of our bedroom, brandishing a weapon. I relaxed a little as I saw that there was no hint of Julie storming out. I decided that it would be best if I waited. After having waited for ten minutes, and still not see Julie stepping out of the bedroom made me wonder what was actually going on. The house was so quiet that I would be able to hear a pin drop. I listened intently for any railing tone that would be hers, but none came.

"Julie," I called out.

But, there was no response.

"Look Julie, doing anything stupid will not help a thing, okay?" I went ahead. "I know you're mad at me. But we can talk it out."

When I still did not get any response, I began to get a feeling that Julie might no longer be in the bedroom. Not wanting to believe that, I shut it out. *Julie has murdered herself in the bedroom* came a voice in my head. I shut that out as well. But, one thing that I could not help but get seized by was my curiosity—It wrapped me in its arms. I could not resist any bit of it. It ran so strong in me that it urged me on, arming me with the courage to make a move and see what was actually up with my irate wife. It had me make a move to the bedroom, but slowly and still holding my fork and knife in my hands—I had to be careful, Julie could still be somewhere waiting to hit me when I least expected it. That was what my mind told me. And, I had no choice than to pay heed to its well-timed advice.

However, all my preparations amounted to nothing. I was bewildered with what I saw in the bedroom when I got there—Julie was not there. My feelings had been vindicated. *Have you seen it now? We told you, and you would not believe us...* my feelings were quick to inform me. My jaws dropped, almost so that I could tell them how sorry I was for not believing them. Then, I quickly realized that my feelings were no humans and would not hear me. But, I did appreciate them by nodding twice, hoping they would be able to see that. I thought they did.

I did not even realize when my weapons fell off my hands and dropped to the floor. The bewilderment that descended on me was responsible for that. But, Julie was no ghost. I was quite sure that I had not seen any sign of her being one since we started living together as a married couple. Not even in our blissful days of high school romance did I notice anything that suggested she was one. Fear gripped me, I must confess—Fear of ghosts. The footage of the numerous ghost movies that I had watched as a child began to flash through my mind. I began remembering verbatim many of the very scary ghost stories that I had read as a kid. My whole body began to shiver at such thoughts. Not even my behind was spared—It started to tickle with fear and awareness all of a sudden. Although what I saw suggested otherwise, I was beginning to give in to the feeling that I was not alone in my home. There were many ghosts—pretty ones and ugly ones. There were those with complete fingers, and the ones with only one, two, or three fingers—All ghosts—and were hanging on all the walls around me, together with those that had bloody faces, including the ones that had numerous heads—

ranging from two to ten in number. All of a sudden, I could feel the whole room getting increasingly infested with ghosts.

"No...," I screamed to shake off the fear that was devouring me. It worked. I felt good again and managed to eke out some courage from within. I took some steps that led me to a little book rack beside the bed that I shared with Julie. I looked for and grabbed a book about ghosts for adults that I had once bought and read. My eyes sped from one page to the next in a frantic search for anything that could suggest that ghosts disappear on mortals when things make them furious. I was so fast in flipping through the pages that I would not even have seen it if it ever existed in the book. My search led me nowhere. I dropped the book on the bed, being convinced that I had searched well, and that what I searched for never existed. *But, what happened to Julie?* This was a question that chimed like a cathedral bell in my head a hundred times.

"Julie!" I screamed. Getting no response from anywhere in the house, I screamed more, "Julie...Julie..."

But, the more I screamed out her name, the more her absence dawned upon me. A running tap inside the lavatory made me run like an athlete at a blistering speed to only to see that Julie was not there.

"Julie, stop playing pranks on me!" I went ahead to scream. "Where are you? We can talk! Remember we were told on our wedding day that all issues can be resolved by talking about it? Where are you, Julie? Where are you? Please stop doing this to me."

The silence from the other side persisted, no matter how loud I screamed. I had given up on searching for Julie now. As I headed for the living room to relax on the couch, I had barely sat down when I noticed that the front door was wide open. It was not the time for me to go out. Lightning had begun to flash. Thunder had begun to growl. Wind had arrived with massive force. I knew this because I was not deaf. It had begun to howl. One thing was clear. Nature was making haste for the sky to pour down rain. Julie had not become a ghost after all. Ghosts do not have to open doors while making their exit, let alone leaving it fully ajar.

This is the end of Julie! came one voice inside my head. *Relax!* another suggested. My tale is still unfolding. Some things are better left alone for now. Instead, let me share one experience of mine in Los Angeles which had me running for my dear life!

CHAPTER FOUR

Twilight had passed, and night had already arrived. It would have been a complete dark street, if it were not for the street lights and a few lights coming from passing cars whose engines droned along. My mouth was wide open. It had to be since I needed more air to surge into my lungs. My nostrils were not enough to do the job—They were simply too small to let in all the air that I needed now. I was being chased by stern-looking men, more than two in number. All of them were bald and were dressed in blue —from blue jeans to blue short-sleeved shirts. Even their sneakers were blue in color. Their bulging biceps would terrify an adult. Their attention had just one unflinching focus—Me. I had something in common with them. And, that thing was focus. However, mine was different from theirs because it was hinged on losing them. I fell over a garbage can as I tripped while speeding past a facility that resembled The Staples Center, home of the LA Lakers, spilling out all sorts of unwanted stuff that it contained. The first things to gush out were semen-filled latex condoms, followed by decayed kitchen leftovers, and all sorts of stinking stuff which amounted to nothing but dirt and filth. I succeeded in disturbing the peace of a colony of American cockroaches—they wriggled out in large numbers. They must have been up to ten-thousand in number. I considered myself lucky that none of them was able to make it into my mouth. My mouth, however, was not spared from tasting something—Some stale milk had splashed on my face from its pack, seeping into my mouth. The taste was sickening. I creased my face in disgust and spat it out quickly Beads of the same horrible liquid, trickled down my face and dropped to the ground. My left hand moved to my face at once and wiped it clean as quickly as it could. Time was what I did not have to waste, for the men were coming right behind me. I could see them clearly galloping like top athletes towards the spot where I had fallen. I saw one of them smile, and I read that to mean that he must have thought I had given up on dashing away from them. He could never have been more wrong. I would never let them catch me. That was what stood so solid in my mind. It gave me the courage to get back to my feet. I did and started running away from them again. I did not need to look back to confirm that those after me were still coming. I could feel it strongly that their lives would never be joyful again if they were not able to catch me. And, I was so determined to make them fail that I ran faster. A vehicle nearly knocked me down—But, I only realized that when I heard its tires screech to a halt. I had been running without watching, completely oblivious of the fact that I was not the only person around who was using the same road.

"Damn you, asshole!" cursed the man who nearly hit me with his Buick . "Stay off drugs if you must use the road!" his sarcastic advice followed. He began saying more, but I did not care to hear more. Who cared anyway? Bolting away was the thing that was of utmost importance in my mind. Haste did not allow me the luxury to talk back at him, since I looked back to see that the men were still running behind me as strong as ever, as if they just started the chase, the determination to catch me still stamped on their faces. I ran on, wishing I had wings to fly, singing one of my favorite songs *I Believe I Can Fly* and believing that it would give me more strength. I had never had to run that fast for so long in my life before. And, it was only a matter of time before the lactic acid started to become my undoing—gradually beginning to build up in the muscles of my hands and feet. The zeal to go on pushing myself was there, but my body no longer proved to be the race car it was when I started off. I was losing speed, and the distance that I had placed between ourselves was getting shorter—they were gaining speed. I did not see what stood in front of me until I ran into it. It actually hit my left leg. I fell, bruising my right shoulder. A brown rat, so big that it would actually pass for a big rabbit, scurried across my face, annoying the hell out of me. "Shit!" I screamed. The rat actually smelt like shit. Being fully aware of what was behind me meant that I had no more seconds to waste. I managed to pull myself up in spite of the pain that shot through my entire left leg, making me grimace. Running as fast as I had wanted to was now no longer going to be possible. I was sure that anyone who might have seen me must have been tempted to believe that he or she had seen a frog—I was almost hopping like one. This further helped to reduce the distance I had placed in front of those that wanted to grab me. I felt them closing in. I kept on moving, drawing the last strength in me. My subsequent efforts proved to be futile. The only consolation was that I was able to prove to them that I was no chicken whom they would pick up with little or no stress—I surely made them sweat before they grabbed me.

"Get off me!" I yelled, shoving their hands aside. "What the hell do you want? Leave me alone..."

"Shut the fuck up, will you?" barked one of the men, his voice deep and thunderous.

But, I went on shouting as I was being dragged away, my body weight seeming like a feather in the hands of those men. It was so easy a thing for their muscular hands, clearly.

"Get off me..." I continued to yell until I got thrown into a van that looked black in color. Its tires screeched hard, and it sped off at once. It was dark inside the van, so dark that I could not see a thing. Silence reigned supreme inside it as well. All I could feel were the bodies of those that had caught me and had completely sandwiched me. The van kept speeding. The 'where am I being taken and for what' questions kept arising in my head, seeking possible answers. But, how was I to know? Only time could tell.

Chapter Five

I was not a man who stole some cash from a store and was on the run. I was also not a man who had raped a little girl of four and got busted, but escaped. And, neither was I a man who had fondled the boobs of a famous singer or actress in Hollywood, and her bodyguards were after me. Those that came after me were no cops...

It all began one night, on a Sunday, which was the final day of a Super Bowl. The New Orleans Saints were scheduled to lock horns with the Indianapolis Colts in the city of Miami. Like very many of my fellow Americans, I was set to see the best of soccer. Although I was not a die-hard fan of either of the sides, I did not need to be informed that the encounter would be very keenly contested and quite entertaining. All news media, the internet not left out, were buzzing with news of the big showdown.

I was on my couch, relaxing in my very spacious and lavishly furnished five-million-dollar condo in LA, the city of dreams. I was smoking a Cuban cigar and lovingly stroking a glass of fine Cognac, from which I took a sip at frequent intervals, filled up from a decanter. I had turned on the TV and awaited the commencement of the big game, when the door-bell rang. So, I got up and walked to the door to find out who it was. I was surprised when I opened the door—it was not the kind of person I expected to see at all. It saw a fat man, but not obese in my opinion. His face was beaded with droplet of sweat, and it appeared flushed, most probably from the rigors of doing his job. I thought his ears were rather weird when I saw them since there were plenty of hair growing on them. That certainly brought pictures of apes flashing through my mind's eye. He wore a black pair of shoes, which looked polished, and he had on a shirt and cap that were blue, while his shorts were black. It was a mail-delivery man that had rung my bell. He smiled when he saw me, and thrust his right hand into his blue bag that was wrung around his shoulders. I could feel the warmth in his brief smile, and I smiled back. When his right hand emerged from his bag, I saw three things which I quickly recognized—a ledger, a pen, and the item that was meant to be delivered to me. I had an impulse to ask the man who it was from. But, then came a voice in my head that buried the urge quite fast. *"Relax!"* it said, *"When you get to the bridge, you cross it."* I understood exactly what the voice meant. I went calm, and I was full of appreciation for the advice that the voice had imparted into my head. I wished it were human so that I could buy it a beer or martini.

"Mail for Mr. Beck," said the mail-man. His tone had a touch of courtesy.

"That's me," I replied.

"Can I see your ID please?"

"Sure."

I did not have my ID at the door, so I had to go in to get it. After getting it, I gave my ID to the man. I saw his eyes meander over the parts that contained my name and my photo, and his bushy moustache twisted sideways, almost making me laugh. He was through within seconds.

"Fine," he said. I could see the satisfaction flashing through his face for split seconds before he returned my ID, which I tucked into my shirt's pocket.

He smiled again and handed over the ledger to me along with the pen. I took them both from him, and I regarded him as one who took his job very seriously, so seriously that he passed for a clown capable of thrilling audiences in a Broadway musical. He peered into the ledger, pointing at the place where I was supposed to sign. I obliged him, signing at the exact spot that he indicated to me. The man handed me my mail with another smile.

"Thanks! Have a nice day," I said, smiling back.

The mail-man responded with only a smile.

The man had turned his back on me and was leaving when I shut the door. I got back to my seat to see that the Super Bowl final was on now. But, the mail had taken my attention hostage. I ripped open the blue envelope, took out the sheet it contained, and began to read what was written on it. It was only after I had finished reading that did I realize that the news of my accomplishments had spread more than I could ever believe. The letter had been sent from Spain. A movie studio by the name of Crème Pictures, based in Spain, had learned of my incredible talent and were interested in me. The letter was so enticing that I read it all over again to be fully sure that I did not pick up any wrong information when I first read it. But, no! I did not make any mistake. The information was the same. The letter was actually a huge offer coming from the studio—I was being wooed to sign up to do a screenplay for a big movie in English, which was titled 'Don't Think You Can Get Away from Me.' I found the title quite intriguing and had the desire to read the story quickly. In my hands was an offer that I could not think of passing away. I could not stop smiling. However, the smiles did not do enough justice to express how I felt. So, I exploded in laughter, which shattered the tranquility that defined the atmosphere in my home. I stood up and mounted the seat I had been sitting on, jumping up and down like the actor Tom Cruise in the Oprah Winfrey show, screaming my head off and waving my hands wildly like a person seriously possessed by the spirits of joy. I felt exuberant as I realized that men and women from far and wide would not mind emptying their bank accounts just to get me on their projects. Crème Pictures was ready to part with a hundred-million dollars for my services. Unbelievable! I was not only moved by the huge amount, but was thrilled by the exhilarating chance to pitch my craft on such a platform that would enable many other European Studios to witness my talent—I was convinced that Crème Pictures would provide me with that platform. They were ready to talk to me as soon as possible. Their letter had an invitation which requested me be present at 6600 Sunset Boulevard, # 302 Hollywood, California, where their executives would wait for me the following day.

CHAPTER SIX

I jumped off the seat I had been bouncing on out of pure joy which had now tattooed itself across my heart. I started jumping up and down again, being so drunk with bliss as if the offer was the first ever good news to have come my way.

"This is great! Fantastic! This is awesome!" I screamed, feeling jubilant. "Hey! Hey! Hey! What is this? Where did it come from?" I asked out of joy, as if I did not know. "Julie...Julie...Julie...You don't want to miss this! You don't want to miss this, Julie...Don't you get it? I said you don't want to miss this..." I began singing a one-line song on top of my voice.

Beck's a jolly good fellow...

Julie walked in due to all the clamor that I had caused and found me busy dancing like a madman. I did not make sense to her, of course. She did not know whether to laugh or frown from where she stood. I invited her to join me, making signs with my left fingers, but she would not budge. She had on a green apron, having emerged from the kitchen where she had been preparing a meal. On her face stood a question that I knew so well—what is the meaning of this? I ignored her and went on singing.

"Stop singing!" She screamed when she could take it anymore.

"O yes! Yes! I have to stop now..." I screamed back. Julie looked at me as if I had gone crazy. The mood she saw me in was quite unprecedented to her.

"Should we see a psychiatrist, Beck?" Julie asked, as her stares sized up my entire frame, as if she had never seen me before. I did not grace her question with a response. I felt no embarrassment too knowing that she did not understand. How would she understand what it was all about when I simply continued to jump up and down like a monkey and keep the news from her? But, she did look very eager to know what was actually going on. "Is it the game?" Julie asked with an unconcerned look on her face. She was no fan of the Super Bowl at all. She would rather cook than spare some time to see it.

"This is marvelous, Julie," I responded, waving the letter in front of her. "This is awesome!"

"What the hell is making your head pop with such joy?" asked Julie as she came towards me.

"This! Julie," I replied, handing her the letter, "This is what is making my head pop with great joy."

I handed her the letter when she got to where I stood and stopped. As she started reading it, I focused all my attention to her face in an attempt to see what her initial reaction would be. I had expected to see a smile light up her face after a short while. But, when that did not happen, I began to wonder if what she was reading was what I had read. Julie read the letter from the very first word to the last without even a grin showing on her face. What I saw on her face was rather shocking to me—disapproval. It stood there very clearly. Looking up from the letter, and she looked straight into my eyes to see how stunned I was and nodded twice. Her nod said it all—what I already knew.

"Are you crazy?" I was forced to confront her, "What the fuck are you talking about?"

"No, Beck. This isn't good. This isn't good for you. Not good for me. Not good for us and your career."

"What the hell does that mean?" Anger made me thunder. "This is hundred-million dollars at stake here, Julie. Are you half asleep now?"

"No, as you can see. I know exactly what I'm talking about," Julie responded, and looked me in the eye in a 'you can't prove me wrong' sort of way.

"I will bet with my life that you don't!" I said.

"Stay away from this, Beck," Julie replied. Her tone was quite commanding.

Mystified, I said, "What the hell's wrong with you?"

"Beck, you're the one who's got a problem here. You are not being able to see beyond the juicy part of this horrendous letter. Beyond this letter is a road strewn with sharp rocks. This road is rich in thorns and thistles."

"Bullshit! That is complete bullshit! How interesting it is to know that I've been married to a psychic without even knowing it," my sarcastic response followed.

"I am not a psychic, Beck."

"Really? How quickly you deny...What then told you that the letter in your hands is bad omen?"

"Instinct, Beck. My instinct! It doesn't let me down most of the time."

"Bizarre! Julie, you're bizarre. Your so-called instinct is bizarre. It makes me sick! It sucks! You are not telling me to leave an offer of a hundred-million dollars to fizzle away just because you've got some fucking instinct? No! You don't want to do that!"

"I wouldn't tell you a lie. You're my husband, Beck. A man I love..."

"Oh...no, Julie. Keep love out of this now. This is money in large sum that we are talking about."

"You talk about money like you've not made millions before. Sometimes you talk as if you're no longer a star so hot right now."

"Yes, you're right, baby! You're right. I'm so hot right now that I got that letter. But as a star, you can be the hottest commodity in Hollywood this minute and be a nobody the next. Of all women in the world, you should be the one encouraging me to grab this offer."

Julie waved the letter. "But not this one, right?" she added.

"Wrong!" I exclaimed.

"Don't accept this offer, Beck."

"I'm deaf now, Julie!"

"Discard it!"

"I'm deaf!" I repeated.

"Throw it away now!"

"I've been deaf for ten years now..."

To me, Julie was a woman very high on crack as far as the offer was concerned. I almost told her that I would be glad to see her check in to a rehab.

"Hello," my voice came on after having picked up my phone. I had to quickly call my agent.

Chapter Seven

I got to the place where I was to meet with the executives from Crème Pictures the next morning. I was informed in the letter that our talks would start by eight o'clock in the morning. It was almost eight, and I felt glad that I had not arrived late, for it was my policy to always take appointments seriously. I pulled up in front of the house that carried the number in the address with me, it was a condo actually. I alighted from my SUV and walked straight to the door and knocked. A tall man wearing blue jeans opened the door for me with a rather forced smile on his face. He was bald-headed and most probably in his mid-forties. I sensed that he was just forcing himself to display some courtesy. It was not a thing that wallowed in his blood, I believed.

"Oh...Mr. Beck!" he said, his thick Spanish accent very audible. "So, my name has spread here like virus?" I muttered quickly to myself, though not audibly. "You are most welcome," the man went ahead to say, as he pointed in the direction that he wanted me to take. I smiled in response.

"Thank you," I responded.

"The whole team is waiting."

I smiled at him again, and walked along, full of confidence that I would close one of the best deals of my career. I passed through an alley to another door the man had pointed at. I knocked on the door and heard a voice say, "Come in."

To my surprise, the room I walked into was quite dark. The air-conditioning system inside was obviously well at work, since I got chilled the moment I stepped inside. The room smelt of lavender. However, there was nothing about it that gave me the impression that it was a boardroom. Just as I was going to ask the man who had directed me, inquiring where the executives were, I heard the click of a switch, and the room suddenly became well illuminated. I could see what it contained now. It *was* a boardroom, but it was strange in its own unique ways.

There were three windows covered with black curtains. Right above the glass round-table was a chandelier, on which three black G-string panties and four black bras hung from. That was rather weird, but I decided that I wouldn't let it bother me. "A man has all the rights in the world to fix his office the ways he wants," I told myself. The floor was neat, had fine wood grains. Ten men, all of whom wore black tuxedos, were seated around the round-table. They were all clean-shaven, no beard at all, as if it had been their plan. Well, maybe it was. None of them had hair on his head too, not even a single hair. I believed all of them were well into their forties, despite their boyish appearances, which could deceive anyone. A spiral-bound document lay on the table. I knew right away that it was the story that I would be asked to develop a screenplay for. 'Don't Think You Can Get Away from Me' was the bold inscription on its hard cover. Seeing that title alone made me feel more confident that I would do a good job. The eleventh person looked out of sort to me—the person had on a mask. Was it a man or woman? I could not tell. I did not see any hint of breasts sitting on the chest of the masked person. The very tight black leather jacket the person wore made it hard for any breasts to dangle a bit, even if they existed. My conclusion was that the masked person must be a man or hermaphrodite. I gathered my attention from the masked person in the room to the ten men who were regarding me highly now. Their faces were very rich in welcome smiles. One of them pointed to a vacant seat I knew was meant for me. I smiled back at them, walked straight to the seat, and sat down.

"I am Mr. Raul. I am Mr. Fernando. I am Mr. Reyes. I am Mr. Gonzalez. I am Mr. Benitez." It went on like that as the men introduced themselves one after another. Their Spanish accent poured out. The only person who said nothing was the one wearing a mask. I took my rapt attention from the mask and focused it on the men again. The meeting got off to a good start with the team telling me how it had been following my incredible progress and had no grain of doubt at all that I was the best man for their project. I was told the budget for the movie was two-billion dollars. The team also took time to explain all that I needed to understand about their offer to me. Mr. Reyes pushed the document on the table to my side.

"That is the story," he said to me.

"I understand," I said, picking up the document and flipping through its pages.

I saw Mr. Reyes point at the person who wore a mask. "Very good writer," he said to me. "Wrote that one."

"He or she wrote it?" I asked Mr. Reyes, curious to know the sex of the person behind the mask. He only pointed at the masked person again, but this time with a smile.

I shot a glance at the person who wore a mask, expecting to hear something, just any response. I took my eyes off when silence was what I got and began to read through the story synopsis. I thought it was great when I finished. It sounded fantastic to me. It had to do with romance between a writer and his agent—romance that later got sour and left the agent boiling with rage.

"Nice beginning," I spoke of my first impression, which came from the first paragraph I quickly read. "I'm excited to have the chance to work on this."

"We are glad to hear that from you, Mr. Beck," said Mr. Benitez, while his colleagues nodded in affirmation. I understood that their nods were a confirmation of what Mr. Benitez had said. Silence consumed the entire room as I went through the document again. After having gone through the document for a while, I raised my head to face the man or woman who had a mask on.

"You're a good story teller," I said with a broad smile, trying to compliment here. However, the smile had to be wiped off my face when I got no reply to the compliment. I had no choice but to withdraw my attention and focus it on the men when someone interrupted my concentration.

It was Mr. Fernando. "Mr. Beck, we can now understand that you are interested in working on that story," he said.

"Yes! I've not really seen all of it, but what I've read so far tells me that this is a story that *needs* to be told," I said quite excitedly, "I feel honored to be presented with an opportunity to be part of this project."

"That is great," Mr. Gonzalez added, "Now, how much time do you think you will need to complete the work? This is a project we would like to get on with as fast as possible. We think three months should be enough time..."

"Give me two," I replied with all gusto.

"Fantastic, Mr. Beck. Your confidence is striking. I guess, I am beginning to see glimpses of why we came for *you*. And, it further gladdens our heart," smiled Mr. Gonzalez when he finished. As I turned to look at the other men, I saw that they were smiling as well. However, the masked man or woman remained silent, showing no emotions whatsoever.

"Get the job done, and you'll get your money, Mr. Beck," said Mr. Gonzalez again.

"I give my clients the best," I replied, sounding confident.

"You have not talked about money, Mr. Beck," said Mr. Benitez.

"That's the easy part." I laughed.

"That is really the easy part," said all of them together and roared in laughter. I joined them.

"Your offer is satisfactory, and I'm ready to roll," I added.

"We are glad to hear that!" Mr. Fernando said.

"My agent will be on this."

"Okay! That is most appropriate, Mr. Beck," Mr. Fernando replied. "You're a smart man."

CHAPTER EIGHT

Even though my discussions with the men had got on well, I was beginning to have one big concern now—It was about the person who wore a mask and never said a word all through. The masked person kept looking at me in such a manner that it almost made me ask whether we had met before. Although I managed to restrain myself successfully, my body language kept asking 'What are you looking at?' All the men put their heads together, whispering things to each other, and smiling as I kept screening the story. I did not hear anything that they said, but I took it that they were summing up their impressions of me. I interpreted their smiles to reflect their absolute confidence in my ability to deliver a good job to them. I also believed in my heart that I had met and interacted with a nice group of men, who were easy to get along with. This encouraged me to tell myself that I had no other choice, but to deliver my absolute best to them. I was hell-bent on doing everything possible to hand in the screenplay of my life—nothing but the very best of my craft.

I was about to tell the men that I would love to take my leave in order to have a talk with my agent, when the person who wore a mask asked me a question, which I considered to be absolutely ridiculous. "*So, you can talk? I thought you were dumb and did not have a mouth,*" I said to myself, inaudibly. It was a stern female voice that I heard—one I thought I had heard before, that of my agent. I quickly told myself that it was stupid of me to think that I had heard my agent's voice! I must have been seriously hallucinating. My agent and I had agreed that I meet with executives from Crème Pictures first and get back to her if I made up my mind to work on their project. This was not the proper way to do things though—Crème Pictures ought to have gone to her first. And, she was supposed to have come with me. But, she had told me that she had to keep an appointment with her physician, one she could not miss about the nagging breathing problem that she sometimes had. I was bent on setting the ball in motion, with or without my agent, having deemed the offer from Crème Pictures as just too good to pass me by.

The woman with a mask began to repeat the question when I did not come up with any answer for her. Of course, I never had one because her question made no sense to me. Of all the questions in the whole wide world, the one she asked was, if I thought that I could get away from her. She continued with her question, and it did not look as if she was going to stop. It got to a point where I felt embarrassed and angry. I looked at all the men questioningly. None of them seemed to be disturbed by the barrage of unnecessary questions that were being thrown at me. I expected, at least, one of them to react against that, but all acted contrary to my expectations, all to my big surprise. They just sat and watched the masked woman throwing her questions at me. All I could wonder was why all of them were most unwilling to say a word against her improper conduct. It almost felt as if the air they were breathing was in her hands, as if she was their mother who would not hesitate to starve them of food and water if they dared to speak against her in any way.

"What the fuck do you expect me to answer?" I finally replied to the masked woman when the anger in me broke out of the lid that I had managed to keep on it, "I don't even know you! You will do this gathering a whole lot of good by keeping that fucking question to yourself!"

I glanced passingly at the faces of the men. I only broke my silence in such a manner so that they would say something in my defense. But again, none spoke a word, making me even more surprised than before.

"You people must be sick in here," I muttered. The masked woman asked me her question again, and I felt insulted. "Mr. Raul," I said. "Please tell this masked thing that I'm not here to take silly questions from her!"

Mr. Raul said nothing. The masked woman continued with her questioning. I further voiced my displeasure, my voice having risen steadily.

"Mr. Reyes, can't you hear her? Please ask her to behave! Is she under the influence of some hard drugs or something? What did she smoke this morning? Can someone here tell me...? I don't know what she's talking about! I don't, I swear!" I was getting agitated, and they could see it.

It all continued to look like only one thing, as if I had spoken to no one at all, and all I said seemed to have fallen on ears plugged with stones. I felt ignored and deserted, and most of all, insulted. "What the hell has hypnotized you all?" I went ahead, yelling, "What the hell is starting to go on here...? Shit! Who's she....? Who's this masked junkie? Wait a second! None of you men wants to talk anymore...? Come on! What the hell's going on here...? Who's she? Can't she shut up for a minute...? Hey, masked junkie woman, shut the fuck up!"

CHAPTER NINE

Something from inside was quick to tell me that it was pointless to call on the rest of the men. The friendliness that they had displayed earlier had become a thing of the past now. The whole room would have been completely engulfed by silence if not for the woman having a mask on—she continued going on with her question, which only got me sick. I could not take it anymore.

"Go to hell, you sick bitch!" I yelled at the woman, and it all turned ugly soon after—All the tuxedoed men pulled out their hand-guns and pointed them at me. It was only at this time that the truth of Julie's instinct dawned on me. I should have paid heed to her warning and not brought my ass here like she had asked.

"Julie, I'm sorry..." This was what came out from my mouth.

"Make no more sound!" thundered all the men. They had all spoken fast and simultaneously, looking very mean at this time, their malicious demeanour very much different from the calm one that I had seen when we talked business.

My mind was quick in telling me that I had hurt no one when I began thinking of who might have planned what was now my reality.

"Take him away," the masked woman ordered.

As the masked woman got up from her seat, her frame suggested that she could be someone I had met before. But, I had no time to process all those thoughts that kept barging into my mind. The ten men, whom I had held talks with, withdrew their guns to where they had pulled them from, while four others, armed as well, entered the room at once and held me. They wore blue jeans like the one that opened the door into this hell for me. All looked as if they had malicious intentions, their bulging biceps and shaved heads only adding to that impression.

"You know what to do," the masked woman said to the four men who had entered the room.

Three of the newly-arrived men left me for the one, who began to drag me away from the room to where I wouldn't know. Knowing full well that it would be the end of me if I allowed fear to consume me, I was bent on capitalizing on my situation. I looked for an opening, and when I saw it, I did not waste a second. Taking advantage of a moment of a slight loss of concentration on the part of the man who was dragging me away to somewhere I did not know, I sent a hard jab to his jaw like I was a Muhammad Ali product, making him lose his balance and drop his gun. I was lucky that the man who opened the door for me when I had arrived was no longer standing there. As I flew through that door before any of my captors could make a move, I heard bullets jamming the door behind me.

"Do not kill him! But make sure you catch him alive!" I heard a voice scream. I would not misplace it—It surely came from the masked woman.

That was how I had started to run for my dear life before I was captured and hurled inside the van.

CHAPTER TEN

I feared the worst when the van in which I was being taken away screeched to a halt after a while. I quickly got dragged out of it into an alley that was faintly lit by one bulb. A stale stench of cigar smoke prevailed in the alley, and it choked my nostrils. Someone kicked me from behind, making me fall to the floor with a thud. An excruciating pain shot through my whole body as I fell.

"Ouch!" I cried in pain, "Where the hell's this?" I asked out of fear, as I struggled in vain to get away from their grip. But, none of my captors was in the mood for questions. "Why are you doing this to me?" This was the question which I screamed, and once again, received no answer. Then, I saw one of the men remove a little green bottle which had no label, from the back pocket of his jeans.

"Leave me alone!" I screamed when I saw him bringing out a clean white piece of rag. I knew what was coming. "Help!" I screamed all the more. But, the help that I needed most could not hear me, let alone come to my rescue. Two of the men kicked me hard on my ass to stop me from struggling. They wanted me to be still, but I kept on wrestling them to free myself. However, their strong hands, which kept me down, made my efforts completely ineffective. The picture you would get was that of a hare already in the mouth of a cheetah and was struggling to get out. The man who had the rag poured a little of the bottle's content into it. I could see the rag heading for my face now, his colleagues pinning me down harder.

"Help!" Another scream flew out of my mouth. But, where was Help? It must have gone deaf, two big stones must have blocked its ears. My eyes shot a glance at the sky full eaten by darkness, and I wished that I could fly up there and turn the switches on so that the street would have enough light to expose my captors. But, alas! The rag was placed on my face muffling up my scream. The liquid felt cold against my skin. I did not even have the time to detect what it smelt like, it was too fast for me. It did its job in the twinkle of an eye—I lost all consciousness.

***

I could feel my eyes twitching a little. When they opened, everything was a blur. It seemed to me that ages had gone past during the length of time that it had taken me to regain my lost consciousness. I was lying on my back, and darkness reigned supreme everywhere. It was hot, and beads of sweat constantly crawled from my head, running down my cheek, and falling from my chin. Stale air was all that I could breathe. Upon trying to move my legs, I discovered that it was not possible—I realized that I had been chained as I heard clangs of metal. The metal that held my legs were hinged strongly somewhere so close.

After a while, when my eyes were wide open, it only felt as if they were not, everywhere being just black. "*Maybe my hands are free,*" I thought, but I noticed that they too were bound to fetters of iron when I tried to move them. How did I really confirm this? Well, I heard the iron cling. My mind was racing fast like a Kentucky Derby horse on which everyone had betted to win, to come up with an idea which would allow me to save myself. *Why don't you use your mouth? It is the only thing you have that is free now...* suggested my mind, and I thought it was absolutely true. If my captors could find a way to bind it with metals, I am sure they would not have hesitated a second. I also realized that no one had taken my cell phone, it was still there in my pocket. The urge to take it out and make a call rose up inside me like a fountain of water. I wanted very much to call Julie, let her know the kind of mess I had fallen into. If only my hands were free. I wanted to tell her to get the cops to free me from this bondage which I could not figure out how I had attracted. I knew that trying to escape from those shackles was as useless as spending time and resources to create an ad that was intended to sell Gillette shaving blades to the Taliban in Afghanistan. Though I knew this so well, it did little to shrink my determination to do something in order to escape. I had to use the only thing I had—my mouth.

"Help" I began screaming began. "Help! Help!" It got louder. But, nobody talked back. The echo of my screams was the only thing that I received in response. "Why are you all doing this to me? What have I done to deserve this sickening place? Help! What have I done to deserve this dungeon? What have I done? Help...Someone please get me out of here! Help! Someone please help me dial nine-one-one."

I began wriggling my body as if that would get any close to securing my freedom. I wriggled hard, pulled and pushed only to make the metals cling louder, and that was it—nothing more. "*This is just a big waste of my time*," I thought. "This is getting me nowhere," I muttered, the frustration quite evident in my voice. The futility of my efforts got me to be calm the moment I realized it. "What's the point in trying when I know that I can't get out, no matter how hard I try?" I muttered again, my voice now had a touch of despair. My mind went blank as I felt a big blanket of hopelessness cast its shroud over me. I was now a man whose life had shut down. Fatigue began to arrest me. I was not supposed to be tired, having just woken up. But, the hands of tiredness arrived from nowhere and began to grasp every part of my body. My eyes were beginning to shut in the thick darkness when suddenly my cell phone rang. My mind sprang back to life and told me that it must be my worried Julie who was calling. I could not help but agree completely with it. No one else but her knew that I had gone out. Oh! If only my hands were free, and I could use them to yank out my cell phone from my pocket. It rang for a while, buzzing inside my pocket, before the silence prevailed once more, and it had me full of regret—I ought to have listened to that woman, Julie. I ought to have paid heed to every word in her warning.

Regret soon became a sea which deluged me. I did not even know when my mouth opened, the words came out, "I'm sorry... I'm sorry... I'm so sorry, Julie. I should have listened to you. I'm so, so sorry... I know you're the one trying to get to me. It's a pity that I can't get to talk with you. I really want to tell you how sorry I am."

Tears moistened my eyes as I spoke, tears which later coursed down my cheeks, and crawled to the back of my ears, creating a mini pond there. Who would say that men do not cry?

CHAPTER ELEVEN

I was about to close my eyes when I heard a door open beside the place where I lay, making it obvious that someone was entering. The lights from a torch brightened the parts of the place that I was being held captive. I looked around quickly and got to know that I was in a place that looked like a basement. I even managed to see two green masks lying on the floor beside me, before the person that had entered, switched off the torch. Total darkness reigned everywhere again. Fear suggested that I begin my last prayers and ask for God's forgiveness for my sins. It went on to tell me that this were my last moments as a living being. It said the person that had entered would just blow up contents of my skull with bullets. It made me freeze. However, I was determined that I would not die in silence if it was indeed true that whoever it was that had come in, had come to ensure that I became a corpse.

"Who are you? It is not a real man that takes advantage of a helpless man who can't do anything to save his life. You're not about to kill me, are you? Listen, let us talk about this. Name your price, okay? I'm sure you don't love to spill blood of the innocent, do you? I know you don't!"

The person, who had walked in, did not utter a single word in response to all that I ranted about, but simply switched on the torchlight again, and quickly pointed it to a corner. I followed the strong beam of light that poured out and saw a wall with 'Don't Think You Can Get Away from Me' inscribed on it.

"Have you seen that?" said the person at last. It was a male voice that I heard—one that was not hostile, but it had a little warmth. He did not sound like a person who was about to kill me after all. Oh...How fear dumps a bunch of lies into one's mind.

"Plenty of times," I replied, "What has that got to do with the way I'm being treated right now?"

"Don't tell me, Mr. Beck, that you no longer understand that those words make up the title of our upcoming movie. You have a deal to do the screenplay, don't you?"

"Like this? In this condition? Who can write a screenplay in this dark gruelling incarceration?"

"I'm afraid *you* have to."

"This is insane!"

At this moment, my cell phone began ringing again. "Please help me out," I said to the man, "I must take the call."

"Ah! That must be your lovely wife whom I plan to sleep with," the man said. I got so angry that I felt like smashing his head against any wall that I could find around me. He noticed my anger and laughed in a mocking manner. The laughter came off his mouth with a message that I could read so well—It dared me to make a move. But, what was I to do being chained like that? "Is that anger that I see, Mr. Beck?" the man continued, "I don't know why some men don't like to hear the truth." My phone continued to ring as the man spoke on, "I don't hide my plans, Mr. Beck."

"I will set fire to your balls for talking about my wife in that manner!" I threatened. The man could see that it was nothing but an empty threat. Very empty, really! A gazelle seized by the fearsome fang of a cheetah must be stupid to challenge the cheetah, when it ought to be begging the cheetah to spare its life.

The man did nothing but laugh again, his laughter daring me all the more to make a move if I could.

"Your anger can't hurt a fly, Mr. Beck. Someone is doing it now as we speak. And, I understand that her boobs are the size of Alabama...so perfect for me. The kind of boobs my hands love to squeeze."

"I'll cut off your fucking balls, I swear!" I thundered.

"Really? I will tell you what I think you ought to know right now. She's got the type of boobs that love the warmth my tongue and mouth can deliver. How about that?"

"I'll feed your balls to the dogs, I swear! Hey! Don't mess with my wife!"

The thought of someone making love to my Julie was so unbearable to me. There was no point imagining it—It would have choked me to death if I had tried. I made an attempt to yank off the chains and metal that bound me to the floor with spurts of strength that I quickly felt inside, which were obviously inspired by anger. I got nowhere, my breathing now hastened, tears flowing down my face and armpits. My phone stopped ringing. Then, it started to ring again.

"I will commit murder, I swear!" I screamed, "Anybody that dares to touch her must die!" The man just went on laughing.

"You make lots of noise for a person who can't move. Oh...what a very jealous man. I see... You want your pie for only for yourself, isn't it? But why don't you love to share your wife? Did Christianity tell you that it's a sin?"

"That's what it is! Nothing more!" My phone stopped ringing.

"There goes the church-man. I guess your pastor told you that, huh...?"

"Not just my pastor. My bible too!"

"Well, I shared my wife and never regretted any bit of it. It brings warmth and peace to the soul, if you didn't know. And, now you know...giving and sharing is love sublime, Mr. Beck. Didn't your bible tell you that? Even your pastor didn't tell you that he has tried it a thousand times...he only kept it secret? You bet he wouldn't want to let his gullible church members know about the sweet little things he does behind their backs, things that refreshes his body and soul."

"Stop lying..."

"That way he will go to heaven, leaving you blind followers to rot in hell with uncle D."

"Stop talking about the Devil!"

"You have no idea what you've been missing, Mr. Beck. You should go on and share your wife. I can assure you it's the fastest way to heaven."

"If that's the only route to heaven, then I don't want to go there! I would rather wine and dine with uncle D at his Pandemonium."

The man roared in laughter. "Its being lots of fun kidding with you," he declared when he stopped laughing, "I must say it's interesting to see you charge like a bull elephant. We have no business with your wife, Mr. Beck." My phone began to ring again.

"Please let me take that call," I screamed.

"We knew she would call you."

"Please...I need to take that call!"

"Don't think we are fools here, Mr. Beck. We have been waiting for that call. You must say what I want you to say to her and nothing more."

"Who are you to tell me what to tell my wife?" I had to voice my disagreement.

"Are you ready to listen now, Mr. Beck?" The voice had changed again. The little tinge of friendliness that it contained a moment back had now given way completely to one that had much malevolence. I would've said a lot more had it not been for a metal that I felt at the back of my head. Believe me; the sense of touch speaks in a clearer manner than the sense of sight. I knew it was a gun that I felt, so I had to stop myself from uttering anything more. My phone kept on ringing. "Are you ready to listen now, Mr. Beck?" The man repeated in a stern voice.

"Yes," I replied reluctantly.

"Good boy...You must tell your wife that all is going well with the deal. Tell her that you will close the deal soon and get back home. Nothing more, Mr. Beck. Do we understand each other?"

"Yes."

The man picked out my cell phone from my pocket. He brought it close to my left ear. Julie's voice was unmistakable. She had already begun to express how worried she was that I had not returned home by then. I was glad that she did not sound in any way like a person whose private parts had been violated. I knew my Julie so well—She would have mentioned that to me first had anything of that sort occurred. She told me that my dinner was getting cold, and I began to speak back. I wanted to say something else—I was tempted to tell her that I was in trouble, get her to dial nine-one-one. But, that cold touch of that gun kept me from saying those.

"All is going well with the deal, Julie. I'm fine, sweetheart. Relax. Don't get yourself all worked up. I will close the deal soon. I'm fine, okay? I will be home soon. Love you too."

No sooner did I complete saying this than the man snatched the phone away from me and put it back in my pocket. He was also kind enough to take his gun away from the back of my head as well.

"What are you doing all these for?" I screamed at him. "Why are you keeping me here? What the fuck have I done to deserve all these?"

"I don't know. You know what, Mr. Beck?"

"What?"

"You simply talk too much."

I heard footsteps once again. As I assessed them, I knew they came from two people. Hands grabbed me once again...

Chapter Twelve

"What the fuck are you do—?"

These were the words that I managed to articulate before I felt something that smelt like a tape seal my mouth. I could only make some incomprehensible animalistic sounds after that happened. I heard myself clearly—I sounded like a whining dog which had just sighted some bones. Thunderous laughter broke off from the men who were present. Their hands raised my head a little after all the laughter had died down. Someone hit me hard at the back of my head—it happened five times. It brought so much excruciating pain that weakness permeated through my entire body now, wearing me out. The light vanished, consumed by thick darkness all over again. I heard footsteps going away and a loud bang coming from the door before I passed out.

***

When I regained my consciousness, I felt someone fondling the pubic area around my waist. I could feel the fingers, however, it was not easy for me to say for certain whether the fingers belonged to a man or a woman. I could not see a face—That would have helped me. The fingers gently moved to my private parts and began to stroke it tenderly, arousing my loins. Within seconds, I had an erection, a strong one. Someone got on top of me, and I felt entering someone within seconds. A dark figure, I now knew to be a woman, was springing up and down on me. I could hear her moaning in varying cadence. In between her stimulating moans, I also heard her mutter the words, "I must take something." And, I did not bother one bit to think about what those words could mean. I was by now already engrossed in savoring the pleasure that was exploding like huge fireworks all throughout my body. I lost all the care in the world about what my ordeal was for, and I urged myself to relax and enjoy the show. I did not call for it. Neither did I see it as good. However, I could not stop it. It only left me with an option that I could not fend off, which was to relax and take it. So, the hands of adultery did not tug at my conscience. Slowly and steadily, we both began to ascend the hill of orgasm. It was only when we got to the very top that I realized that what I thought had been going on was not actually happening. It was when I got to my peak and climaxed with a loud scream that I fully emerged from the mists of drowsiness. It was still dark everywhere. I thought that I had been dreaming. But, no! A woman had actually sat on me and made love to me. I felt a disconnection from my private part as she got up. A little semen crawled down to my groin. I felt her move away from me. The heels of her shoes made some sounds that were headed in the direction of the door. I wanted to pounce on her and stop her from leaving. But, what could I do when the chains of metal still held me to the ground like an African slave in a ship headed for the West Indies? My mouth was no longer sealed, of course, so I screamed at her.

"Who are you? Why did you do that to me? What do you want from me?" My voice could not do a thing. She did not even bother to speak back to me. The resonating clicks from the heels of her shoes were the only sound that came as a response, and it continued towards the direction of the door. Only within a few seconds, I heard them no more. The door had opened and closed. I knew that she was gone. Tears rained out from my eyes, as I rued the loss of my hands and legs to fetters of metal.

The door only opened again after what seemed like half an hour had passed by. Incoming footsteps followed in a swift manner. From the sound of the footsteps, I could gauge that there were more than one person entering. My heart was sunk in the fear of what next would be done unto me.

"What do you want again?" I screamed, trying in vain to free my hands and my legs. "What do you guys want again? Have I not been enough of a sex toy?"

"Leave me alone..." I screamed when I felt a pair of hands hold on to my head. "Leave me alone! Leave me alone! Haven't you all had enough of me?"

"Of course, we have had enough," laughed a male voice.

That laughter made me feel like a piece of shit. I hated being helpless. I could feel pangs of anger shooting up through my body. It got me feeling like strangling someone or poking my fingers very hard at someone's stomach, never relenting until his guts spill out. The anger made me forget my condition and try to spring up, only to realize again that my ass was kept kissing the floor by the chains.

"I believe your wife can't come close to making you feel as nice as you felt a while back," came one voice.

"That amounted to an abuse of my right to choose what I want. I'll sue your ass for that!"

"Abuse? But you enjoyed it, didn't you? It refreshed you, didn't it? Many pray for that sort of abuse all over the world. You did enjoy it, didn't you?"

"I don't know..."

"He's a pretender."

"I'm not a pretender. I love being faithful to my wife!"

"Then answer the question. Did you not love all that pleasure while being chained?"

"It is all clear that he did. You don't need to ask him any further. I believe, from now on, he will always demand the show from his wife like he's had it—the chain style."

Thunderous laughter exploded, the resultant echo extending it. I heard voices that made me know that there were all men around me.

"You must all be men," I said in the hopes of getting a final confirmation.

"Yeah!" replied one of them, "What's your fear, buddy?"

"Help!" I screamed, "Somebody save my ass..."

"What the fuck is wrong with you?"

"You think we're gay, and you're afraid of your asshole?" Loud laughter exploded.

"Don't worry, Mr. Beck. We love to do it with women as much as you do. The chain style..."

"Help! Some gay men are about to violate my asshole...Help! Help..."

"He doesn't believe us!"

"Next move?"

"Show him what we've got!"

"Leave me alone..." I shouted in response, "What the fuck do you want again?"

That was all I could say. Their hands suddenly came upon me, gripping me hard. I feared for my asshole and the large quantity of blood it risked losing. I struggled to save it—but to no avail. My mouth got sealed like before. The hands that held me would not still leave me. I felt some of them on my ass, opening my pants. I wanted to beg them to take it easy with me but realized that I could no longer utter anything meaningful. I saw the light from a torch flashing, concentrating on my ass. However, it was not enough to dispel the thick darkness still hung above. Fear now had me in its bowels. My body stiffened when something made contact with my ass. I had expected an erect male sexual tool in search of my asshole. But, this was not to be—I only felt a pinch instead, which made me wince. I now knew that it was a syringe that poked me in my ass. I shut my eyes to fend off little sting that I felt as the syringe stood on my ass. The torch was switched off when it was all done. The syringe had slipped off the hole it made in my ass. There were no more hands pinning me down anymore. Total darkness reigned supreme once again. The footsteps began to fade away in the direction from which they had come. I was already feeling drowsy when I faintly heard the door being opened. Sleep had, by now, stolen much of my sense of awareness.

Chapter Thirteen

My head was resting on top of the steering wheel of my black SUV when I woke up. There was no trace of doubt in my mind that my captors had bundled me into it after being done with me. I actually felt strong and good. Remembering the assault that I was subjected to, I peered into my private part. "*Wow!*" I thought. It had been cleaned up and perfumed. I got a pleasant whiff as I sniffed. I was even more surprised that there was no pain in any part of my body despite the fact that I had emerged from hell. I was dumbfounded only until I remembered about the injection that I was given. Its aim must have been to restore me back to a sound physical, psychological, and emotional state, I concluded. I tried to figure out, without much success, what my captors had achieved with my incarceration. I thought it very necessary to quickly take advantage of the freedom I had now, before they changed their minds. I turned on the ignition and got the engine of my car roaring. I was driving home when I noticed that a sign had been placed right on the dashboard in my car. It was inscribed in such a small font that it did not catch my attention earlier. I pulled up and looked at them closely only to see the same words that I had seen over and over again—"Don't Think You Can Get Away From Me."

"Silly words," I said, not giving the sign a thought. I brought the engine of my car back to life again and got rolling home. After the ordeal, I had been longing for home, which felt like heaven.

It was four at night on the dot when I arrived home. It felt like I had left my home for ages. When I alighted my car, after having driven it into the garage, I found Julie standing right there in the living room with her arms extended, waiting to grab me and cling unto me. Oh sweet, Julie. She had been awake. Her eyes were wide open due to the surge of joy that coursed through her. And, they carried only one expression that I saw clearly—I missed you.

"I missed you too, Julie," I said, walking straight into her arms, and getting locked in a warm embrace that none of us was eager to break off until a few minutes had passed by. Julie withdrew herself from me slowly. She still stood close when she was done. Her glances ran from my head to my feet. I knew she was sizing me up.

"You look great, Beck. But why did it take you so long...?" she asked and gave me no time to respond before flooding my face with kisses. I had no choice but to reserve what I wanted to say. The kisses came in large numbers, and my own lips had to get to work, reciprocating what her lips were doing to my face. The richest man in the world is the one with a lovely wife like mine, I concluded in my mind. The flood of kisses we planted on each other's face gradually began to get smaller. We were slowly getting tired of kissing now, our faces already wet with a sea of saliva, our breaths, running out.

"Getting the deal done was not a piece of cake," I replied at last. Julie's hands were now placed across my shoulders, while mine held her sumptuous waist, pressing her succulent ass a little. I felt good feeling it. Why? Simple! It belonged to me! It still does!

"I'm sorry I tried to stop you with my wrong instinct." Julie's apology stung my ears and tore my conscience to pieces.

"Don't worry about that...Show me the perfect woman in this world, and I will leave her for you," I said in my desperation to make Julie feel good. This way, I hoped to keep her away from suspecting that anything ugly had happened to me.

"Did you close the deal?"

"What else should you expect? My agent will carry on with it."

"That's great..."

"Thanks..."

"Your dinner must be a lump of snow by now. I must warm it up for you."

"Don't worry, Julie. I don't mind eating it that way."

"Are you crazy, Beck? It must have gone very cold by now."

"Don't you get it? Julie, I want nothing more to stress you up. I see that my long absence has done enough of that. I'm eating it cold."

"Good night dear..."

"Go to bed, Julie. Get some sleep, alright?"

"Okay."

"I will eat the delicious food you cooked for me after taking a shower. And then, I'll join you in bed, okay?"

"You haven't even tasted it yet."

"Did we get married today?"

"Yes, we just did. Two minutes ago," Julie said with an inviting faint smile that flashed across her face.

"Nope! I am well aware of what my lovely wife can do in the kitchen." I smiled.

Julie laughed. I savored it all, which showed in my quick smile.

"Beck, you're so wrong, baby," she replied with a smile, trying to be humble, "I'm the worst cook in America. Go ask somebody."

"No way...Julie is a renowned a chef! When is your TV show starting? I heard eighty million Americans can't wait to begin watching it. Our Black president and his wife inclusive. Three million more, worldwide, are getting ready to tune in. What are you still waiting for? Come on...Bring it on..."

Julie giggled and looked me in the eye before her face brandished that sort of a broad and warm infectious smile that singer Whitney Houston would always be remembered for.

"I don't know what you're talking about, Beck."

"Stop pretending!"

"I very much wish I knew."

"I am sure you do!"

"Honestly, I don't!"

"Stop lying like a little girl."

"Stop pulling my legs like a little boy who is up to something!"

"Okay...what do you know then?"

"It's simple! I know that I love you, Beck."

"That's great, I love you too."

"Thanks, my sunshine."

"I'll be with you soon."

After giving me another hug and planting a brief tender wet kiss on my jaw, Julie headed for our bedroom, leaving me wondering if I could ever bring myself to let her know the truth, especially about what that woman had done to me in the dark.

Chapter Fourteen

The last thing that I wanted to do was let Julie in on anything that would make her sore. After taking a quick shower, I ate my ice-cold meal of fried egg, potato chips, and chicken-ass stew. I went straight to lie beside Julie in the bed as soon as I finished. She pulled me closer to her breasts, full of warmth, after landing a kiss on the tip of my nose. Julie held me in her arms like I was the blood her heart pumped, the air her breathing depended on, the apple of her eyes that would remain even if life ceased to exist. My eyes were closed now immediately in relief as my body touched the bed. I had not felt what I felt now in what seemed like centuries—It felt as if I was being caressed by heaven as I was being fondled by the warmth and tenderness that Julie's body exuded, with every single heartbeat of hers. However, this bliss that the bodily closeness brought me could not thrive freely—My mind was not a place where one could truly find absolute peace and tranquillity. Julie must have thought that she had cuddled me to sleep when she began to sleep off without a single care in the world, like a child that was not even a year old. But, I was a man, lying still and wide awake, a rattled man determined to keep his wife happy.

My Julie was a smart woman, for sure, and I would be the biggest fool in America to harbor any strand of doubt about that. I knew the questions that she would ask if she did not see me start my work the next day. Only the heavens and I knew really well that with what the brains behind the so-called Crème Pictures had put me through, I would be the biggest fool on planet earth to still believe that I had an agreement to do a screenplay for them. Going back to them, under any circumstance, was more than a million centuries away from my plans. But, I had to start writing something the next day, for Julie's sake. I had to do anything to prevent her from suspecting that something was amiss. If I let her suspect something was up, she would not stop searching, probing, and prodding.

"I see you're working on it," she said to me the next day, all smiles, upon returning home from shopping for groceries when my fingers hit the letters on the keyboard of my laptop.

"I have to," I said, and I went on typing.

Julie did not get to keeping the things she was carrying in her hands—two colorful polythene bags, fully filled with the groceries. She walked straight to where I had been scripting my phony screenplay and gave me a sloppy kiss on my lips, which made my fingers stop. The fact that I was really writing nothing that was of any value was a very heavy load that weighed down my conscience, making my mouth not too welcome as that of Julie. I was lucky that she did not bother to ask why it was so. It was not that she did not notice it, but I guessed that she must have accepted herself to be the reason—having come to distract my creative exercise.

"What's the title?" she asked, her eyes aglow with lots of interest just like the sun.

"You should be knowing that by now..."

"Why?"

"You saw it in the letter, didn't you?"

"I forgot."

"'Don't Think You Can Get Away From Me. That's it."

"Intriguing! This must be a piece of cake for you."

"I will awe them with my very best."

Julie laughed out loud. "That's my man," she said, her sense of pride in me pouring out like a thick cloud of smoke from a chimney, doing nothing else, but billowing up the sky.

"I have to get back to work now. I was given three months to deliver. But I chose to do it within two."

"That's okay, Beck. I guess it's time to leave you alone. Writers love to be left alone, don't they?"

"It helps the creative process all the way."

"Fine, here I go."

I could gauge from the way in which Julie stepped off, doing a little cat-walk like a super model on a runway, that I was the biggest trophy in her love-life.

CHAPTER FIFTEEN

It was the same man who delivered the letter I got a month later, the same man that had delivered the offer from Crème Pictures, which put me through the mess whose aftermath now hung over my life like a dark cloud. It was disgusting to set my eyes again on the bad news courier as he handed me an envelope.

"What is it again?" I grumbled upon shutting the door after collecting the envelope. I had decided against ever meeting with any of those callous people that claimed to be the executives of Crème Pictures, no matter how lucrative an offer they might come up with. I was in agreement with my agent about this, having spoken about my ordeal with her. She had sympathized with me, stressing on the urgent need for us to discontinue with further interactions with any of those Spanish men and their masked woman.

***

We were in my agent's office in Los Angeles, which was very spacious and well-decorated. The air in there smelt of a sweet fragrance of which I did not know the name. Her four blonde female assistants were very busy—Two were reading manuscripts, while the other two were taking calls—each of them a young lady sitting at their own cubicles. Hanging on one of the blue walls in my agent's private office was a gigantic wrist watch that was too big to be worn on any hand. I had actually wondered what made my agent prefer that over a wall clock the very first time I had stepped into her office. The office had a large wooden table on which many sheets of paper lay in a heap. Apart from the biggest leather seat, on which my agent sat, there were three other smaller ones. A desktop computer and a laptop were also on top of the table. There was also a mantelpiece behind the seat on which my agent sat, stacked with books that had glossy covers, obviously authored by her clients. Titles like 'Gone with the Stars', 'Eloping with the Devil', and 'Kiss of Death' quickly caught my attention. They had not been there the last time I had come around.

"I'm sincerely sorry about what you had to go through, Mr. Beck," my agent had said to me, "If only you had waited for me to come with you." Her beautiful blue eyes shone. She had on a short black skirt, and she wore a blue-striped white turtle-neck shirt on top. Her shoes were black and had long heels.

"You were to see your doctor that day, remember?" I was quick to respond.

"If only you had decided to reschedule your meeting with them...I mean scheduling it on another day, a day—"

"I know exactly where you're going," I interrupted my agent, "You are wishing that you had gone with me, right?"

"That's it."

"That would not have made any difference, my dear. Who knows what would have happened to you had you come with me..."

"Maybe I would have been raped too, isn't it, Beck?"

"Yeah..." My agent looked at me and smiled. "No one can do that to me and get away with it," she said gently

And, when I told her about the woman with a mask, she smiled again. "Strange things," she said, shaking her head and smiling again, "Can this world be an interesting place without such strange things happening?"

"What are you talking about?" I really could not help but ask.

"She must have been a woman on a mission."

"How?"

"Beware of deceits. Beck, did you ever offend any woman who did not truly forgive you?"

"Not in this world."

"But in planet Mars, right?"

"Stop kidding about this now..."

"You may keep denying it, but the truth remains that you're so attractive that many women who can't get your attention can plan such a thing. What do you think, Beck?"

"That's absolutely ridiculous! I'm very much tempted right now to believe that you're out of your mind."

"I love to face things the way they are, Beck, and say them the way they are. I believe many women in America are dying to have you in their beds. Come on, Beck! Don't tell me you've suddenly forgotten that you're a charming man with a very attractive square jaw. They all are dying for a piece of you! You don't want to crucify them for making your nude body the object of their fantasies, do you? They love you! They think you're one of the sexiest men alive." I was so astonished at how my agent talked. I couldn't believe my ears.

"What kind of a talent and literary agent are you?" I had to ask.

"One of a kind, Beck."

"Yes, I truly believe that. But don't make me think otherwise."

"An agent that's not afraid to tell her clients the truth."

"What truth?"

"Oh.... never mind," my agent was quick to say. "Some of those misplaced words we sometimes speak," she further said with a smile that was a bit sly. "What about your wife?" she went on to ask.

"Even if I did offend her, I swear she would not have gone to that crazy extent for a revenge."

"How sure can you be about that?"

"Stop kidding."

My agent laughed. "Have you considered getting the cops to sniff around for you?" she asked, "I mean getting those guys arrested? You could bring on the Los Angeles Police Department."

"I want none of those guys meddling into my affairs."

"Why?"

"Let the LAPD mind their business!" I lied. I did not want to involve the cops because I did not want the news of what happened to me to go public in any way. It was my chief goal to make sure that Julie did not get to know about any of this. "Let's talk about the woman with a mask," I continued, "Why did you say that she must be a woman on a mission?"

"Never mind, Beck. I was only thinking aloud."

"What mission do you think it could be?"

"Let's talk another day, Mr. Beck. I've got piles of manuscripts to read. Besides that, I will soon be on my way to getting some money that is due to you and some other of my clients. I also have a lunch date later with a New-York-based editor that's currently here in L.A."

That was it. We never had the chance to talk about the masked woman owing to my agent's extremely busy schedule for the day. She was a young woman having long wavy blonde hair that went on to touch her shoulders. She was quite tall and had long attractive legs and was born and raised in New York.

***

The mail that I received was from them again, Crème Pictures, just like I had believed. I began to read the letter that I found when I tore up the envelope.

Hi Beck,

It's been so long. I kept saying that you would not get away from me. But you never took me seriously. A turtle never gets away from its shell. I'm glad to inform you that I have succeeded in taking something away from you. I'm so glad that I made love to you recently. Tasting the splendor around your groin was a special treat—It is the best thing I've ever done in my entire life. Thanks for being there for me when I needed you badly. Please find a document enclosed with this letter for more information. What gave you the guts to think that you could get away from me? Have a nice day, my love. There is really nothing like Crème Pictures. I made it all up to achieve my greatest life ambition. Have a nice day, my love. I can rest now.

Trisha. [The masked woman]

I could not believe what I had read. So, Trisha was the masked woman? This question popped up in my mind and unsettled me at once. Getting to know that Trisha had been the woman that raped me was so disturbing.

"You idiot!" I screamed, referring to Trisha, as if she stood close to me, "Stay away from me! Leave my life alone! Can't you understand that?" I screamed further. There was no way Julie would not have heard me loud and clear had she been home. However, on that day, furniture and other stuff in the living room were my only companions. Scrappy, our little dog, ran into the living room alarmed by my scream. It stared at me like it understood what I had screamed about. Then it mounted a couch, lay down, and looked at me again in such a way that seemed to show that it was telling me that it would all be fine in the end.

"What the hell do you know, Scrappy?" I said to it. Scrappy barked twice in a way which I could understand so very well—It was telling me that it needed something to eat. Feeding a dog was not my priority now. I was very eager to find what Trisha had left for me in the document that she said was enclosed. I quickly reached for it and began reading it. I felt okay until I got to the part where I saw the word that confirmed it all. My head felt as if a sledgehammer had crashed upon it from a skyscraper. I went numb completely, from my head to my toes. It was as if time had stood still for me, and my heart had stopped pumping the red blood that it is known to do. I was still alive though. I knew this because my eyes wavered again to the spot where the all-important word was. I saw it again but told myself that it was not true. If there was anything I wanted to believe at that time, it would never be that the one who conducted the test was right. I tried forcing myself to believe that the person was totally wrong. But, the more I tried to tell myself that what I had seen was wrong, the more its reality kept resonating within me.

"It's not positive!" I wailed, in spite of the fact that the document in my hands said it was. "No...This is not happening to me...No! No...Trisha! You are not pregnant by me! You bastard! You evil! No! No! No! Not for me.... No! Not for me..."

I tore the pregnancy test result into pieces and tore the letter. The envelope that contained them was not left out. I set them all on fire. Tears spilt from my eyes as I watched the smoke rising from the burning papers, the fire eating them up fast, bringing back to me the memories of how it all started. If only someone had not gone away, away from my life.

Chapter Sixteen

If only Julie had not left me upon learning that I was hell-bent on writing my eleventh story. If only she had stayed with me and persevered a little longer. I wondered if it was a crime for one to aspire to have one's story used for a movie by a Hollywood studio. My first story had been a story about a young girl who came to planet Earth from the moon. She had lots of money and wanted to buy up everything that all the human beings owned. However, all humans disagreed to sell their belongings to her, and she began to unleash the full weight of her might on the world. It became her mission to conquer the world and own everything in it amidst fierce resistance from brave men and women in the world. I had titled my story 'The Clash' and had mailed it to Columbia Pictures Executives, hoping that they would love it. I only received a reply after a long while. My talent and effort were appreciated, but my story was rejected. I swore never to give up, strongly believing that it was only a matter of time before my dream would come through. So, I mailed another story that I had written to Paramount Pictures. This one had been titled 'Species'—it was the story of the coming of time when man would begin to copulate with robots and produce unique hybrids, which would be capable of doing so many things that man cannot do. Nothing but rejection was what I received again. I was told that no studio would ever love to work with 'Species.' However, I shoved my failure aside and kept on trying.

"Die or keep trying!" I kept telling myself again and again, the phrase being the stimulant that I got addicted to in order to be able to press on against all odds. My resolve was, however, getting tested in a stiff manner. Julie had been the one carrying us all that time—the sales job that she had before we got married was getting the bills paid. We hoped that my attempts would fetch me a deal quickly, one that we expected would catapult us into a better life. We even reached a time where the lean amount that Julie earned got strained so much that she began to see me as a heavy burden on her financial shoulders. That was when she started to see my insistence on writing to earn a living as a waste of precious time—time that ought to be spent doing jobs that would yield quick cash.

"It's not going to work this way," Julie kept telling me, "These bills are popping up. We can't keep up with them like this, I swear to God. Are we not going to have a baby? I want to get pregnant soon! That would mean more bills. More bills, Beck. Don't tell me this ambition of yours has got you castrated. We just have to make some changes in here. Sit up, Beck! We need more money in here!"

"I understand..." This was all that I could say.

"Oh no, Beck! You're not going to keep telling me that you understand and still have your ass at home, trying to write twenty-four-seven!"

"I understand, Julie. I really do."

"I need action, Beck. Action!"

"Okay. I will swing right into action from tomorrow."

"Now you're talking like my man."

I bowed down to her pressure and took up a part-time job in a large boutique where I sold clothes for a female reality-TV celebrity, who was six years younger than me and was named Chelsea. I only did this job for three hours a day since I still wanted to have a large chunk of time to weave stories for movie studios, even though it felt nice to be making some bucks, which I channelled towards the running of our home and life together. But, the rising cost of living later proved that I needed to cut down more on my writing time, work more hours in the boutique, or pick up a second job in order to raise the amount of money that I earned. Julie's pressure came at me again, but I had become an impervious rock now—most unwilling to budge even when it made no sense for me at all to continue to try to sell a story. My tenth story had just failed at this time. So, Julie would not hear that I was bent on writing and working on my eleventh story. In her judgment, I was a lazy man, very blind to reality around me, reality as bright as sparkling stars hanging in the sky. She had had enough of me.

CHAPTER SEVENTEEN

My tenth story, 'Twisted Mission', was a story about a-nineteen-year-old Nigerian suicide bomber, named Hakeem, who was trained by Al Qaeda operatives in Yemen and sent on a suicide mission to France. He was specifically instructed to target French immigration officials that were in charge of handling the deportation of many a Roma from their ramshackle residences. Hakeem was about to detonate huge explosives that were strapped to his body, when something that had never been known to strike a suicide bomber before, struck him—Love. It was love that arrested his suicide mission. Hakeem saw and fell in love at first sight with a gypsy girl who was being deported. That was how the life of all folks, which would have been blasted out of existence, got saved. It then became Hakeem's mission to locate the gypsy girl, whom, he felt, could not be more than twenty years old. It was love. What a feeling. That was love! Instead of detonating explosives, Hakeem began to sing 'It must be Love', a love song recorded by a famous American country music artist, Don Williams.

Hakeem knew that the girl would either be from Romania or from Bulgaria, and he was determined to do whatever it would take to track her down, only to let her know that he loved her so much. However, upon choosing not to detonate the explosives, Hakeem had dared to disobey his mentors who had a lot of influence on him, and was being hunted quite seriously for destruction.

I saw a copy of The New Yorker magazine in my closet two days after I had finished working on 'Anatomy of Their Fury', which was the title that I gave to my eleventh story. It was Julie who had bought the magazine. I picked it up and flipped from page to page in search of something that would arouse my interest. I found nothing until I got to the section on fiction. It was the title of a story in there that aroused my curiosity at once. I found it captivating the moment I set my eyes on the words that made it up—'When Love is Angry'. Being lured in by the title, I started to read the story. The story arrested me right from the very first word. Its first sentence consumed me. And, I was totally enthralled by the time I had finished the first paragraph. Dropping the story was no option at all. It made for a delightful reading experience. After having read only about three quarters of it, I was mesmerized by it. I was never going to stop now. Just then, the thoughts began to spring up in my mind, suggesting that I send a copy of my eleventh story to The New Yorker's fiction editor. A frown descended on my face at once—It said it all. I did not fancy the idea one bit, being already stuck on targeting the major Hollywood studios. I got back to reading the story in the magazine. *Try it now! You never know what might happen! Try it now! There are many paths in which a dream is actualized! Try The New Yorker! Try The New Yorker!* These thoughts were not ready to relent. They kept hitting me and striking me, kicking and eating into my concentration to the extent that I could read no further.

"Shut the fuck up!" I screamed out loud at them as if they were humans. They died down shortly after, leaving me with enough peace to get on with the story that I was so interested in reading to the end. But, I had only read another paragraph of the intriguing story when those thoughts struck again, rising and falling in my head, swinging and mingling. I got completely distracted and looked up from the story without a hint of delight showing on my face.

"Fine!" I said, finally relenting to their pressure. "If that is what it will take for you guys to leave me alone...It's worth a try. I will try it! You all must shut up now! Shut up..."

It was almost as if those thoughts could hear me. They did not bother me again and I read through the rest of the story in peace.

I sent a copy of my eleventh story to the fiction editor of The New Yorker by email the next day, even though I did not believe it to be the right thing. However, that action did not stop me from mailing another copy of the story to Paramount Pictures again. The studio's response came to me after three weeks— It presented nothing different. It was the same response that I had come to be so used to—"*Nice piece! But, we feel this is not fit for our current plans. Thank you so much for thinking of us.*" I was convinced that I had written a great story that a studio ought to pick up for a movie. I was convinced that I had strived to produce my absolute best even when things were at their absolute worst. These convictions led me to think of sending my story to a different studio. All the while, I never thought about the submission that I had made to The New Yorker even for a second, as I was not expecting anything good to come from there. Why should I? They do not even make movies, do they? It was after eight weeks had passed after receiving the response of rejection from Paramount Pictures that things began to change. I had gone online in search of information about a Hollywood studio I could send my story to, when I had a sudden hunch to check my email account on Google.

"What else is going to be there other than stupid junk mails?" I protested at first, "What else...but mails from the ever-inventive advanced fee fraudsters from Nigeria, Europe, and Asia? Anyway, let me just have a look. It's been long since I checked my mail." When I signed in, I saw that I had ten messages, and one of them was from The New Yorker.

"Time to see another rejection, The New Yorker style," I said and laughed a little, "Well, let me see what they actually have for me. Surely nothing good can come from those guys..."

I clicked on the subject of the email, which was 'OUR RESPONSE', and waited for the message to show up. Once I began to read their response, it got clear to me that I had been wrong all the time. Of course, I knew that they were not going to offer to make a movie based on my story, but offering to publish it was enough to gladden my heart. However, no offer of any amount of money was made. I knew The New Yorker had a wide reach and enjoyed huge readership. Publishing my story would mean that lots of people would be able to see my art. I quickly replied, telling the editor how glad I was to learn of their interest in publishing it. I could not wait for it to run. I felt as if CNN and Fox News were about to beam my artistry to millions of TV screens across the world. It took some time for the reality of this matter to begin sinking in on me. I had not known the magnitude of what I had achieved until my story began to be serialized in The New Yorker. It felt like an accomplishment having it there.

"Yeah, now lots of people will get to know about Beck's talent!" I kept saying, as I walked around my home, drunk with joy—the jubilation was overflowing. I could not contain it, of course. Scrappy kept looking at me like I had gone crazy, as I mounted my bed, springing up and down, tossing pillows around, and screaming my head off. "Beck's got talent! Beck's got it...Come on now, everybody... Come on now! Beck's got it! I got it going on right here..."

Wait a second! My jubilation had been premature. Something much bigger was on its way.

Chapter Eighteen

I just ought to have taken a little sip and delayed the party—Getting my story published was just a little scratch on the surface. I did not know it until Paramount Pictures gave me a call. The executives there had seen my story run on The New Yorker, and they were well aware that lots of readers, with numbers probably running into hundreds of millions, liked it very much. The reviews that I saw were very strong. All of them were just so fantastic that I nearly got tempted to say they were all a bunch of lies, made up by some seasoned literary critics who just wanted things to swing in my favor. But, the whole truth, and nothing but the truth was that my story had become a huge hit. This made the executives at Paramount Pictures suddenly see a goldmine in it and want to acquire it for a movie project. Mr. Ken Shades, who was one of the executives at Paramount Pictures, gave me a call from there. "We've thoroughly examined your work, Mr. Blades," he said, "And we think it is excellent. Very well written, Mr. Blades!"

"Are you talking about 'Anatomy of Their Fury'?" I asked, as if I did not know.

"Sure. The masterpiece. It'll make a grand picture, and we are very much interested in making that happen."

"That's great," I replied, "Get on with it."

"We would like to start by talking with your agent."

It was almost as if the amount of joy that I felt inside was going to explode when I hung up. I considered receiving a call from Paramount Pictures a huge achievement. I screamed so loudly out of joy that I lost my voice. But, there was no one else at home to celebrate with me but Scrappy. I decided to go out of my extremely miserly way to get two packs of nice and delicious dog-food for my dear Scrappy. That choice took a hundred-dollar bill away from my pocket, enough to get us fed for three weeks. But, who cared? It was my conclusion that Scrappy, the ever-bubbly brown dog that stayed with me throughout the very rough times in spite of being fed only once a day, deserved a special treat—the very best a dog can get.

I got a call from a woman the following day, an agent, offering to provide me with professional representation. She said that she had discovered that I was a very good writer. Since I have never had an agent before, I was quite excited about the prospect of having one. However, I decided to put my answer on hold, only to check out her profile. She was twenty-two and awesome, having great deals running for her numerous clients who were high-profile screenwriters, novelists, playwrights, Hollywood actors, and presenters. What a league of very talented people she had brought into the fold at such a young age. I thought her feats were quite fantastic. I would have been a lunatic to let her pass me by. I placed a call to her L.A. office, letting her know that I was very interested in having her run my affairs. I signed the agency agreement papers she forwarded to me, and she has been my agent since then.

I was now quite an acclaimed writer, and I imagined that there would be a future for me which would require me to be doing screenplays. So, I went ahead to read up quite a few materials on screenplay writing. I further satisfied my appetite to learn and hone my skills by attending a number of creative-writing workshops, whose key emphasis were on crafting compelling screenplays. I thought that I had been dreaming when my agent gave me call a year after I had become her client—she was the harbinger of the cheering news that she had been able to secure a deal for me to do the screenplay of my own story which Paramount Pictures had now purchased. I exploded in laughter upon hearing the news, tears of joy wetting up my eyes.

"I had always sensed that a time like this would come...But not this fast," I said to my agent, completely overwhelmed.

"Congratulations, Mr. Blades," she said before going on to give me some advise that I could not help but appreciate, "For you to keep going places, you've got to keep learning new things. Don't ever think that you've got the magic touch. No one has! There's really no such thing. One gets better by working hard and by never being complacent, and by moving on to bigger themes each time one writes..."

She had handled my interests well and in a professional manner, letting me in on the big sum of money that was waiting to become mine in a week's time. The demand for my talent was not about to let up in the least. More studio executives kept swarming around my agent like bees, dangling juicy deals, all in their desperate bid to have me write stories and screenplays for their next movie projects. The whole thing overwhelmed me. I would have died if I had to accept all the offers. Working nine to five, seven days a week, would not have been enough to complete that much work. It was indeed a very sweet feeling to be so hot in Hollywood. And, I kept feeling Bosco Jude bursting out in a long and loud laughter, being full of joy that I had made it at last. Who's Bosco Jude? Be patient! It's time to delve into my background.

CHAPTER NINETEEN

My full name is Beck Blades. And I do not have a middle name. My buck-toothed Dad said that it was not necessary when I had asked him why he did not give me one at birth. Mom had agreed with him. Their names? Never mind. I loved calling them Dad and Mom. And, I still love to. Dad was a tall and burly blonde. Mom was a blonde too, but she was slim and really pretty. Surprisingly, I am no blonde. I wondered sometimes as a kid what must have happened to my hair.

"Mom, did you make a plan with the doctors to dye my hair black when I was born?"

Mom only stared at me, her mouth-agape and eyes wide open. I could not read her eyes for information then, but I now know that it showed how weird she thought it was to hear that kind of a question from a kid of six. However, she did not stop at her flabbergasted look. Mom loved to tell Dad about these things.

"Go and find out about the science of genetics, Beck," Dad had said to me when Mom had told him, "Or make sure you do well in science so that you can go ahead and study genetics. Then you will understand why your own hair is black..."

Dad loved talking about science even though he did not receive education beyond junior high. I thought that he ought to have gone ahead and become a professor in one of the branches of science. Leaving all those prospects, he became a street gangster, and later married Mom as a repentant sinner who was converted by some Christian missionaries. Mom and Dad's commitment to the affairs of our local church was outstanding. Their dedication to things related to Christianity never betrayed any trace of the fact that they had a dirty past. Their 'Praise the Lord' screams were always the loudest in church. They wanted me to be as spiritual, attend church on all the Sundays of every year, as well as memorize all the verses in the Holy Bible as clearly as my name.

"Sin is the one thing that shortens the long hands of God from reaching man with his goodies." This is what Mom and Dad told me a million times while I was growing up. I had always had a question then, which I could not ask for the fear of Dad kicking my ass. All I wanted so much to ask them was why the both of them strayed into lifestyles that do not please God as youngsters, when they knew so well that God's hands would be hindered from delivering the goodies to them.

Mom and Dad were experts at presenting themselves as saints to me. But, their pasts took up the nature of pregnancy in the sense that it could not stay hidden forever. It was a thing that they could keep from me for only ten years. Grandmom told me everything, whereas granddad acted as if he did not know anything. Dad was into a lot of drugs. It was only thanks to the missionaries, who helped him come clean, that he was able to earn the title of ex-junky. And, mom loved to roll with guys that did drugs. It is not a big surprise now as to how she met Dad. Dad loved going on trips to Vegas whenever he was a little high, so that he could catch some fun with the daughters of Eve who fuelled the pleasure industry there. Mom used to be one of those daughters who traded pleasure from juicy spots between their thighs for dollar signs. Dad used to love those spots more than anything else once he got high, especially on crack cocaine. And, that is how I was formed to begin my journey into this world. Mom later made contact with an organization called Hookers for Jesus, founded by a former hooker, which aimed at taking hookers off the streets and into the tender loving care of Jesus, who brings peace that surpasses all understanding. That was how Mom was saved. She began going to church, where she met Dad, and they struck a romance. Somewhere down the line, my issue had to pop out. Mom had informed Dad that he had got her pregnant on one of their many nights together in Vegas when their libidos were absolutely uncontrollable, surging up like a fountain. Mom said that even though she had aborted many babies, some forces, she could not explain what, held her back from getting rid of me. It was thanks to those forces that I was born, otherwise I would have ended up as thrash in a clinic where babies are butchered. Mom had her hooker friends take me to a foster home as if I had just dropped from the sky. And, she had to go to the foster home later to fetch me. DNA tests were handy to prove that she was indeed my parent. Even though Dad was a man who was very much in love, he still ran DNA tests for an answer that he needed. Only after the results confirmed it to him, did he believe that he was my Dad.

Unlike most other kids, I had the special privilege of seeing Mom and Dad get married. I was glad to know that I had a Mom and a Dad after all the rooms, walls, smells, and the entire world of foster home, which I grew up in, had drummed it into my head each day, for six years, that I was an orphan. I posed with Mom and Dad, the flashes from those cameras nearly blinding me. I noticed that it was not a wedding that the whole of America knew of. But, it recorded enough attendance from many Christians who either attended the same church with Dad and Mom, or the ones who worked in the same soybean farm with them. I saw Dad blow Mom a kiss on her lips. "What's that?" I had said to myself, thinking that Dad was about to swallow Mom. I almost stepped off from where I stood to kick his ass with my left leg. I only relaxed when I saw him take his lips away from those of Mom. I expected to see Mom crying, but to my surprise, she was laughing. She was extremely happy. I saw the two of them cut a tall wedding cake to the admiration and applause of everyone in attendance. Then, Dad picked up and carried Mom in his hands, with Mom kissing his right cheek without a care in this world as to who was watching. I thought they were being promiscuous in the eyes of a crowd. But now, I know better. They were simply showing off public displays of affection associated with weddings. I must confess that when I had turned twenty, I noticed that most couple who did that on their wedding day started cheating on each other once their wedding ceremonies became history. I did not fancy that. Julie had once asked me why I left all the kissing to her on our wedding day. I told her that my style was to reserve it until we got into our bedroom.

You're welcome to delve more with me into my background! My tale is truly far from being over.

Chapter Twenty

My Mom had to take a break from Vegas, and she returned to Nebraska when I got big enough to make her tummy bulge, throwing her out of business. That's how Nebraska became the place of my birth. 'Live-and-die-in-Nebraska' was my life slogan until fame opened its doors unto me. I never wanted to leave behind this part of America that I loved so much for anything less. Nebraska, my Nebraska. Nebraska of agrarian economy, home of rocky mountain oysters and calf fries and cowboy caviar delicacies, rich in soybean cultivation, having safe quiet streets, on top of which lies the open-wide sky. Nebraska frees one from urban stress, while infusing a nice scent in its breeze and offering the sound of melodious chirping birds. Both Mom and Dad hailed from Nebraska, and I met Julie there as well. Julie's mother had divorced her father and returned to Nebraska from Texas after having won the custody battle for the two-year-old Julie, against her often unstable and alcoholic father. A court had ruled that he was not fit to properly discharge his fatherly responsibilities towards the little Julie.

I was not good at math and science in school, and it made Mom and Dad mad at me. They even went ahead to tell me that I would not amount to anything in life because of this shortcoming of mine.

"Let me tell you where the real deal is, son," Dad used to say to me constantly, "It is in excelling in the sciences and in math. You can be nothing worthy of praise in life without excelling in them."

"Yes, he's saying the truth," Mom often supported Dad this way, "Literature and the arts won't give you a good prestige. Channel your interest in them to science and math, Beck."

"Mom," I called.

"Yes," Mom responded.

"Dad," I called again.

"I'm listening," Dad said.

"So, could it be right to say that the two of you are failures now?" I asked them.

"Why should that be of any concern to you?" Mom quickly responded. I saw that Dad was going to reply in the same manner, but Mom had beaten him to it.

"I know the two of you never excelled in math and science," I answered.

"Shut up!" Dad had screamed at me, his eyeballs dilated so wide that I thought he would strangle me.

My dad in his pure form was crude and brutal and was even capable of killing, but for the sake of Christianity which came to rule his life. He knew that he had a reputation to protect before the Reverend Pastor of our church and the other church members. I knew that he would have been hitting me hard all day for the kind of questions I loved to ask him—questions that pointed, in one way or another, to his ugly past. He did not want to appear as a sinner before the Reverend. That was it. It was not as if he truly gave a damn about all that Christianity had to teach. However, the missionaries thought that they had truly converted a soul. They couldn't have been more wrong. Even Mom would have long ended up as his punching bag if not for the prying eyes of our church members. The savage beast in Dad was very much far from being gone. On a certain day, when our Reverend visited Mom and Dad, I could not help but laugh, though not openly, of course, at the way they both ran up and down like little rats, all in a bid to impress. Dad went as far as cleaning up the couch with his ass. Smiling at our Reverend, he said, "No more dust on this now, Reverend. Make yourself comfortable, holy man of God."

"Only God is holy. Thanks, Mr. Blades," replied our Reverend. And, while Dad cleaned up the dust with his ass, Mom had already scurried to the kitchen. I wondered what she was up to, after having told me that it was a day to fast. Dad had the supreme authority at home to declare any day of his choice a day of fasting. He always said that fasting was quite essential to cleansing us and scraping away blotches of sin on our souls. Hunger was dealing with me severely. So, I was quite sure that no one would blame me at all for not being able to restrain myself from salivating when Mom dashed back to the living room, her face full of ravishing smiles, with a bowl of fried turkey that could not have weighed less than ten pounds. All that for the Reverend? That too on a day of fasting? Wow! The insides of my belly wobbled. They growled like a bull dog that had charged. I had seen that meat a few minutes before our Reverend came visiting. It had been whole, and now parts of it were already missing. A day of fasting indeed! Mom and Dad must have helped themselves and thought that I would not find out.

"Praise the Lord," our Reverend kept saying as he devoured the rest of the meat, rolling his lengthy tongue from side to side, occasionally casting me a glance, much to my annoyance.

"Amen and Amen and Amen..." Dad and Mom chanted in response.

"Teach a child the way of the Lord," said our Reverend, when he was done, only cracked bones remaining in the bowl, "I hope you're doing that to Beck."

"Always," Dad was the first to respond.

"He won't depart from it," added Mom.

"Says the good book," our Reverend replied.

"A family that fasts and prays together is the apple of the Lord's eyes," said our Reverend when he got up, farted twice, and was about to leave. But, you should have seen Mom and Dad, they were something else—They even chanted "Amen" when gas escaped from the Reverend's asshole. What the hell were they thinking? They welcomed it as if the Reverend had sprayed a little bit of pleasant-smelling celebrity fragrance in our living room. Wow...

I often wondered how long it would take to expose all the pretence from the deacon whom I called my Dad, and Mom, the deaconess.

Dumb, later, became my second name, the reason being that I consistently failed to excel in math and science. It did not take a long time before I was given a third name by Mom and Dad. It was "Empty-shell."

"What the fuck's your name, son?" Dad would ask, mocking me.

"Empty-shell," I would answer, pretending to like it very much.

"Now fuck your fucking monkey ass and tell me your name, son," he would often add.

"Empty-shell."

"What's your motherfucking name?" Mom would say.

"Empty-shell," I would respond without having a choice. And, it was during this time in my life that I knew that using the F-word freely was not a big deal at all. As long as I did not use it in our church, it was quite alright. I gleaned that from the best couple in our church—Mom and Dad—according to our Reverend Pastor.

My new name made me craft a short story about a boy who became successful and famous after people had said that he would amount to nothing. I had titled it 'In Spite of All.' I went through my story at least ten times when I finished writing it in order to catch any errors that might have gone unnoticed as I wrote. I had heard about the importance of going through a story again, after it had been written, in my literature class. My final judgment was that my piece was quite good. It gave me the confidence to give it to my elementary school literature teacher to take a look at it. Her name was Miss Florence.

"Good Morning, Miss Florence," I said once I got inside her office with two sheets of paper that contained my story in my hands. Miss Florence was always kind, gentle, and receptive. She smiled at me, while her eyes hovered to the paper on my right hand. She was an affectionate tall woman of twenty-six, had a round face, with shapely lips, black hair, and a jaw with sparse hair growth. I thought that she must have been half a man because Dad had told me that only men carried moustaches. I believed that completely because I had never seen a hair grow on Mom's jaw. Seeing those of Miss Florence, however, made me know that Dad was not correct.

"Good morning, little Beck, how are you today?" Miss Florence greeted me.

"I'm good, Miss Florence."

"Could I be of any help to you?"

"Yes, Miss Florence. I've just written a story..."

Miss Florence loved to read out stories from books to us in class. She loved to read us stories from books like *Peter Pan*, *The Wizard of Oz*, *Oliver Twist*, *Little Red Riding Hood*, *The Famous Five*, and *The Adventures of Tom Sawyer*. She encouraged us to keep watching *Sesame Street*, saying that it was good for us. I agreed with her because I immediately got hooked when I saw my first episode of the show, falling in love with its characters, especially when Michael Jackson came on as a guest. It was quite an educative and an entertaining show. I even watched it a few times as an adult. Old habits often do not die, do they?

"Oh, that's great," said Miss Florence the moment I told her that I had written a story, "That's fantastic, Beck. And I guess you want me to take a look at it?"

"Yeah." I said nervously, while handing over my story to Miss Florence.

She had been writing something in a diary when I came in. So, that had to wait. Miss Florence began to read my story immediately. I waited for her, observing her face for any trace that would enable me to figure out how she liked it. Miss Florence kept reading to me. Her face was blank and showed no expression of any kind. I expected to see her smile if my story was any good. So, when her face showed nothing, I concluded that I had not done a good job after all. It was only after Miss Florence had finished reading my story that I saw her face light up with a smile. She looked me in the eye and said, "This is brilliant, Beck! I didn't know that you could do something like this. It's a fantastic piece! Can I keep it? I want to read it again and again."

"Sure."

"This is great, Beck. Keep it up!"

And, Miss Florence was not the kind of person that would just do nothing more.

Chapter Twenty One

Miss Florence did not just stop there, truly. I only got to know that when I heard people talking about my story. She had sent it to the editor of the school's literary magazine that was called 'Spate.' My story got published and won an award for the best story of the year. It brought fifty dollars into my pocket. I was full of joy and immensely proud of my achievement. However, I never told Mom and Dad about it, knowing full well that they would have no words of encouragement for me. I did not go ahead and write more stories as people might have expected of me, in spite of the accolades that heaped on me in school as a result of my little success. Mom and Dad kept drumming science and math into my head each time I returned from school. They kept me struggling with them. It was excruciatingly hard because God gave me no endowment for them. I tried explaining to Dad and Mom that I wasn't born to be good at math and science, but they would have none of that. They were quick to compare me to Bond, the son of our family friends. Bond was a kid with precocious talent for anything related to Information Technology. Dad and Mom were so proud of Bond that they talked about him so often that it made me feel as if I had no gift at all. If only there had been a legitimate way to get Bond and make him their son, Mom and Dad would not have hesitated to exploit it. Unfortunately for them, Bond's parents were alive and well. Had they been dead, Mom and Dad would have seriously considered adopting Bond. And, that would have really made me more of the junk-child in the house.

"Look at Bond. He's so good at Math and Science. He will get a job in Microsoft or Google one day, and will rule Silicon Valley." These were the words that Dad and Mom kept speaking which really left me feeling worthless, as if I was nothing more than just a piece of trash that God had just dropped into this world.

I was beginning to believe that writing was something that was not worth taking seriously until I learnt from Miss Florence that Bosco Jude would be coming to my school. She also let me know that she had sent Bosco a copy of my published story. Bosco Jude was a famous American novelist, hailing from Little Rock, Arkansas. He had many titles to his credit, ten of which were bestsellers, all already sold to the Hollywood studios for movie projects. Bosco was out on a reading tour of certain selected schools.

"I never knew that he would even find time to read your story," Miss Florence went on to tell me, "I sent it to him because of my conviction that it deserved the attention of someone as renowned as him. And he sent me a heart-warming response. I'm sure that you must be interested in knowing what he has said."

Miss Florence was absolutely right. I was thrilled that she had gone to such an extent for me. I found that very encouraging. That alone reinvigorated, a little, my lost zeal to go on writing.

"Yes, Miss Florence. What did he say?"

"He said, and I quote, 'This kid, Beck, has shown amazing promise in this piece. I think a kid born to rule the literary world has been evading our radar. Thank goodness that I have been lucky to witness only a bit of the vast brilliance that is yet to come from him. I look forward to meeting with this budding genius.'"

There was no force capable of convincing me not to take writing seriously when compliments of that magnitude came through to me.

Chapter Twenty Two

I made it my mission to present Bosco with another story by the time his tour would bring him to my school. Home had become the worst place for me to write because Mom and Dad would tear up anything they saw me scribble if it wasn't a bunch of numbers and symbols. No creative writing of any sort, no drawing, no sketching, became the military decrees that I had to live with. My storytelling capability was a lamb struggling to grow up, while Mom and Dad, a pair of lions, were determined to see that it never became a sheep. I knew that I had to be inventive, take some risks in order to escape their siege. Instead of trying to write in the comfort of my room, I began sneaking inside the garage and writing there even though it was not a good enough place for such an activity. However, it was quiet, the noise rarely filtering into it. Dad did not come in there much ever since his car, an old red Mercedes Benz, broke down and remained a relic of a lost age in there. The garage had a foul smell that was strong and repulsive, but I did not care one bit. All that mattered to me was a cover, away from the prying eyes of Dad and Mom, under which I could craft a story for the eyes of novelist Bosco Jude. I finished writing a story which I titled 'Genesis.' After reading it over and over again, I thought that it was good enough and took it to school the day Bosco came around.

Meeting Bosco was a terrific experience for me. I took lots of pride in the fact that I got a chance to shake his hands. I took a good look at him—His grey hair was overgrown, his moustache a little bit bushy, and a rather short man. He wore black jeans and had a red-stripped green shirt on top. When my glances fell on his feet, I saw that he wore a pair of brown sandals that did not appear fanciful in any way, let alone expensive. But, I was not surprised that he looked a bit shabbily dressed. Dad had told me long ago that writers were the worst dressed people on planet earth. He even went ahead to say that they lacked any sense of style, speaking with an air as if he was a fashion icon himself. I did not care about Bosco's appearance. I thought his intellect was what mattered. He sure had more than enough money to fund the launch of any clothing line and buy lots of collections from designers, but I thought clothes were a long way down in the list of his priorities. My interactions with him informed me about where his actual priority lay—He got fulfilment from inspiring kids and getting them to shine like a million stars with their gifts. No amount of wearing designer clothes would even come any close to doing this for him.

When Bosco read my new story, he thought that it was great too. He did say something which showed that he knew what I was going through at home. "Don't worry that your mom and dad are not on your side," he had said to me, to my astonishment. Who could have told him? Was he good at reading minds and far into the lives of folks? Was he a psychic? I could answer none of these questions. My conclusion was that his IQ must have been more than one-hundred-and-sixty-five for him to have detected that I had problems at home. However, the length and breadth of it all was that Bosco opted to follow me home without my asking for it.

"Come on," he had said to me, "Let's get going." He got into his car and waited for me to get in. I hesitated for a while. It was not that I was not excited to have a ride back home with a famous writer. But, all I could think of was how uncomfortable Dad and Mom would feel about it. "Let's get going, Beck! Come on!" Bosco further urged me.

"I don't care!" I murmured to myself and hopped into Bosco's car. Its engine roared to life at once, and we got rolling.

"I would love to see your parents," he said to me. I became glad he said that.

"Are you a psychic?" I asked. Bosco only laughed. His laughter showed that he already knew why I popped up such a question.

"Yes and no! I'm not one because I'm not in practice. However, I am because that stuff flows in my blood. Never mind, Beck. I sensed you're oppressed. Like I said, it is in my blood. I felt so much oppressed energy flow from your home the moment you came close to me. Your energy is alive, but not enough to completely repel the strong force coming from your parents. Being the channel through which you came into this world gives them some advantage for now. Let me talk to them. Whatever is meant to be will be when the time comes for it to be."

CHAPTER TWENTY THREE

Smiles, as wide as the length and breadth of the whole of the United States of America, would have been lighting up their faces if it were Bill Gates that had followed me home. It would have been the same if it was the founder of Google, that of Facebook or Twitter or any CEO from Silicon Valley. Dad and Mom would have popped many bottles of champagne even if it would mean that they would have to take a loan to do that. I saw their faces crease in displeasure when Bosco introduced himself as a novelist. Dad and Mom rarely read about writers. So, there was no way that they would have known that Bosco was a novelist of distinction. They did not think Bosco to be worth dipping his lips into even the cheapest wine or any other kind of cheap drink which we had at home. They detested him the moment he introduced himself as a novelist. Bosco became their enemy, who, they believed, had been making me stray from the path that they had chosen for me. It was as if Bosco had spoken to no one at all when he went ahead to tell Dad and Mom that they had a budding literary genius in me. Some hostility started to hang in the air the moment he had introduced himself. He told them how wrong it was to despise my gift just because it was not in line with their expectations. He voiced his conviction that I would go places as a storyteller. He demanded that Mom and Dad should encourage me. However, all Mom and Dad did was run their stares all over Bosco as he spoke. I am sure that they must have thought, judging him by the way he dressed, that he was wallowing in abject poverty. I saw Mom frown hard after taking a look at Bosco's hair. I could understand what her frown said—"A person who can't even afford to fix his hair is talking about the genius in our son"—That was what it said. Mom and Dad found Bosco's presence so disgusting that none of them spoke any word in response when he finished speaking. Silence dominated the room as if no souls were present to break it. I was immersed in growing discomfort. Bosco's visit had turned out to be one big farce that lacked the right sting that could change the minds of Dad and Mom. It was a drop of water that came face to face with a huge impervious rock. I wanted Bosco to get up and step off. I felt that he did not deserve the humiliation he received for my sake. He got up as if he knew what I had in mind and spoke of his intention to leave. His words were once again met only with silence. But, he was not a man who would be perturbed by the very cold reception that Dad and Mom had presented him with. He still smiled in spite of it all. He did not leave without letting Mom and Dad know one more thing—something they did not want to hear:

"No human hands are big enough to cover the sun and stop it from rising in a youthful morning," he began, "Your son, Beck, is the sun," he concluded and threw me a glance before he walked off quietly. His last words only inspired me all the more. I wished that I could run away from Mom and Dad's presence in order to see him off and let him know how sorry I was for the huge ridicule that he had faced. However, Dad had glowered at me, which was a strong enough warning for me to not step an inch away from them. He went to peer out of a window, a look of savage cunning on his face, watching Bosco prepare to leave, having got the engine of his car roaring. The unexpected awaited me as the sound of Bosco's moving car faded away from our hearing as it moved away into the distance.

***

"Get on your knees. Fast!" Dad snapped the moment he saw that Bosco had driven away. I had no doubt about who those words were intended for the moment they had been said—None but me.

"Are you deaf?" Mom added very quickly when I hesitated for a while, her voice quite shrill. It was after Mom had thundered that I quickly got on my knees. "Throw your hands up and keep them there!" Mom said again, looking stern and authoritative as if she was a senior military personnel barking commands at her subordinates. Dad had run off while Mom spoke. I did not know about his mission...well, not until he appeared with a huge stone that had plenty of rough edges. That was when I got a sense of what I was in for. My heart quaked with fear. Dread engulfed me, dilating my eyes. I almost thought that my own father was about to stone me to death.

"Dad, have mercy on me," I screamed.

"Shut the fuck up!" Dad screamed back at me, looking as menacing as a tiger in front of a lamb that is so close to being mauled by it, Dad the tiger, and I, the lamb.

"Shut the fuck up!" Mom waded in. And, even before I knew it, her right hand landed on my face, very strongly. The moment I received that slap, I was blinded. I screamed out in pain, trying to open my eyes immediately, but seeing practically nothing but stars spreading out and about like fireworks. It was only after a few moments had elapsed, though not quickly, that I regained my vision. My hands clutched my face as tears trickled down my eyes, coursing down my cheeks. Dad spoke again, his anger fulminating.

"Throw your hands up," he screamed. I quickly complied, disregarding the pain in my face. Dad went on to place the stone on my hands. It was so heavy a stone that the excruciating pain drifted from my hands to my back and my spine. It got my whole body shaking as I wept, but Dad and Mom were not in the mood to show me any mercy.

"The next time you bring a disease in here, you'll be dead!" Mom said, looking absolutely furious.

"I will never do that again...," I pleaded as pain ripped me through like an earthquake had once ripped through Haiti.

"You wouldn't bring anymore infections into this house, will you?" Dad asked.

"I won't..." What else could I have said?

"Good boy," responded Dad with a mischievous smile on his face, while all the while Mom stared at me like a vampire who had seen blood sprinkle out of my neck.

Dad relieved me of my pains by taking away the stone from my hands. The sudden relief surged through me, however, a relief so short-lived that it had gone like vapor—the pain from the heavy stone was about to replaced by something else —I was about to be a frog for a while.

"Your hands to your ears now!" Mom commanded. I complied fast fearing that another one of those blinding slaps would be on the way if I didn't; clutching my right ear with my first finger and the thumb of my right hand, with the first finger and the thumb of my left hand doing same to my left ear. "Now sit on your heels!" Mom barked. *Had Mom ever been an American Marine?* This was a question that sped through my hurting mind, one that I could not care to give a thought, not even for a second. I had to comply with Mom's order, even as fast as lightning, if I could.

"Now start hopping," came Dad's commanding voice. I began to hop with my hands strapped to my ears, repeating what I was asked to say, which was, "I will bring no more infections and diseases into this house." The burning pain spread through my body again within seconds, as if I had been set on fire with huge quantity of gasoline. I started to cry as I looked at Mom and Dad, forgetting that I had words to repeat. Instead of sympathy, I got struck by one harsh reality, which showed nothing but the fact that they were impervious to my agony. They only counted as I jumped, with tears fast pouring out of my eyes, until I had jumped a hundred times. That was my frog-jump experience. Unfortunately, even that was not enough for my parents and did not bring my ordeal to an end.

I received the beating of my life after my frog-jumps. I would have cried my eyeballs out if it were possible, having been hit hard with a baseball stick several times on my legs.

"Never bring such infections back home again," Dad said in a menacing rage as he kicked my ass several times with his right leg.

"Never bring such a disease back home again," Mom added, kicking me simultaneously with her left leg. I sustained injuries that I was warned never to speak of. On no account was I to let any member of our church know what had actually happened to me.

"What happened to you, Beck?" Mom and Dad would ask me in a rehearsal scenario they quickly set up. My answer, without a doubt, had to be the one they had chosen.

"I fell off a tree," I had to say. I had to say this, loudly, to their hearing, a hundred times before they were satisfied that it had been stamped onto my brain, and that I would be able to spill it, even while asleep. This was the answer that I was made to give not just to our church members, but anyone who would bother to ask.

I was taken to a hospital. All what Mom and Dad told the tall thin doctor, who treated my bloody bruises and stony weals, was that I was a stubborn child who would not stop climbing trees in spite of their warnings. The doctor did not ask how the fall from a tree gave rise to multiple weals and bruises. He was no foolish doctor that would just believe my parents' cock and bull story. Even a person with no rudimentary knowledge of any thing in medicine would have quickly discerned that I had not fallen off any tree. The initial expressions on the face of the doctor gave away his deep-seated doubts. They were even more pronounced in his eyes when he looked up from one of my bruises and into my eyes. Perhaps, he must have concluded that the true story behind my very many bruises was not his business after all and must have thought it wise and most appropriate to concentrate on what should be his business as a medical personnel, which was for me to get well. So, he initiated the treatment at once. I wanted to let out the truth, but I dared not, dreading that Mom and Dad would kill me. *Speak the truth! Speak it now! Speak to this man! Speak and let the world know your troubles! Let the world know the hell you've been through!* Several voices suggested all these and many other things in my head, voices I could not obey, even though I very much wanted to. It was like my lips got sealed with a tape the moment I tried to open them. That moment also coincided with the time Dad and Mom shot glances at my face. Wow! Who could ever say that glances cannot issue threats? I could literarily read those threats in the glances that Mom and Dad suppressed me with. "You wouldn't dare! Speak a word and have your mouth roasted in big fire! Don't even try it!" Those were the words, and many more, that their glances beamed like a huge billboard. I could not believe that Dad and Mom would lie that way against me in spite of all the holiness that they portrayed in church on Sundays. Dad read out portions of the scripture more than every other member of our church. Our Reverend preferred him doing that the most number of times. He could quote the Bible, from Genesis to Revelation, and as the Sunday school teacher often said, his favorite portion of the scriptures were the teachings of Jesus on true repentance, honesty, and forgiveness. Mom always led the praise and worship sessions with a voice that often sounded like it was owned by angels. They were the holiest couple of our church indeed! Our Reverend Pastor was the most gullible man I had ever seen. He was a short and thin man of African American descent, having a moustache that could aptly be called a thick forest of hairs. I still wonder how his wife came to allow him to carry such a bushy beard, which must have contained enough lice, mites, and little cockroaches. Who knows? Maybe he succeeded in convincing his wife that his spiritual inspirations came from there, as I noticed that he would not speak words of prophecy without pulling at his highly unkempt beard, parts of which had black and white beads attached to them. He had an empty brain that could not pick up the slightest signal of hypocrisy that happened right under his nose.

By now, my mind had already been made up to never forgive Mom and Dad. But, each time I went to church and heard our Reverend Pastor talk about forgiveness the way Jesus taught it, I saw the urgent need for myself to forgive, even if my parents could not do it. This I had to do quickly. Not forgiving was becoming much of a heavy burden weighing my life down, stealing my joy and inner peace. I had to let the baggage crumble like a stack of cards.

Chapter Twenty Four

When I recuperated, I went back to school after hearing enough warnings from Dad and Mom about never to indulge in creative writing or bring home any asshole like Bosco again. They actually called him that. Bosco was a big asshole as far as they were concerned.

"What is creative writing?" They had both asked me together when the answer to their question had already been forced on me.

"A thing of the devil," I had been taught to say.

"Is it better than anything in this world?"

"No."

Mom and Dad even threatened to withdraw me from school if I did not heed their warnings. I went struggling, without success, to be a brilliant kid in Math and Science. I never stopped having horrible results. It was not just happening for me. I just didn't find interest in those subjects. Mom and Dad thought that their harsh approach would get me to strangle my love for creative writing, but they were wrong; and that too on a colossal scale. All they kept doing was making my resolve to write get stronger. I kept reading all the more, honing my skills, and getting better at writing. Being a voracious reader gladdened my heart. The school library became my monastery, where I worshipped books. I shared my ordeal with Miss Florence, who urged me to never let my storytelling skills die.

"Come on, Beck, you're born to do it!" she had said to me, "Keep writing at all cost." Her words, I was quite sure, were such that would have made Dad and Mom get her into their list of people they hated most, after Bosco Jude of course, if they had heard her.

I wrote stories secretly and found out that I was improving beyond my wildest imagination. Miss Florence was always ready to help me out with her comments and critiques. But, I was an entirely different person at home—A kid

Mom and Dad wanted, a kid who had banished every urge in him to pursue writing. I always grinned with delight as Dad and Mom smiled each time they came into my room, and saw that I was reading my Math and Science books. Their hearts must have weighed a thousand pounds owing to the big joy they received when they saw me studying those books.

"Good boy!" Dad would say, "Now I can sleep with both my eyes closed. Yeah! I can now begin to believe that you were made from my sperm."

"Now we have a son!" Mom would add. "Now I can believe that it was actually you who came from my womb."

"Keep it up!" both of them would say to encourage me.

They did not get it. They did not know that those were the times that I was busy organizing my thoughts, gradually drawing new story concepts, bit by bit from inspiration. This was the way I had to keep going in order to sustain my passion for creative writing. This went on even when I got into high school and met some folks who loved to write as well. Though I was not excelling in Math and Science, my parents got deceived into eventually believing that I was really giving it my best shot. They held on to the conviction that time and a lot of effort from my part would turn things around.

Luckily for me, my communication with Bosco did not shrivel to death because of how my parents had treated him. We remained in touch. Reading his letters always made joy and inspiration blossom in my heart like flowers in spring. He kept on urging me to write, especially when he learned that I had got into high school. Nothing could contain his joy when he found my stories, the ones he subsequently read, were getting better. He pointed out how he loved the intelligent twists that were becoming the hallmark of my stories. I was overjoyed when Bosco mentioned that he found my stories quite interesting.

My relationship with Bosco remained alive and booming until the very day that he had to leave me. I had received that letter from him, never doubting that there would be more to come. It had the usual tone of his earlier letters— encouraging and inspiring—but it was particularly moving and touching. He wrote about the regrets that had tortured his life without a sign that they would fade away someday. What struck me most was his pain of not having a son or a daughter that was ambitious. All his children had turned out to be drug and sex addicts who would never let a day pass by without injecting heroin and spending any dollar they had to have perverse sex with anyone that was willing. Bosco had ended his letter this way:

Story writing can get you to shine like a star for all eyes to see if only you will keep doing it and never give up. I will only find full joy in death the day you will take up your reserved place amongst the very best.

I deciphered that Bosco must have been dying as he wrote to me when I read the concluding part of the letter. I broke down in tears, which dropped to hit the letter in my hands, so much that it got it completely soggy. It was only a day after I had received this letter that I heard Bosco Jude, my literary father, to have passed away. Testicular cancer saw to that. I only wondered how he never looked sick, not even a bit, the times that I had met with him. His demise left a huge void in my life but set my eyes much more firmly towards achieving my dream, as his voice of guidance seemed to whisper to my hearing each day, as though of distant thunder.

CHAPTER TWENTY FIVE

Fame and wealth meant that I had to leave my beloved rural Nebraska home for L.A., the city of angels. I held Scrappy, my only companion, in my hands, as three men whom I had hired, gently carried my few valuable belongings into their van. I had also decided not to take any of what Julie had left behind—Some of her shoes, clothes, jewelry, lingerie, and perfume—Things I concluded that she did not really have a need for. Why would she have left without them if she did? And, she had not even bothered to come for them ever since. Scrappy was filled with a sense of frisky nervousness. It felt so uncomfortable at the fact that it had to leave the only home it knew ever since it was adopted by Julie. The men finished carting my stuff into their van, hopped into it, and were off to my new condo in L.A. However, I was not interested in leaving right then. It was morning, and I had a flight bound for L.A. in six hours' time. So, I had enough time to wallow in nostalgia. It permeated me so much that I almost had tears in my eyes to show as proof. It got me to turn back immediately. Distance had completely absorbed the van from my sight, and I was left facing my home of many years again. Somehow, I suddenly began to see it as a relic of my past struggles and ordeals that should not be allowed to slip off my hands. After a moment of thought, I came to a conclusion that I would make a move to buy it from the owner if he ever made a move to sell.

Little did I know that the five-feet-six-inches Texas blonde had come around as time went on. She still stood tall, looking ever sweet in the Levi's blue jeans that she wore, and had a skimpy blue shirt with splendid yellow stripes on the top, which did not do a good job of covering her belly button. I could see a bit of her blonde pubic hair, a few strands, peeking their heads, right under her belly button, enjoying some fresh air. Her hair was nothing less than one that must have had the very best of touch from a seasoned stylist; long, shiny, curly, angelic, and dropping on her shapely shoulders. Her adorable long legs were rested on a nice-looking pair of black shoes, which had long heels. I could easily have called her a sexy super model. But, had she been stalking me all day? What would she want right now? No wonder Scrappy had been trying to wriggle out of my hands. It already knew that someone was around, someone it was really fond of. I wondered who that could be apart from Julie. Julie had been long gone from my life. I concluded that it could never be her. It was only when I turned back that I realized how wrong my conclusion had been—absolutely wrong. She stood at the exact spot the van had been, staring at me as if she could never have any air to breathe without me. Scrappy really wanted to free itself from my hands, its wriggling and whining were now ever determined. I gave it its freedom. It began wagging its tail as it quickly ran to Julie, who bent down and lovingly picked it up, beginning to stroke its long ears.

"Hello," she said to Scrappy, "How have you been?" She went ahead in that tone that I had not heard for quite a long while, which I have to confess that I had missed.

"You can see it's been having a swell time," I replied on behalf of Scrappy, who quickly found comfort in Julie's hands.

"I can see that. Its skin is so bright...A well-fed and healthy dog."

Julie kept lavishing attention on Scrappy, and I smiled a bit. What precipitated a smile on my face was the fact that I saw that she had got stuck. She did not know how to begin speaking of why she had come. I made up my mind to get her talking.

"You didn't come around to get all sentimental about a dog you abandoned, did you?" I asked with the sole intention of prodding Julie to say something. Julie put Scrappy down the moment she heard me, as if what I had said was a pin that had stung her skin. She looked up at me. Her face held an expression—a tender mix of remorse and determination.

"I'm sorry," she whispered under her breath.

"It's not all about the dog, is it?"

"Beck, I'm sorry." There were tears in Julie's eyes now. But, her voice sounded choked with tears.

"Nobody loves to go back to an abandoned desert unless news begins to make the rounds that the desert has suddenly turned into a huge ocean swarming with lots of fish. Look Julie, I did all I could. I placed a call to Texas, spoke with your father. He didn't know where you were…"

"I went—" Julie tried to speak. But, I felt that I had more to say, and that she had to let me finish. So, I was quick to interrupt her.

"I called your mother," I interrupted her and continued, "and she too was absolutely ignorant of your whereabouts. You know that you got your Mom and Dad worrying, Julie? They were out to get the cops and declare you a missing person."

"They didn't have to do that eventually. I got in touch with them…I told them that I was doing quite fine where I was. Yeah. I had kept it a secret. I did think that telling them was not a good idea because, I thought, they might disclose it to you." Shocked, I only stared at Julie, totally stunned by the words that had left her mouth and had stung my ears.

"You hated me that much?" I asked, trying hard not to be moved to tears.

"Beck, that was then—"

"You left, not minding the prevailing inclement weather, not minding that you might come in harm's way, not minding that we've come a long way. Julie, you brought tears to my eyes…lots of tears, Julie…I thought you were long dead." Tears slowly made its way out of my eyes.

"Beck, I was stupid. I was under a lot of pressure. Pressure ought to have made me focus, but I folded. I was in New York, somewhere in Manhattan…I moved in with a female friend of mine."

"Time proves us wrong sometimes. It proves us right sometimes."

"I shouldn't have stepped out of that door."

"But you did out of your own will. It was your decision."

"I'm sorry, Beck. I was just stupid…"

"We do stupid things sometimes…"

"Mine was very stupid. But, let's leave that aside…Congratulations, Beck! You're the man of the moment. Even the wind peddles your fame around."

"Thanks. Hard work eventually pays those who can wait as long as it takes. Things do happen when hard work and constant perseverance come face to face with the grace of God. It is time and chance that happen to men. The Reverend Pastor of my childhood church used to say this a lot. And I believe it."

"I see complete truth in it now."

"You've not come to simply congratulate me now, have you Julie? What else do you want us to talk about?"

"Us..." Julie uttered and cried a little bit before she spoke again, "I'm really sorry. I never thought about how horrible what I had planned was. I just went on with it. It haunts me now."

"Oh...How circumstances bring pressure that makes us crack in spite of our promises."

"Yeah...Beck, I know I promised to be by your side always... Please forgive me, I'm human after all...I'm sorry."

"Yes, we humans are full of frailties..."

"I want to get back to being what I used to be to you, Beck. Do you want me back, Beck?"

I could not speak. I was numb for about three seconds. Memories of our sweet high school days descended on me. Memories of our wedding day also came around. I recalled my marriage vow. Voices erupted in my head saying, *"She's being a nice woman, loving and caring. Have you forgotten so soon?"*

I did not forget. I thought I still loved my wife in spite of what she had done to me.

Chapter Twenty Six

It happened that my relationship with my agent took on a twist—It became romantic with time. I had not planned on it, and never did I think for a second that it would ever come to that. It just sprouted like a seed thrown into a soil that had external conditions which were perfect for the germination to occur. I was lonely. My agent was young, sizzling, and sexy. She was the only one whom I was close to. She was lonely as well, without a man, and she needed me. My agent had told me that she once had a boyfriend, her age then being nineteen and her boyfriend being the sweetest thing in her life. Her boyfriend, Carlos, aged twenty-one, an American, but originally from Mexico, had dropped the bomb half an hour before they were supposed to be wedded—Carlos had ditched her for a man. She never knew that Carlos was bisexual and had been dating a man alongside her. My agent told me that she had been shattered, her world went upside down, and that she swore never to have any love affair with any man again for the rest of her life.

"Beck, I was a deflated balloon," she had said to me, "I got messed up. The clock of my life stopped ticking. I was really hurt, Beck. I thought that my heart was going to stop beating at some point. It seemed like a sharp sword had passed through it. Beck, I went through hell...for giving my heart to that shit of a man...who couldn't even choose between being gay or straight."

My agent would have kept on keeping to her decision religiously, had I not become her client by stroke of fate. She let me know that I was the missing man that had made complete joy elude her. The joy that her tremendous success in business could not bring along. She told me that she was my Eve, and I, her Adam.

"I am a diabetic patient now, Beck," she had once said. I was shocked to hear that, pity filling up my heart, until I heard her speak further.

"And you are the insulin I can't have enough of." I giggled at first. Good sense of humor, infectious one, I thought. I had to laugh, and I did, very loudly.

"I see. That's quite interesting."

"Not as interesting as you, Beck."

Saying that I did not find her extremely attractive would amount to nothing but a lie. I would have cried like a little girl, developed bulgy eyes as a result, if she had in any way not meant what she was saying. And, if I would have to play her a song by a Black American recording artiste, begging her, if she had woken up the next day and said that she wanted me like oxygen no more, it would have been R. Kelly's 'Radio Message'. I felt pure bliss the moment that she told me that her life had been one of total hibernation until I had come along announcing spring. We just hit it off, developing a love affair before we even knew it.

"To fall in love is what everyone is in need of. Life's too short to live alone, Beck. I need someone to call my own. And that's you. I'll care for you, and you'll care for me. Our need for each other will live forever. Shower me with your love always, Beck. Always... Thoughts of you run through my head and make me always want you around. Let's stick together forever like magnets and grow old together. Just you and me, Beck."

Those were her lovely words that came before our first kiss, which held onto my heart, refusing to let go. She invited me for dinner in her condo one day, as our relationship progressed. I felt obliged to honor her invitation. One of those things men do for love, isn't it? One strong attraction that I had, apart from her, was a balcony in her residence, which offered a magnificent lush-green hilly view. My agent had a taste for good furnishing. I noticed it the first time I stepped into her condo—nice looking blue settees, chandeliers, blue curtains made of fabrics which I admired very much. The rug on the floors was beautiful, and its color was also blue. The kitchen and rooms were quite spacious. All the walls were blue, and so were the sheets on all the beds. I could not help but think that my agent had a special attachment to the color blue. And when I had asked, the answer that I received was exactly as I had thought.

"Yes," my agent quickly said. She laughed aloud, obviously excited that I got impressed enough to ask, "Don't you know, Beck?" She talked on gently, her voice enchanting. "There is something about the blue color...It's so tender and beautiful...Don't you have a favorite color, Beck?" I had never fancied having one.

"No," I replied. My agent threw me a glance that said that I was strange.

"Hey, give me a break here," I said, going defensive, "Not everybody has to have a favorite color."

"It's no good that you don't have one, Beck. Blue is so nice and romantic...I had to drum it into the head of the guy that decorated my home that it was going to be blue all the way."

"So, why not all blue in your office?"

"Beck, office is for business. Any color will do there."

"No wonder all your under-garments are blue in color," I added and guffawed. She was excited to hear me joke. I knew this because she smiled and looked me in the eye and said, "Smart guy...I thought you would never notice...It's actually nice to be blue down there, frankly, if you know what I mean..."

I nodded in the affirmative to indicate that I did understand what she talked about.

"Come on, Beck," said my agent, who was wearing a blue dress so faint and short that it left very little to the imagination as far as her body was concerned. After she had finished setting the table, she walked towards me, her face aglow with a smile. "I made a nice meal for us. Ready for some sea food? It's all ours, sugar..."

There was music which gently enhanced the romantic atmosphere that I understood my agent had taken her time to put in place, music that I thought was apt for our rendezvous. I loved it. My agent was already singing by now, and I could not help but join her.

Love comes with a good meal
And brings the heart a good chill
A woman in love cooks her man a good meal
And keeps him yearning for the thrill

And, it was while I sang that I remembered what the day it was. I had not realized since the break of dawn that it was the fourteenth day of February, Saint Valentine's Day.

The meal exuded an alluring aroma, and I could not wait. My agent got to where I sat, pulled me slowly to my feet, and so close, that my chest got rested on her boobs, her teats spraying impulses down my groin in a flash. She softly kissed my cheeks, her left hand, so warm, slid straight to my waist, and I was now heading for the table that was in a part of the condo that would have been totally dark if not for light that came from a number of well-arranged candle sticks, which stood on the table.

"I know you're a busy professional," I said, "How do you find time to cook?"

"When a woman cares a lot about her man, finding time to cook to his taste won't be a big deal at all...Unless she hasn't been bitten enough by that bug called love...The lyrics of the music I'm playing for us say it all...A woman in love cooks her man a good meal..."

"That's nice...Yeah...I appreciate every bit of that...That's great..."

When we were done with the meal, which I thought was superb, particularly the shrimp and tasty sauce made of Mexican chilies, I got pleasantly full, having drunk sumptuous amounts of alcoholic red wine as well. We moved to one of the couches in her living room.

"Let's make it fast, okay?" said my agent. I, being slightly tipsy, did not understand her.

"What's that?" I asked, as my belly churned a little bit.

"Is it not time that we take this stuff to the next level?"

"Do you mean what we've got? Us? Our relationship?"

"Of course! I do..."

"I must confess that I've been thinking of it." I was not lying at all. I really did think that my agent was awesome.

"Not as much as I do, Beck..." she said and moved gently until she was seated very close to me, so close that I got a whiff of her body perfume. Its name was GLO, she had told me once.

"But would it not be nice if we take our time?" I responded gently, smiling at her a little.

"You need me, Beck, don't you?" she said. Her tone held allure so strong and arresting that I would not have been able to say no, even if I had wanted to.

"There's no doubt about that," I responded, my answer being one I couldn't afford to withhold. It was like I had been charmed by something much stronger than her physical beauty, something sweet I really had no words to describe.

"And I need you too...So, what should we be waiting for? I understand that you're not exactly divorced yet. But you can get that done in a jiffy."

"In a jiffy?" I asked, being very surprised to hear that. "I'm no divorce attorney," I went ahead to say, 'But I know that securing a divorce is no piece of cake."

"Not in your case, Beck. Your wife was callous enough to leave you, and without even a single word. It's been quite some time now that she has disappeared on you—Three years, if I still remember correctly." My agent knew all these because I had told her. "You don't even know if she's still alive," she further added.

"I very much doubt that she is."

"You've got no proof that she's still alive."

"Yes...All my attempts to establish contact with her came to nothing. It was nothing but a futile exercise that had me dripping with frustration. Where the hell *is* she? My single status just has to end," I said, feeling quite sure that even if Julie were to still be alive, she did not care about me anymore. I did not see how I needed the services of a legal practitioner to get on with my life. "It's time for action..." I said again, absolutely convinced it was time that I moved on. I could see my agent smile. I was so happy that she wanted me like bears want honey. She rested her head on my waist, her face looking up as she stared at me, full of longing in her eyes. She did not have to speak a word before I could tell what she needed. I brought down my face a little so that my lips could locate hers. It all started there. Soon, we were reaching out for succulent spots on each other's body with our ever-adventurous fingers, turning the heat on. Not even an earthquake or a tsunami could have stopped us.

My plans to marry my agent had advanced quite a bit. We had arrangements to have some A-list Hollywood celebrities as our wedding guests.

"Paris Hilton is number one on the list," my agent had said.

"Yeah..." I voiced my agreement because I thought that the wealthy and successful celebrity would love to party hard even at sixty. We thought of Lindsay Lohan and found her very qualified to make it to our list too.

"What about the President of the United States?" I asked my agent.

"Oh sure!" she said, "Why not?"

"That won't be easy though..."

"Yeah...I know, but we can try. I think some strippers and pole-dancers from Las Vegas will also be required, won't they?"

"I'm not comfortable with that," I disagreed. "What do we need them for? Our wedding is not going to be turned into a strip club. What the hell are you thinking? What the...?"

"Making marks, making our wedding the talk of LA, Beck. Let's have some strippers come and spice things up a little bit, if you know what I mean..."

"Yes. I know what you mean! Who doesn't? But, what else can they bring on other than ass, boobs, and seduction? No, I don't like that idea one bit!"

"Our guests will *love* all that you've just mentioned. Don't you think so? Ass...Boobs...and the adorable art of seduction."

"Only some of the men."

"No, Beck. Have you forgotten? You ought to know how it is...People in America are of different sexual orientations. Some lesbians might turn up, even bisexual men and women."

"For our wedding dripping wet with strippers!"

"No, Beck. Do not see strippers as being dirty. They are workers doing their legitimate duties. These girls are the bomb! Eyes roll to wherever they display their sexy stuff. Come on...You know what I mean...Their smiles, turning and twisting and shaking...Delicious, isn't it? Not everyone can pole-dance. Can you, Beck? Give strippers some respect. They've got skills."

"We're planning a wedding no more, but a wild party in which orgies of damn dirty sex is going to linger."

"It's a wedding, Beck. One of a kind! Trust me."

"I don't see the President fitting into all this."

"Well, let's forget about the President."

"What?"

"Relax, Beck. I will work it all out with the wedding planner that I'm about to hire. You now see why you don't have to worry about a thing?"

"Yeah, a professional will soon step in," I said. But, I knew that I was never going to have any wedding planner parade strippers in our wedding.

"Beck, what problem do you have with strippers anyway?"

"Were you once a stripper? I wonder why *you* like them so much."

"I've never been one. What's your problem with them? Some men can't do without them."

"No! Don't even go there!" I yelled, obviously angry.

"I'm sorry your mom used to be one, and you feel so bad about it because you think strippers are dirty worthless whores who live for nothing else but the penis, and..."

"Cut that off!" I yelled again when I could not stand what more my agent had to say. She was right, absolutely correct. Mom's past made me ashamed of myself. Being an ex-stripper's son was a scourge on my consciousness. There was no way that I would watch strippers do their thing without seeing my Mom in them, which would strike me as rather very disgusting. Neither of us talked after I had yelled. My agent knew that I had got very angry. She looked me in the eye. I could see that she had now realized that her words had loaded my heart with thickets of thorn.

"I'm sorry," she said after a while, "I promised not to talk about it after you told me. I've let my tongue get loose. I'm sorry, Beck. Please...I'm sorry. It was not my intention to hurt you in any way."

"That's okay. We all make mistakes as humans." I took a deep breath and exhaled heavily before I spoke, the anger I felt having fled.

We concluded it there, but I was still not comfortable with the idea of flooding our wedding with strippers. It was to be a wedding in which millions of dollars would be spent. It was also in our plan to fly to an exotic location in India for our honeymoon. My agent pressured me to get her pregnant. But, I stood my ground. My adamant stance against having strippers at our wedding was rock-solid. It was not in my style to take an unborn child to the altar. Thanks to those that manufacture condoms that we had it going on in the bed, the couch, the bathroom, and even in the kitchen, without creating a new human being.

"Why can't you do without that rubber?" My agent had asked me one evening we were on the verge of making love. I knew what she was talking about, but just feigned ignorance. She loved to call a condom 'rubber.' She would sometimes call it latex or sheets.

"Rubber?" I said and looked her in the eyes, languid with the urge for us to get on with what we were out to do. "What rubber? There are no tires in here," I spoke again. She looked at my face. A frown of disapproval appeared on hers as soon as she did. And she was quick to speak.

"Don't give me that look, Beck, like you don't know what I'm talking about..."

"What?" I asked, pretending to be bewildered, and acting ignorant as much as I could, to convince her that I honestly did not know what she had meant by rubber. She doubted it and struggled to bring herself to believe that I truly didn't know.

"Why do you love to use sheets all the time? Sheets! Sheets! Sheets! Rubber! Rubber! Rubber! I'm talking about condoms, Beck!"

"Oh...condoms..."

"Why do you love them so much? Or do you think I'm not clean? Like I've got something? Like HIV? I'll prove it to you, Beck! I'm healthy! Not a trace of that hellish nonsense in my blood! You've got nothing to fear. First thing tomorrow, I'll get that test done!"

"No...No! You've drifted far away...So far away...My reason is simple! They are much better than the real stuff."

"You mean using them is sweeter?"

"Absolutely!"

"I can't believe my ears...Beck, you're strange!"

"Now are we going to get on with catching this fun or suspend it? Take your pick!"

"Let's get it on, Beck...Take me to that height like you always do..."

Though I felt hurt when Julie left me, I did not find it comfortable to see her as a demon. Which woman is perfect in this world? This question raged in my heart. It tolled in my head as loud as a cathedral bell. I did not find an answer to it. Though my agent had been faultless so far, all loving, caring, sweet, and romantic a person, I knew that time would burst forth like a butterfly and prove that she had her faults as well.

***

"I'm sorry I hurt you," Julie said again, and began to walk away with her baggage. Scrappy ran after her. It got stock-still after a little while and kept looking from Julie to me, wagging its tail intensely, obviously torn between taking a decision on whom to follow. Then, it concentrated on me with a stare that said, "Are you coming or what?" I did not talk back to Julie, as I ignored Scrappy. I did not make a move to go after Julie. I had not taken any decision by now, let alone a firm one. But, time seemed to be melting away fast. And, in what seemed like no time, what Julie and I had going for us, constituted a huge force, and began to lure me fast.

"Not so fast, Julie," I called out behind her, "Don't think you can get away from me."

CHAPTER TWENTY SEVEN

My mind was also made up on how I would let my agent know my new resolve—
I planned to send her an email. Julie had already lost hope and kept widening the
distance between us. I ran after her. Scrappy ran along, barking as it did.

"Julie...Wait for me..." I screamed. She stopped exactly the moment she heard
her name and turned back. Though distraught, she was an angel before my eyes. I
was glad to be running to an angel. I grabbed her waist immediately upon getting
to her. She yielded completely, throwing her arms across my shoulders, her head
across my left shoulder.

"Please come back, Julie," I said, "I need you back."

"Thanks, Beck, for giving me the chance to be better."

Julie broke down and cried. There was nothing that I wanted more than to
have her move to L.A. with me. The love we used to have, being at its strongest
again, surged forth with the force of a huge storm. I was glad that Julie found my
shoulders worth crying upon. She cried like a little girl. I consoled her while I
fought hard without success to keep my emotions from overwhelming me. Little
drop of tears escaped my eyes as a result. I looked for Scrappy and saw that it was
standing close to us, watching us, thrilled, its tail wagging with a breath-taking
speed—A thousand times per second, I believed. Even dogs get excited when love
gets stronger. That's what Scrappy had taught me. I looked up at the sky and saw
a gathering of clouds, and I wished that I had a ladder that would take me there. I
needed to reach the sky so that I could squeeze out the moisture from the clouds
and pour it on Julie's face, which I saw were demarcated into unequal parts by
tear marks.

"Your shoes, your clothes, and some other stuff that belong to you," I said
gently to Julie, "They are still in the house. Do you care about them anymore?"

"Not really...Why do you ask?" Julie said, not crying anymore now. Crying seemed to have refreshed her, as she suddenly beamed with liveliness, smiling most sweetly, as we remained physically entangled within each other's arms.

"I'm in love with your timing, Julie. Perfect! L.A. is our home now. I've moved."

I could see a little smile flicker on Julie's face, one that hid the profound joy inside her sparked by the breaking news of my switch from Nebraska to L.A.

"I love Nebraska, Beck. But L.A. is wonderful..." Julie said, and without a single care, laughed out loudly. Her mouth was so wide open that I could see all her white teeth gleaming. I could not help but laugh as well.

"You still care about them?" I asked when the laughter had subsided, "Your lingerie and other stuff of yours are still in the old house."

"Let those that will need them cart them away."

"Come on, Julie! You're so crazy. A woman doesn't leave her lingerie behind. Come on..."

"And what if she does?"

"Well, I guess some rats will come and make big holes in them. That's it!"

"I guess it's time to let the rats take care of their business, while we take care of ours, Beck."

"Ours?" I asked, not knowing exactly what Julie had meant. "Oh!" My voice howled a little, as I thought I knew. "Our business is that we are moving, right?"

"Remind me, Beck. When did I last kiss you?"

"Now...I really see...where you've been heading to. Not bad, actually. I—"

"You still haven't given me an answer."

"That must be when man still lived in caves and ran around naked in the jungle."

"It's been ages since we last kissed, right?"

"I've just told you that!"

"I want to catch up with the old times now."

"Old times? Look, Julie, my real business now is to see if you can fly on the same plane with me to L.A. today."

"That can wait."

"Old times are calling me right now. Yes...I hear you calling, old times...from your cradle in my fresh memory. Beck, do you still remember how much you loved me gently kissing the tip of your nose? I'm ready to bet with my whole life that you still do."

"Who's ever going to deny that? Well, not me!"

"Beck, I know your mind is wandering."

"Don't tell me that you possess psych powers now."

"Let your mind rest, my love. Beck, let's take it back to those sweet days, our high school days. Hinge it on that day in which you shared the dream that you're living today...with me."

"Yeah...I know it so well...Give me a kiss, Julie. A gentle one, right at the tip of my nose."

"No."

"You are just joking. You will not deny me, will you?"

"I will."

"You must be joking. Tell me you're joking."

"You're blind, Beck. Can't you see that I am?"

It felt quite nice, rekindling that moment in time, that September evening that kept spreading a damp chill like it were a nozzle.

Julie and I got on with it. She definitely did more than kissing just the tip of my nose, making Scrappy, who had watched all the way, almost jealous.

"It will be so wonderful if I can get on the same plane with you," Julie said, disengaging from my grasp, when we were done wetting each other's face.

"You have been dreaming! Now reality beckons!"

"There should be a way!"

"All we can do is to try..."

I sent my agent no email like I had planned earlier, after I had thought that it was best that I see her. So, I went straight to her office the next day in the afternoon. She was all smiles, as if she had seen a goldmine, the moment I stepped in.

"Hello, Beck, how are you doing?" She asked, her tone all vivacious. "Take a seat. One moment please, while I get you something to drink. She had barely got up from her seat when I spoke.

"This is not the right moment," I said before I got seated. Her face dulled a bit, all its earlier shine, half gone. She looked me in the eyes, and on her face there was a confused and questioning look.

"What are you talking about?" she asked.

"I know you've been so nice and so sweet to me...You've been there for me. We've shared lots of fantastic moments, most of them sexual in nature...I—"

"What the hell are you talking about, Beck!" she asked, the warm glow that I saw in her eyes when I came in, now vanished.

"I'm sorry I'm right here and about to drop the bomb..."

"What bomb?"

"I'm sorry, okay? I'm sorry it just turned out this way..."

"You're sorry about what? Beck, you're not really talking!"

"I'm sorry about the bomb that I've got to drop right now."

"What bomb?" My agent asked again. She had peered at me like she had never seen a man properly before.

"The bomb about us, I'm sorry."

"What about us?"

"I'm sorry, but our relationship has to end."

My agent stood up quickly the moment the revelation hit her. She left her table in thought, turned her back to me, and began to stroll around, keeping her head down. I could see the pain that my decision had brought to her. It was evident in the very slow agonizing steps that she threw as she sauntered. She then grabbed her head with her hands. I could feel her deep disappointment before her hands dropped from her head all of a sudden.

***

"Please tell me you're joking," she said after a while without looking at me, stopping her stroll.

"I wouldn't be here if I was," I replied, feeling a little guilty.

"Do you think you know what you are doing?" she asked and gently turned to face me. I could see neither fury nor displeasure from the look on her face.

"I do," I replied. "I'm sorry I've got to do it. I'm really sorry."

"Who's doing this? Who's she? Who's he? Are you gay, Beck? Or bisexual?" She spilled these questions and turned her back at me. She had only taken two calm steps away to where I would not know, when my reply made her stop.

"Her name is Julie," I had said.

"Your wife?" she asked without turning to face me.

"I'm sorry we have to split."

"No problem, Beck. Things do happen," my agent said. She turned to me and smiled, her twinkling gaze making me feel as though I was being x-rayed. "Can I at least give you a last kiss?"

I did not think that was bad idea at all. If that was the compensation she really needed, it was one that I was willing to give from the very bottom of my heart.

"You're as free as the air," I said.

My agent then came close to me and brushed her lips with mine, gently at first, very gently, before she quickened up, her lips probing, massaging, and digging, until mine emerged and embraced it. She was hungry, as if her mission was to eat up everything in my mouth. Her tongue went on a wild wet adventure in an enclave that would be my mouth. It got very wet quite soon, so filthy wet that I had got aroused before I even knew it. Now, I really got to know where it all was going to lead us. I had to pull myself back to stop us from slipping further into any act of sexual nature.

"Thanks," my agent said to me as I stood up to leave, her eyes and labored breathing saying that she wanted more. I left her behind, having a big erection under my pants. I saw the looks on the faces of her assistants who saw me leaving. I could read those looks so well. Looks that said, "Now I really see what went on in there..."

I was stunned to see that my agent took it all very lightly. I had expected her to create a belligerent scene in which I would be struggling to save my head. In her email to me the next day, she said that it was quite alright that I had decided to leave her for my wife. She said that she was a fan of men who went back to start loving and cherishing their wives after having fallen for the temptation to go astray. In her opinion, such men are much better than those who continue to flounder in adultery. My agent said that she was irrevocably committed to respect my decision completely. *Wow!* She went about handling my interests in her agency most professionally, like she had always done. It all looked great.

I had moved on, piled my attention on my work and on my wife, catching up with our very romantic past, loving to kiss her ten times each day, never intending to stop until the sun fell down from the sky. Love and a good life flourished at home. I would not have noticed if the world had suddenly ground to a halt. Julie made me understand one day that she wanted to have a baby. "I think I'm ovulating, and you've got sperms. So, let's make it happen, Beck," she told me. I wanted to have a baby too. So, her words sounded like music to my ears. We had to commence what we had to do, first with foreplays, for we had all the time in America and indeed the world, to fully explore each other's body, our tongues and fingers running wild after we had tossed each other's clothes apart.

"What...are...you still waiting for?" Julie said in between her erotic moans. "Is it...not time...for you to get to work?" I ignored her, being fully engrossed in getting very naughty with her boobs. Her pointed teats and ass looked very new to me as if I had never seen them before. *Wow!* Julie, being out of clothes, looked more beautiful than ever. I wanted to pick up my camera and film her exotic body, but she, at the time, was not up for it. All she wanted was for the show to progress, being all wet and ready.

"Beck..." she called, her voice a gentle, teasing, and inviting one that arrested me. "Please Beck, go ahead and get inside me...I can't wait any longer..." Julie went ahead to say. What I could not do too was wait any longer. My tool was already very hard, bobbing its head, and telling me that it had long reported for duty. So, I started working with my engorged tool without any further delay, all to Julie's delight. She quickly turned into an animal in bed, going wild as she yearned for more, begging me to do all I could to stop myself from reaching my peak. "Hold it, Beck...Please don't get there now..." she continued to whisper as I pummeled her as fast as I could. I was tempted to call her a wild, wild bitch. But, she being my wife, I could not. *Where did she learn to be like this? Had she gone to Vegas to work as a hooker all the while she was not with me?* I discarded these questions from my mind very quickly. I did not care. I was enjoying Julie in her new explosively intimate form. I continued to work, digging her, and savoring all of it. Julie, at a point, exploded with a scream. She tore through the skin of my back with her long fingernails in the process. I hardly felt any pain because it was at this point that I had a rush of pleasure surging all through my body, as I came inside her. I shuddered all over. "Come on, Beck! Come on..." Julie encouraged me, massaging my turgid ass with her sweet fingers. I felt like I had been drained completely when I was done, every bit of semen in me having been emptied into Julie's tank. Julie planted a wet kiss on my lips, got her sweaty body off the sheets and was on her feet. Her only mission, like I thought, being to go for a shower. She began to leave, as I remained in bed, exhausted, languid with post-coital contentment, and very much interested in dozing off. Julie looked back at me and blew me a kiss.

"Great," she said to me and lept up and down a few times like a tap dancer. And, there was a smile that came upon her face, which said one thing that I understood very well. In that smile were these words—'Thank you so much for a job very well done.' I soon began to hear her taking a bath, the water sprinkling upon our Jacuzzi. I wanted to forget about Julie for a while and take a nap, when she poked her head out of the door that led to the lavatory and smiled at me. *What the hell was wrong with Julie?* I smiled back at her, not knowing that my smile was going to urge her to do more. Julie got out of the lavatory, her body wrapped in a white towel. Only her shoulders, her head, and her legs were left uncovered. There were beads of water and bubbles all over her face and hands. I saw an inviting smile on her face that made me wonder what more she could now be up to. I looked into her eyes, and they were telling one thing—*Come on, Beck, it's no longer time to keep lying on that bed...Come on...*

I ignored what Julie's eyes spoke to me. This was after I had told her with a clear look in my own eyes that I intended not to get off the bed.

"You know what, Beck?" Julie gently said to me, the smile on her face still remaining.

"What?" I said, yawning.

"Do not attempt to sleep off, Beck. You're butt-naked."

"Go tell that to the whole of America now," I replied, 'What's wrong in a man of my status sleeping butt-naked?"

"That...wasn't what I was trying to say anyway. I was just thinking if..." She said suggestively.

"What?" I demanded.

"Beck, I must first let you know that..."

"Julie, what are you talking about?"

"No...I must confess this."

"What?"

Julie only laughed to see me so confused. And, when she finally stopped laughing, she looked me in the eye and said, "No vibrator works better than your tool, baby." I laughed and cast a glance at my now flaccid tool that had earned me credit.

"Get the hell out of here, Julie," I said with a smile when I looked up at her. I actually felt quite thrilled about her confession though. I laughed again. "Get out, you spoilt thing" I added.

"Beck, I was thinking—

"Get off and take a shower, Julie..." I interrupted her. The smile vanished from Julie's face. She looked for a while like I had hurt her with my dismissive sentence. But, she smiled again, determined to say what she wanted to.

"I was thinking...if..."

"Go ahead," I spoke to encourage her, "I'm listening!"

"If...you could come butt-naked with me...to the Jacuzzi..."

Having said that, Julie looked me in the eye with her smile getting bigger, letting her towel drop to the floor. She gently walked back into the lavatory, daring me to say no with her eyes, smiles, and all that I saw when her towel hit the floor. I must confess that she looked like a complete new person, as if I had never had her before. She appeared so lovely and unexplored. I could not wait to explore her. I had to leave the bed to be with her in the foam-rich Jacuzzi, butt-naked, of course.

"I was going to ask who gave you the power to resist my charm," Julie invitingly said to me when I joined her. I was at one end, while she was at the other. She slowly crawled to my end, rested her back on my chest, my arms now sprawled across her chest. I kissed her head and the back of her neck a little, making her giggle a bit.

"I thought I could," I said, rubbing her stomach gently.

"Now you know you can't," Julie said and cast some foam upon my head and face.

"Did Las Vegas teach you the much that you know now?"

"No."

"Great."

"You deserve the best. Don't you like me like this, Beck?"

"I didn't complain, did I?" Why on earth should I? Not every man in America can boast of a wife as sweet as mine. "You're wonderful," I further said, feeling very good about Julie.

"Thanks. You're wonderful as well."

"I must be on drugs and need to check into rehab, Julie, if I say that I don't love you. When I look at your lips, I see a honey-coated chocolate."

Julie giggled.

"I love you too," she replied, taking her left hand backwards and picking up my tool, which was getting ready for duty once again.

"That's great..." My verbal response went off.

"We're talking too much now, are we not, Beck? So, I decided to act against it."

"Yeah..." That was all that I could say now.

I noticed a new wave of vigor surging through me. Julie was all open and more than willing. And, we started to proceed again, right inside the Jacuzzi. Julie was very glad after a month had passed. She had news, a pleasant one that made a fountain of joy erupt from my heart—Julie was pregnant. I was thrilled at the prospect of becoming a father, oblivious to the fact that my agent had been up to something. My agent's name? Trisha. The masked woman.

CHAPTER TWENTY EIGHT

You might wonder why Dad and Mom hated anything that had to do with creative writing with such a strong passion?

"I warned your father to keep off, but he would just not listen. He said writing was his life," my grandmom began telling me as she talked about Dad. She was big, but not beefy, and she wore big glasses. She had said that Dad had set his goal, very early as a youngster, to be a successful writer. But, he kept having hellish experiences in the hands of well-established traditional publishers in America, who were some of the big names in the global publishing field. Dad's experience with many literary agencies was no less hellish. Rejections flooded him and drowned his enthusiasm to persevere. Frustration dragged my father into sending his first and only novel entitled 'The Devil in Writing' to a print-on-demand publishing outfit based in Raleigh, North Carolina, which he saw online. The publisher had rolled out a fantastic plan to distribute Dad's novel worldwide and pay him a royalty of ten dollars on each copy of his book that would be sold. Dad was glad. He went about showering curses on agents and publishers who never thought that his book was worth publishing all the while. It took just three months before Dad began to see his book being listed by major book distributors and retail stores worldwide. He thought that he had made it at last until he got a shocker that he never actually recovered from. His book indeed had a worldwide presence and had even made it into the bestsellers' lists. Trying to contain the joy Dad experienced was like trying to contain air with bare hands. He was the happiest man on earth. However, he must have been the happiest man already in a mess—His book was on the shelves, online, and selling, but he continued to experience a lack of money. No dime ever trickled down to him as royalty. He had failed to see the bold handwriting on the wall. How could he? How could he have done business with a publishing outfit that did not even have a land address in

Raleigh, North Carolina? An outfit that had no real human beings to pick up telephone calls? Well, that was Dad's story from my source, my grandmom, of course. She did not hide it from me when I secretly had to ask her why Mom and Dad could possibly be so mad at me for loving to write. Despite her almost completely dry, wheezy voice, she spoke very eloquently.

Mom had no such experience as Dad. Her only problem was that she was a staunch follower of Dad. She would put her hands in a red-hot furnace if Dad had done so, or even test the depth of the Atlantic Ocean in the Gulf of Mexico with her two legs at once if Dad did it. She would also not mind cutting off her hands if Dad had cut off his own hands. Mom was a fanatical fan of Dad, extolling his entire penchants, mentality, and idiosyncrasies, very sheepishly and blindly, as if she never had even a little world of her own without Dad. Grandmom told me one more thing about her son. It was Dad's hellish experience in publishing that made him hate that field so much. It made him believe that the only place he could find solace was in the company of junkies. Eventually, narcotics became another world which he knew.

"Heroine, marijuana, methamphetamine, crack cocaine, and all other killer substances became his companions and made him their prisoner," grandmom said with a tinge of pain evident in her voice, "Narcotics became his mother, father, brothers, and sisters—his whole wide world. That was how he went off with some thugs and rarely remembered the home he came from. He only returned sometimes, once in six months, looking gaunt and dirty."

I could feel the pain that grandmom felt as she spoke. She did not stop there. She scratched her grey hairs, twitched her wrinkled face a little, and braced herself up to speak further.

"Writing has never been kind to us, son," she had said to me, staring at me like she had wanted to swallow me with her eyes, whose attractive glow was not diminished one bit by age.

"Grandmom, do you expect me to believe that?" I said in response, feeling a little angry because of her comment.

"Believe me or not, if you travel down that road long enough, you will understand."

"I've always believed you, Grandmom. But, not this time."

My grandmom shot her shoulders up from the seat she had been resting them on, as though what I had said had launched a number of sharp pins in there, which had pinched her. What was amazing was how fast she did that, as if she was still a teenage girl of fourteen. Her eyes sized me up all over. She rested her back, on the seat again, a little slowly this time, taking a little time to draw some air into her lungs, and said, "Little boy, what do *you* know?"

"A lot, grandmom!"

"Impossible! You were only born yesterday."

"What? I'm twelve!"

"Even at twelve, you're just beginning your journey in this world. You're still fresh, son. You've not seen anything yet. What do you know? Nothing! So, shut your young mouth up and listen if you care."

"What about granddad? How come I've never heard him say that writing has never been kind to us? How come he keeps quiet and rarely talks? He has never answered any of my questions. Does he not know a thing?"

"Son, your granddad, my husband, sometimes becomes dumb. His own father had died a miserable writer. There comes a time when a man knows so much about what haunted his ancestors and still haunts his descendants and resigns completely to not even speak of it. He just won't talk, so stop bothering him with your busy inquisitive mind, Beck."

"What are you talking about?"

"Beck, have I told you something about my own dad?"

"No, grandmom. Please tell me."

"He was a journalist."

"I know about journalists, grandmom! They write."

"That's right, son. My dad was the type that dug up issues, sensitive and dangerous ones and wrote about his findings for the world to read."

"That sounds so exciting."

"My dad was smart, famous, and fearless, and would go to any extent to dig up facts for his stories. But..."

"But what?"

"He could not escape the bullets..."

"What!"

"The bullets of the assassins stopped him. He got shot in Moscow. Right on the forehead. It had happened on a morning when he was off to work, getting to the root of the high-profile murder of Vladimir, the Kremlin's fiercest critic of his time. There were clear signs that the Kremlin would be implicated in my dad's investigative journalistic work."

"Kremlin! I know about the Kremlin. It's the place where those in charge of Russia work from...The president and his team!"

"Smart boy! I'm glad to know that you've been reading up these things. Writing does us no good."

"That's not true!"

"Oh...you stubborn thing! When will you learn?"

"Grandmom, did *you* ever write?"

"I did. Only a little though! I had to disengage from it to spare myself the misery. I'm ninety and still alive because I was not stupid enough to tread the path that cost me my dad."

"Grandmom, only God decides who dies and who lives, not writing."

"You're so stubborn! That damn old black Pastor in that damn old church has been feeding you, right? I see...Do you know how my mom died?"

"How?"

Grandmom went on to tell me that her mom committed suicide. She had hanged herself on a tree after facing numerous bitter rejections in the hands of publishers and literary agents, and after having burned all the manuscripts of her many works in anger, which was fueled by frustration. However, she had forgotten one in a train, a novel. Intrigued, I could not keep myself from responding fast. A question popped up in my mind and tortured my curious mind to mere shreds the moment I considered not voicing it. I very much had to.

"What was the title?" I had said.

"What a title. Oh...What a title... 'Hang Myself.' That was it."

"Ouch," I cried.

To be honest, I thought it to be the most intriguing title that I had ever heard, as though it never sounded grim to me. Grandmom went ahead to tell me that her mother was in the habit of writing her residential address on every page of her manuscripts. A very thin, silvery-haired little girl, stunted, having big eyes and ears, and extremely long, curved finger nails that touched the ground, according to grandmom, brought back the manuscript.

"This happened three years after the script had gone missing, and my mother had killed herself," said grandmom, with little tears in her eyes. "It was very early in the morning of a wintry Sunday that the girl brought me the script, while I was yet to emerge fully from the mists of sleep."

It was clear to me from simple logic that the little girl could bring the manuscript back because of the address it contained. What I could not understand, however, was how the girl got inside grandmom's bedroom. Grandmom's account was very shocking, I must confess. She said that the strange little girl returned the manuscript and vanished into thin air without uttering a word, that she must have been a witch, and, therefore, needed no address whatsoever to be able to trace anyone in this world.

"Where is the manuscript?" I had asked grandmom very quickly, being very curious. "Can I read it? Did you read it, grandmom?"

"Speak no such nonsense before me again!" My grand Mom vociferated. "How could I have kept it? Such heinous evil! I never wanted to! Not even if I hated the air that I breathed so much."

"Now I know where you're going, grandmom. You dug a hole and buried it somewhere, right?"

"Who told you that?" replied grandmom as her eyes dilated, the surprise that she got from my knowledge of that fact being responsible. She stared at me as if I were some creature alien to planet earth, or possibly a wizard. "Beck, you're right," she went ahead to utter. "I'm sure your granddad didn't tell you a word. So, who did tell you?"

"I just guessed. Where's the spot?" I replied, "Can we dig it up?"

"What for? It's gone forever! Who would want to relish any memory of that evil?"

"What happened?"

"I couldn't stand the continuous ominous presence of strange-looking birds with ten wings and ten eyes each, which had no business circling day and night over the spot I buried the manuscript. So, I had to dig it up and burn it!"

"That was cruel, grandmom. Oh no! Why would you?"

"If being cruel to evil is a crime, then I would love to spend the rest of my life in jail. Now I have two things to say to you, Beck! Shut up and listen to me!"

Grandmom got to the tail end of her story by telling me that her father stole a book that belonged to a wicked wizard. He had seen the book hanging mysteriously from an apple tree as he took a walk one evening and had decided to take it without an iota of regard for anyone who might have kept it there. He was lured in by the insatiable appetite for the written word that was the book's title— 'Touch Not'—and this made the wizard cast a spell on him and on the generations after him, who would ever venture to write their ways to success. It was a complete myth, a sensational, but ludicrous, legend without a shred of a fact—That was how I had regarded grandmum's conclusion, but only in my mind. I never had the courage to let words leave my mouth and express how I very much did not believe her. That woman was ready to give me a dirty slap if one word in ridicule of her conclusion would have ever come out of my mouth.

CHAPTER TWENTY NINE

Spell or no spell, I am not a happy man now. I kept boiling with the urge to seek revenge. I wish to kill Trisha. I do have the resources that will enable me to execute the murder as perfectly as possible. I can kill Trisha, and not even the FBI or the LAPD can sniff out a thing about it. But, no! I do not want to get rid of my own unborn child. No! I do not want that kind of blood in my hands. My conscience keeps telling me how wrong it is, how God disapproves of murder. But, what Trisha did to me was nothing less than a murder. I am as good as dead. Never in my life have I fancied the idea of having two women becoming pregnant for me at the same time. I never fancied the idea of having a child out of wedlock. But, here I am facing that reality. I vowed never to have a child the way Dad and Mom had me. How could I hold my head high and speak strongly against their having me out of wedlock? Trisha has stained my life. I blame it substantially on fame. Trisha would most probably not have known me if not for my fame, and if I had not become a writer. Fame, you are no longer honey, but thorny. You used to be the honey, but now, you have turned into vinegar. You have robbed me of peace and joy. You have brought crisis to hold sway in my mind and life.

Julie is one person whom I do not wish to hurt by letting her know what Trisha did to me. I am a rock now that has been shattered to pieces. If only I had listened to Julie in the past, and not written my eleventh story. If only I had obeyed Mom and Dad, fame would not have come in to destroy me by scattering my seeds to two different women.

Julie placed my food on the table with a smile that showed how glad she felt doing that for me. That food is my favorite. She had taken her time to prepare the soybean stew, full of fried turkey and potato chips. Julie believes deep down in her heart that I would enjoy it like before. But, she does not know how wrong she is. She believes that I am happy, rich, and fulfilled now that I am a renowned writer.

She is right. I just won an Academy award for best original screenplay that I did for my story, *Anatomy of Their Fury,* the movie version of it. It is now a huge box office phenomenon, somewhere in the region of hundreds of billions of dollars worldwide. But, I am a broken man, dripping with regret. Julie will forever keep wondering why I had to do what has stepped into my mind right now. People's minds do change, do they not? Well, they sure do. I believe it is the exclusive preserve of a man or woman to change his or her mind as he or she wishes. I have now changed my mind. Julie must not be around when I plan to do my thing. I had to finish my meal in a hurry. I am getting away. My destination is anywhere quite far away from home. Julie must not know it. A horrendous thing has claimed my life. Fame and writing, I hate you! I hope all the people on earth will understand that it is natural for me to be sad now. Well, if not everybody, I hope that at least few people will understand. I want to be happy. And, happiness for me is making sure that Trisha tastes from the chalice of my revenge in one way or another.

I do understand completely that my decision may sound extremely foolish to many folks. Many folks who would advocate that I hold out, that I continue to hang out with fame, now my greatest enemy, in spite of the crushing blows it has dealt me with. I am sorry. It is my fundamental human right to choose to be foolish when I deem it very necessary. What else can make life a sweet experience if what one has vowed in his heart never to become, chooses to defy his resolve and eventually manifests? Nothing! I told Julie that I was going for a walk. Anyone has the right to call me a stupid man for what I am about to do now. Do I give a damn? Not really! I am going to act in search of peace. *You, my conscience, leave me alone! Stop rattling your million voices in my head! Stop quoting me the scriptures! I am deaf to forgiveness now! Preach that to the air! To the sky! To all insects! Why did you not preach forgiveness to Trisha when she felt that I hurt her? What I am about to do is none of your business! Leave me alone...You cannot stop me from inflicting revenge on Trisha. She must not have me to introduce to that child in her belly as its father. This revenge must be sweet. Oh...Julie, I love you, and I will continue to do so. Your darling Beck has nothing against you. I hate to do this to you, but some things just have to be done. My right hand will shove a metal into my mouth and pull the trigger to end it all. This is it!*

MY ELEVENTH FICTION STORY

PROLOGUE: THE V1B6F3 VICIOUS ATTACK

Their act had been perfected, a product of three experts on a deadly mission—a deadly pathogen now prowled around the world, a product that was more than just a mere pathogen. It was not a virus or a bacterium. Neither was it a fungus. You can be sure that one thing was ingrained in its DNA. And, there was nothing else except complete annihilation. A very virulent strain, cultured after a long time of painstaking work backed with steely resolve never to admit failure. It was cultured to ravage, cultured to conquer. "God is great! God is great!" These were the chants that rented the atmosphere as they left the mouths that produced them. There were smiles all over the three faces that were there, very wide smiles. Everyone took off their white lab coats immediately after the deed had been done, and busy hands were seen no more in the laboratory. A sense of having accomplished the mission hung everywhere like grape branches heavy with lots of fruit. The men embraced one another so tightly that they seemed like lovers who hadn't seen each other for a very long time.

"God is great!" said one of them again, as he roared in thunderous laughter, threw his hands up, and jumped up and down as if he was an elementary school boy whose father had just returned from work with his favorite cookie biscuit.

"The enemy ought to have known that no one messes with us and gets away with it," another added.

"That is right!" said one of them, "Strike at the heart of the enemy once you can! God is great!"

"God is great! God is great! God is great!" The three now began to chant. No one was happier than them. The depth of joy that they experienced was just unreachable. It is funny how joy can mean a lot of things to lots of people.

The element of surprise will never be in a hurry to cease to exist in this world. No one can disprove the fact that change is the only constant thing in our world and have any degree of success doing that. Surprise has this enduring character of change. It sneaks in on us and often leaves us wondering how we never saw it coming. But, it wouldn't be what it is if we saw it coming. Its soul and essence would be dead once it becomes easy to predict the time of its arrival. Its joy always overflows whenever it takes us unaware. It knocks at our doors at its times of choosing, to continue to let us know that we cannot always be aware of all things at all times, or to make it abundantly clear to us that when we think that we are in control of all things, we are actually not. That when we think that we are secure, we are most certainly not. Surprise makes us know that when we think that our enemy is completely shut out, we could be wrong. It comes to us uninvited. It walks into our lives and our world without its footsteps being heard. It can jolt us up from our sleep and awaken us to the harsh reality of danger if it chooses to do so. What can it not do without our knowledge of it? There is nothing you can cite as an example. We cannot know if, when, and how it will choose to strike. Otherwise its name will no longer be what it is. The best way to take your target by surprise is to make sure that it does not see you coming. And, that was exactly what the brains behind the V1B6F3 pathogen did to ensure that any trace of smile faded off from all the faces in the world.

This became the case from the United States to the United Kingdom, from Canada to Germany, from France to Russia, from China to Australia. The whole world began to feel the heat. World leaders were feeling the pinch. Globally, ordinary people were worse off. The Food and Agricultural Organization and, indeed, the whole of the United Nations had lost their sleep. Agriculture ministers from every single sovereign nation in planet Earth were running about like a bunch of big rats in garbage cans, coming together, huddling up in cozy conference rooms, and brainstorming, just to conceive and adopt the best of the variety of ideas on the way forward. However, this was to no avail, as the conferences always ended with the delegates working away without a workable idea. The best plant pathologists and researchers of the world were caught in their slumber. The whole world was looking up to them to come up with a quick solution when they could not even figure out a single one. Their professional qualifications and all their groundbreaking feats had been awesome until now. However, the V1B6F3 had proved invincible and had rubbished them all. It had left these men of science wandering around the best equipped labs available throughout the world, only to appear lost and generally confused, not being able to distinguish their left from their right. The V1B6F3 made them run around these labs with creases as thick as the Great Wall of China, well-manifested on their terror-stricken faces. Large beads of sweat were trickling off their bodies, which together emitted a stench as pungent as a garbage pile. The whole picture was that of a gathering of professionals who suddenly had become childish amateurs in their established trade. One would capture it aptly by saying that all of them looked like kindergarten children who were in pathology labs for the very first time.

"I must confess that I have never seen anything like this before."

"You are right! I have never seen this throughout my practice."

"Where could this have come from?"

"This thing has defied all my attempts to identify it."

"Is it a microbe?"

"Do you think I know?"

This virgin situation had struck, and had compelled them to sound deflated, awful, and ridiculous.

"But you've always known the answers."

"I can guess that you now know better. I used to believe that you are very smart. What has happened of late?"

"Now you know you have believed wrongly. Don't ever take such a dangerous risk again."

"I will be sure not to, that is if the world survives this invasion."

"Yes, I understand you outright. No life, no research, no pathology..."

"And no science."

"My Nobel prize award is in tatters. I wouldn't have accepted it if I had known that this stalemate would come over to defeat me."

"Oh...Professor...Why are you talking like this? Have you forgotten that not knowing what will come up next is common in this practice?"

"Please pardon me for forgetting it so soon."

"This thing spreads at an alarming speed."

"I cannot say whether it is a virus or a bacterium or a fungus, even with all my knowledge..."

"Resignation is calling me now."

"This is serious! How then are we supposed to find a remedy?"

"You had better ask someone who should know."

"And who would that be if not us?"

"Anyway forward? You have one?"

"I am empty."

"That is it! Empty! We are all empty."

"Hey! Let anyone amongst us who is not empty and has the way forward speak!" The whole laboratory suddenly assumed the silence of a graveyard. If any of the pathologists or other sound minds of science that were there had dropped any pin to the ground at this time, it would have been heard loud and clear like the blast of a bomb.

The V_1B6F_3 showed no mercy whatsoever as it unleashed the widespread carnage it was genetically engineered to deliver. It was furious. It went about its business just like California wild fires, without an atom of any respect or regard for any of its targets. It made sure that ugly sights were left behind in its destructive trail wherever it visited. Farmers all over the world were being rendered absolutely helpless by its brazen attack. They could do nothing other than moping like wretched imbeciles as their livelihoods got swept away. All they could see were their labor, talent, touch, and expertise, that used to put big smiles on their faces, infuse dignity in their character, and got them laughing to their banks, being nothing but a big disaster.

There were dark-brown spots on leaves and stems of growing plants which eventually got them to dry up. Some plants had been afflicted with stunted growth in their vines. There were reduced branch formations in trees which quickly caused leaves to be unusually small. Distorted leaves with significantly reduced sizes, wilting and eventual death of young stems and leaves, very weak stems prone to breakage by a slight breeze because of the cankers created on them had also become commonplace. Blighting of leaves, gums issuing from stems that finally became dead, lesions on leaves that substantially reduced surfaces available for photosynthesis to occur, and lesions on roots affected all the crops. Tuber crops were afflicted with cracks, soft, dry and spongy rot. Withered leaves were everywhere. Maize cobs were reduced to galls that were nothing but a bunch of spores. Many leaves carried brown spots with yellow streaks on them as well. It was really horrible! One thing that was not lacking was the presence of seed-borne spores that attacked and killed young seedlings. Yellow leaves flourished and were very busy falling off. Totally mottled, stunted, and scorched plants were among many more of the things that turned out to be uncountable. They were just ubiquitous. Counting them would amount to an attempt to count the number of stars in the sky with frail naked eyes that were heavily infected with glaucoma.

It, therefore, came as no surprise at all to have gaunt-looking wild, domestic, and farm animals roaming about endlessly with fast-diminishing hopes of finding what used to be readily available food. There were mews, brays, bleats, and lots of other sounds that go synonymous with animals. The only thing different was that this time, they were fueled by hard-biting hunger. How would they find life in planet Earth to be interesting when the V_1B6F_3 had made grass so scarce for the herbivorous ones amongst them? And, with the herbivorous animals finding it increasingly hard to scoop out any blade of grass, the carnivorous ones became faced with big threats to their existence. In this situation, who would then dare to ask dairy cows why their udders had gone dry without any drop of milk? If there was no grazing, there would be no milk for sure. I am sure that any farmer that would even attempt to harbor such a question within the confines of his mind must be seen by the cows as a selfish fool that only deserved a hard knock of their hooves on his groin. So, animals started eating up other animals whom they would not have eaten if all had been well. It became common to see big cats, like lions or cheetahs, in pursuit of small rats or lizards, thereby making the small wild cats starve so badly. It was that bad. Even animal carcasses became very rare soon, and so the vultures felt the heat as well. Prices of the very scarce food crops rose so fast and aimed for the sky. And, only a psychiatric hospital patient, whose case was beyond the ability of medical science to comprehend, would attempt to announce that there was abundance of animal protein. The dream of an automobile world completely driven by bio-fuel was shrinking fast, now hanging by a loose thread that was thinner than the legs of a mosquito. Hunger and starvation were flexing their big biceps with reckless abandon. And, therefore, the human race had no other choice than to drift to the track of extinction at the lightning speed of Formula One cars.

In The Beginning Was Jazi

The V1B6F3 had brought disruption upon Jazi's design. It brought the smell of death to diffuse at very high speed. However, Jazi's handiwork was not for hunger, starvation, and anguish, and gnashing of teeth to dwell freely in. He did not make the world so that fear and hatred would be visited on it at the volition of any man. From the very beginning, Jazi's spirit had kept on hovering over the surface of the deluge and formlessness that were covered in darkness. He did not think it right to leave the mass of darkness and water to remain just like that. Enormous love streamed through his heart as it always did. "There is something good to do with this," he said to himself gently, "I want to pour all my love into this thing that I will make."

Jazi also wanted to make another thing, something so wonderful to be made out of his bountiful love that it would stand out and be left in charge. He embarked on this work at once.

And right after that, something called light came into existence. It stood out clearly from all the darkness that used to be, with an awesome piercing and far-reaching illumination. Darkness and light mesmerized Jazi after he had separated them. He went on to assign each of them different times to reign, and day and night came into existence. The Light held its sway during the day, and darkness did the same at night. No confusion about the roles for these two arose at all, for Jazi's work was a full epitome of order and arrangement to the very core. The water in existence began to move. A portion of it moved up and the other portion moved down. And that was how empty space began to exist between the water. This space became known as the sky. Water below the sky began to move and gathered in one place, allowing dry ground to appear. Jazi kept on falling in love with his progress so far. The dry ground he named 'land,' and the water he named 'sea.'

The dry ground began to show the appearance of all sorts of grass and seed-bearing plants. Assorted trees with seed-bearing fruits began to appear, each capable of producing the kind of tree it came from. They all began to multiply. All the water became filled with fish and other marine creatures. This huge presence of myriad aquatic life looked good to Jazi. He went ahead in his growing joy to cause the sky to be filled with birds of different kinds. It felt gratifying to watch them fly about. And, then came the turn of all small animals, wild animals and livestock, each capable of producing its own kind. They all emerged from the ground, all sorts of beasts, and began to multiply. Jazi was not going to leave it all like this. One more thing was needed to bring his masterpiece to completion. Then at last, the outpouring of his endless love accumulated to give rise to humanity. That meant that the first man and woman began to walk the surface of the earth after arising from dust. They had the capacity to multiply as well. This was Jazi's way of putting his beloved humanity in charge of his beautiful creation. He crowned his work with love and constantly made sure that it always was a source of delight to him. He also left a web of interdependence, which he expected all he had created to subsist within and have everlasting peace and harmony. Man was dependent on plants and animals for food, and animals were dependent on plants and other animals in turn. The crops were dependent on man and animal feces for nutrients essential to their growth, and animals and plants depended on man for their tender loving care.

KWAME AND THE VOICES

Kwame had grown up in Shonga. He had turned just a year old now. And, this was when he began to hear lots of voices whose origin he never knew and could not discern. Being more of an introvert, he naturally kept this burdensome development to himself. He was simply under attack by these voices that were in fierce contest for his attention and companionship.

Antagonism and rivalry are stark realities of existence. These two will never go away from the theatre of life. It has been observed that the relationship between cats and dogs uphold these two aspects. Human existence and interactions are huge arenas where antagonism and rivalry act out their various scripts on a daily basis. Political campaigns make a great picture for these, and politicians act these out perfectly. Desires of the spirit of a man and those of his flesh are constant rivals that will never end their rivalry until a man's flesh returns to dust from which it arose. Good and evil are also no strangers to rivalry and antagonism. They are fierce rivals, always in constant battle within human minds, heads, and hearts—Battles for who will win over human faith, who will keep humans under control and get them to become handy tools with which to give rise to destruction, or peace and harmony. Battles for who will determine the path in which human destiny shall head. Fierce battles always rage between these two that hate each other so much. Good and evil always go out and about in search of fertile grounds with lots of opportunities to establish their intents. They love to leave no vacuum at all with a passion. Either good reigns, or it is evil which does so. These two had now found a fertile ground in Kwame.

"May evil reign all the time!"

"Evil is good!"

"Allowing evil to reign all the time is a sweet experience that the sweetest of honey cannot equal."

"Kwame! Do not mind them!"

"Doing what is good is always the best!"

"That is a lie, Kwame! Do not fall for that deceit!"

"Evil is good."

"Do not mind them! Evil is horrible!"

"Look, Kwame! You must know that doing evil is not good."

"That is a lie! They are only trying to keep you away from doing what is good! And that is doing evil! Do not listen further to what they are telling you."

"No! Kwame! Do you want the worst things life can bring? I'm sure you don't. Always choose to do what is good. Evil is the way forward for destruction and damnation!"

"Kwame, choose evil and live, for the path of doing good leads to destruction."

"Doing evil brings great joy to a man's heart!"

"Doing evil brings prosperity the way of a man!"

"That is a big lie, Kwame! Don't ever take that! Does that sound like the truth? It is certainly not!"

"I am telling you the whole truth, and nothing but the truth. Doing evil is the only way a man finds fulfillment in life!"

SHONGA

Shonga typified the very simplest of primitive existence—a place whose inhabitants needed no more than one look to see that they were exceedingly dependent on nature. They felt quite at home with nature, just like the Bushmen of the Kalahari Desert, depending largely on fishing and gathering wild fruits, nuts, and other products from forests which made up much of the landscape. Within these forests lay scattered human settlements that had nothing but thatched houses for homes. Houses were built from materials that came from the branches and leaves of trees, ones that could very easily be blown away and carried about like dust in one sweep should they ever exist in hurricane-prone areas. The men, women, and children wore no clothes. Not even the young men and women amongst them wore any clothes. All they did to cover a bit of their nakedness was to coat their private parts with hides of varying thickness, made from the skin of animals, mainly antelopes. They cared less that the rest of their bodies were uncovered. Bare-chested men and women simply went about their businesses. They moved around dangling breasts and buttocks everywhere with absolutely no instance of promiscuity ever rearing their ugly heads. Shonga was one of the most isolated places on earth, located in the western region of Africa, that was yet to know even the least of incursions of civilization. A long meandering river, which lined some paths in the forests, was the only source of water for these people. This river mainly teemed with catfish. But, it also had a huge stock of other marine creatures like crabs and lobsters. This was Nature's way of supplying abundant nutrition to its people.

Cases of snake bites were quite common, however, the people were well armed with the knowledge to gather herbs, and squeeze and apply liquid from them into the wounded area to secure complete healing within a matter of seconds. The people of Shonga had never heard of anything called an electric bulb—None of them had ever seen it. The presence of one would be dreaded a lot, avoided, and would be regarded as strange and dangerous. They would say that Nature had gone crazy, that it had suddenly succumbed to the desire of inflicting harm upon them. The people of Shonga had no choice than to rely on sunshine during the day to do all their chores before it got dark. The arrival of darkness meant that all the major chores that were undone before its arrival would have to be put off until the break of dawn of the next day.

The people of Shonga had quite distinctive eyes. They were unique in the sense that they had eyes which allowed them to see clearly even in pitch-dark nights. This way, lactating mothers would not need sunlight to feed their little ones. The main source of energy for these people came from firewood which the trees in surrounding forests provided them with. However, no one could afford to light up firewood for anything else other than cooking, after which the fire would be quickly doused off with water. It is true that the people of Shonga had trees all around them, which should have meant that firewood was a commodity that was never to be found lacking, but it was not easy to come by. Getting firewood meant undertaking risky searches deep inside the forests. Many parts of the Shonga forests were inhabited by man-eating tigers, huge beasts that weighed up to one-hundred-and-fifty pounds, having beautiful stripes weaved around their massive bodies, which would not hesitate to attack and kill anyone that came within their strike range.. They would normally appear very calm, as if they were unable to hurt a fly, until the arrival of any trespasser. That is when they would quickly put aside their often-deceptive calm mien and demonstrate how swift and ruthless a killing machine they were. Many of the people of Shonga had fallen prey to these tigers on a number of occasions. It happened at such an extent that the number of people getting attacked and killed rose so high that it no longer was a thing that brought so much pain, sorrow, and a deep sense of loss. After all, girls of Shonga were very fertile and were well able to begin reproduction at the age of ten. The high birth rate in Shonga meant that women gave birth at a rate so high that their population would still be exploding even if the tigers stepped up the frequency of their attacks by encroaching into places where the people actually lived. This was Shonga...before the $V_1B_6F_3$ invaded it.

THE BIRTH OF KWAME

A young girl of twelve had wandered very deep into the forests one day. She had gone there in search of firewood, which was becoming quite scare—not because of the tigers, but because of the V1B6F3 pathogen. She had not realized when she had stepped into the territory where the tigers were in charge. She was cold with fear when a big male tiger charged towards her at the speed of lightening. She almost passed out. However, instead of going for the swift kill and tearing her into pieces, as tigers would naturally do, this tiger grabbed the girl by her waist and dragged her further into the forest. The girl was by now overtaken by very close shadow of death in whose hands she was now, and upon whom her fate was inextricably dependent on. She barely breathed as the tiger dragged her on.

Upon reaching a certain point, the tiger stopped. The beast had handled the girl in such a manner that only a little blood spilled from her. And, that too came from the contact that her legs had made with shrubs as she was being dragged along—She only sustained a few bruises. To the utter surprise of the girl, a strange and swift metamorphosis descended on the tiger. The girl watched, terrified. The tiger's body assumed the shape of a man. As the girl stood helpless, the man focused his attention on her. The girl was too dumbfounded to even scream. The man before her had bushy eyelashes, one eye, two noses, and one excessively hairy ear. His chin was full with a bushy beard that was around twenty inches long. Strangely enough, he had two penises. The little girl could see that the man's transformation was not complete, for only the fore limbs of the tiger had turned into a man's hands while the tiger's hind limbs had remained. The girl finally let out a scream when a tremendous fear, which had gripped her, had compelled her to do so. That was all she could do before the anomalous creature pounced on her. The girl screamed all the more as the horrendous show went on. But, not even a soul heard her. Screaming was useless, as the arrival of any help was as impossible as candle wax not melting in a furnace. The man took on the form of a tiger immediately after he was done and ran away, leaving the girl in such a shock that it left her speechless. Silence was the best place she could find solace in. She got up to her feet after a while and began to walk back where she came from. She did not speak about her ordeal with anyone. Her strange copulation experience soon brought about conception, and that was the making of the beginning of Kwame.

The remarkable pregnancy that had brought Kwame into this world lasted only three months. He was born while his very young mother was in search of firewood. The pregnancy suddenly ran its full course, as the labor pains set in. The mother was able to gather a few leaves together unto which she pushed out the baby Kwame, who arrived into this world sucking his thumb, looking very calm. His mother didn't care about the danger which the tigers' presence posed. Her previous experience might have contributed to such bravado in no small way. She lay beside the little Kwame, watching him and recovering from the exhaustion she had earlier known during the course of her delivery. Three tigers came close to Kwame as he lay on the leaves. It was curiosity that had brought them. All they did was sniff at the little baby before striding away, not even attempting to attack his mother. They all left with a clear impression that the baby would make no good meal—it was visible in the frisky nervousness that the tigers showed off as they left. Little Kwame only smiled in response before he began to suck his thumb again. Then, he laughed, all to his mother's consternation.

Kwame was surely an unusual child—beginning to walk and talk only a month after his birth. There was nothing he loved as much as going inside the forest to gather firewood with his mother. His mother was not comfortable with this, but Kwame would not stay back for her to go alone. He had the surprising desire to go alone when he was only two months old—that was something that his mother never saw coming. Kwame's quest met with her strong objection. However, Kwame was not the kind of child who could be stopped once his mind was set on something. He was quite an obstinate child. He would cry all day with the voice of a forty-year-old man. He would stop at nothing to make his mother's day a miserable one if she continued to object to his decision. This included refusing to eat for many days at an end, with his mother begging him to no avail. It got to a point that his mother had to give up on stopping him. Kwame was, afterwards, labeled an evil child by his mother, and she left him to do as he wished.

"After all, only I know how I got him into my womb," she said to herself one day. She noticed that Kwame returned more joyful each time he went to the forest. And, he always returned with lots of firewood, which surprised his mother. She could not fathom where from Kwame got all the strength to carry large logs of wood. It then began to dawn on her that there must be more to her son than that which was meeting her eyes. This idea got stuck right inside her mind and made her wonder about it. But, what more did she not know? She could not just figure it out yet.

"I have a destiny I love so much," Kwame announced to his mother one day. His mother was sitting close to him and ought to have heard him clearly, but she had been carried away with the thoughts of how strange his son had grown to be lately. So, she did not hear Kwame.

"Mother, why are you not listening to me?" Kwame went ahead, rousing his mother back from her sojourn of thoughts.

"Sorry, Kwame, I was far away."

"I know..."

"Did you ask me any question, son?"

"What were you thinking of?"

"I was thinking about you..."

"That is fine, mother. I said something which I would like you to know."

"And what is that?"

"I have a destiny I love so much." Kwame's mother was rattled at once. She threw a glance at her son, one that carried a shock, bewilderment, and surprise.

"Kwame!" she screamed, "What do you even know about destiny?"

"A lot."

"That is a lie. You are too young to know what destiny is."

"Well, I know about it because I am already old enough to know about it."

"Kwame, your destiny is to start being like the children of your age."

Kwame laughed in response, his laughter full of disregard for what his mother had said.

"Why did you laugh?"

"I laughed because you lied, mother."

"How?"

"I am much older than them."

"Shut up, Kwame. You were all born the same day. Your destiny is for you to start behaving like them."

"That is a lie."

"Look, Kwame! They still suck their mothers' breasts. You never even sucked mine for a second."

"I think that is great."

"You demanded adult food the day you were born. You started chewing leaves since you were born with a set of strong adult teeth in your mouth which made me fear for my nipples."

"That is why I tell you that my destiny is different from what you think it should be."

"And what is that thing you call your destiny?"

"I love it so much."

"You have said that before with a smile on your face."

"My destiny is to wage war against evil forces that don't even mind killing innocent children to achieve their aims."

Kwame's mother kept silent as she lost her thoughts in wonder as to what her son meant.

Kwame held onto his affirmation every day. He kept on speaking about what he believed his destiny was, until he became a year old. His mother was nowhere to be seen then. She was not supposed to be seen around after Kwame had become a year old, having served her purpose as the chosen channel to set the stage for Kwame's destiny. Death snatched her away peacefully while she was sleeping, the night before Kwame became a year old. It was then that Kwame became a full-time forest wanderer.

KWAME AND THE VOICES

"Kwame, make sure you make proper use of your resources!" the first voice banged on Kwame's head one day.

"You wouldn't be so foolish to do that, Kwame!" came the second voice, "Don't ever use your resources! Make sure you don't!"

"Those terrible liars are back, Kwame! Ignore them! Use your resources. It is only in that manner that good prevails over evil."

"Hey, Kwame! Do we need to be telling you right now that these voices talking about good are the terrible liars? You are quite sensible. We trust that you understand that not using your resources would be the right choice."

"No, Kwame! Using your resources is in line with your destiny, which you love so much! Don't listen to the pack of liars that flocks your mind."

It was then that Kwame's response suddenly came through for the very first time. He had been extremely agitated by the voices that kept battling inside his head. "No!" he said to the voice that spoke to him last.

"Kwame! What did I hear you say?"

"I said no!" Kwame continued, "I have now realized that I must keep my resources to myself! They belong to me alone!"

"Yes, Kwame, we know that. But—"

"I have decided not to use them," Kwame interrupted the voice that spoke.

"That is bad, Kwame! You have allowed yourself to be deceived by evil that wants nothing good to prevail!"

"Leave the boy alone! He is a wise boy, and he has chosen to do what is right!"

"What he thinks to be right is wrong!"

"You would do better to respect his decision!"

"No! We will never do that! Kwame! Think about the destruction you will encourage by letting evil prevail! Please change your mind!"

"I will never do that," Kwame responded.

"Kwame! We are sure you don't understand what you have decided."

"I do!"

"Your decision is evil!"

"Who are you to tell me what to decide?" Kwame screamed in anger.

"Hey! Will you leave the boy alone? He has made his decision and that is final! Isn't it, Kwame?"

KWAME THE VOICES THE ENCOUNTER

Kwame's clutched his head with his hands. "This is too much!" he wailed out of agony. His eyes were shut in pain. He had obviously been rattled by what he was going through. The tone of distress was deep-seated in his voice, and it reigned like a king. Kwame had been wandering in the forest when he was compelled to act this way. Being in a lot of pain, he went on to scream further.

"Leave me alone, all you voices that want good! I have decided on following the voices of evil!"

"Come on, Kwame...What has gone wrong with you?"

"That is none of your business!" Kwame replied fast, screaming it out loud.

"You ought not to take such a stance."

"Didn't you hear me?"

"Come on, Kwame. You must denounce your present stance."

"I said it is none of your business!"

"You can't do that!"

"Says who? Tell me!"

"Kwame, you must know that you were not created to make a decision like the one you have made."

"It is my decision! I made it! Nobody else made it! Who are *you* to tell me to abandon it?"

"We have to tell you because you were made to do good and not evil."

"To hell with all of you then!"

"What did you say?"

"Have you all gone deaf?"

"This is not you, Kwame. Do not stray into the path of evil and destruction!"

"Why? It is the better path!"

"Oh Kwame, shake off all the evil. Now! You have to discard all those liars that are telling you that your decision is the best!"

"And what if I don't?"

"Kwame! Remember your destiny, the one you love so much?"

"What I remember is that I never had one!"

"How could you have forgotten so quickly?"

"Forgotten? I never even had one!"

"You are to get rid of evil, Kwame!"

"Now I remember my destiny!" Kwame suddenly announced after a pause.

"That is great!" replied the good voice almost in sense of relief.

"And that is to shut down all the voices in my head, except the ones that bid me to do evil."

"Kwame, you don't want to do that!"

"Leave me alone! Go away!"

"Shut up, you deceptive voices! Can't you hear the boy? Are you all deaf? Leave him alone!" butted in the evil voice.

"Yes! Tell them to leave me alone!" Kwame urged.

"Carry on, Kwame!"

"Thank you!"

"Don't ever allow anybody to tell you to alter your decision."

"I am going to stick to it!"

"That is great! Evil is good, Kwame! Uphold it!"

"That is a lie, Kwame! Do not do that!" the voice that advocated good tried again.

"You again? Will it take all of you a century to understand and respect the boy's wish?"

"We must respect no evil wish! Get out of our way!"

"We are not going to do that," responded the evil voice.

"The boy needs to be restored to his original state. Get out of the way!"

"We are going nowhere!"

"Get out!"

"You can try all that you know, but you can't push us aside!"

"Get out of the way!" the voice repeated.

"No!"

"Get out!" it went on, its tone becoming sharper with every entreaty.

"No! We are going nowhere! Kwame is our home!"

"Let go of the boy..."

"No..."

"I am going to follow the voices of evil inside my head..." Kwame wailed, "That is my destiny..."

Kwame had held onto his head all the while the voices had throbbed in it. The voices vanished as soon as he had decided on his new destiny. But, suddenly his body began to convulse, making Kwame lose his balance. His feet trembled as if the ground on which he stood was being unsettled by a massive earthquake, whose epicenter was not more than five inches away. It only took a few seconds for Kwame to fall down, his mouth hanging open the way in which the mouth of a hippopotamus does sometimes. "Leave me alone..." he began to utter slowly, "I have made it clear that I stand for evil...Evil, I love you...I will hang on to you forever, the way a little monkey hangs on to its mother's back." The convulsions, which had earlier taken hold of Kwame, drifted away in a flash. His manner of breathing suddenly changed its pace—It went from being very fast and labored to becoming gentle and hardly noticeable. He became calm. Kwame was gone...It was not that he died, but he transited. He went into a state of trance.

Silence took over. Silence prevailed in such a degree that the sun could almost be heard moving in the sky. Even the other ever-present inhabitants of the sky—the moon and the stars—would be heard trotting about had it been night time. The convulsion struck Kwame again and made the silence, which had taken charge, know that it was not possible for it to have such a privilege forever. Kwame's body began to wriggle about as a result of this, and it simply shattered the silence that existed earlier. The crackling sound of dry leaves and twigs began to rise, and it spread quickly. Then, it permeated the atmosphere as Kwame's body began to roll about, damaging young seedlings in its course. It was only the huge trunk of a baobab tree that could stop Kwame's body from continuing its rolling spree. As Kwame hit the tree trunk, he stopped rolling at once, and all the spasm in his body was now gone.

Kwame spotted something move, and it was nearing him. As it came close, Kwame was surprised to see that it was a creature that resembled a half wolf and half man. It had seething eyes and fangs that gleamed. Here and there, he could see a pale flash of skin that was otherwise clothed in green leaves.

"Who are you?" Kwame spoke. No answer came. The creature ignored Kwame and continued to move around, its hooves pounding on the ground. Kwame began to scream, "Who are you? What do you want from me? Who are you? I owe nobody...What do you want? Get away from me!"

"No one runs away from his destiny," the creature finally uttered, having stopped moving about.

"What do you want from me?" Kwame screamed again.

"You can't let this happen," wailed the strange creature.

"What do you want from—?" Another fit of convulsion came down on Kwame even before he could complete his sentence.

"You are to save humanity and not help in destroying it," said the creature again, after which he transformed completely into a wolf. "I am from Jazi, the supreme god of love and humanity."

Kwame's convulsion vanished at the mention of Jazi, and he was transferred back from his trance in the blink of an eye. He rose slowly, looking around in a confused manner, throwing fear-laden glances all around him. His hair had got covered with soil, dry leaves, and roots, and it appeared extremely unkempt. But, all that didn't matter to Kwame for his whole attention was captured by the wolf before him, which transformed into a man whose two legs were, however, those of a wolf. Kwame wondered what this kind of creature could want from him.

"What is it that you want?" Kwame asked in fear, which kept creeping further into him and shook his legs. "Why have you chosen to come to me? Who are you?"

"Do not be afraid," said the man-wolf, "Your time has come."

Then an ethereal voice came along, so loud that Kwame got startled when it descended.

"I have seen the plan of evil to ruin my creation. But, I also have a plan."

The man-wolf quickly went back to its wolf form and vanished with Kwame in a second. A slight breeze started blowing as it happened, tickling the leaves and branches as it began to gain speed. Its speed grew so fast that it could no longer be called a breeze—it had turned into a wind, a strong one and spinning one. It made all the dry grasses, leaves, shrubs, and other dry matter whisk up and mold into a spiral. The shape rose high and vanished into thin air.

HAD TO RETURN

Kwame had to abandon being a forest wanderer because he had to return to Shonga quickly. It was most necessary that he did now that the V1B6F3's rampage could not help but continue to leave the world destitute. A strong wind came around and shook the trees so much that all their leaves danced about vigorously. The cloud gathered in the sky, and it was followed by rain. Even though it lasted for only five seconds, it was quite a heavy rain—one that brought back the calm which it had uprooted earlier.

Right at the spot, where Kwame had disappeared with the strange creature, lay a ball of human flesh surrounded by layers of leaves. This fleshy ball had fallen from the sky with the rains. After a few moments, the ball began to unfold gently like a blossoming flower, yielding a crackling noise that is most commonly heard whenever fire consumes a bunch of dry leaves. As it unfurled, it gradually became clear that the ball was unfolding into a creature that looked very much like a human being—A male. His hands shot out first, followed by his legs. Finally, his head emerged along with the rest of his body. He looked all bloated, with his stomach protruding just like his buttocks. The whole body was twenty-feet in length together. Kwame used to be fair in complexion. But, he had now returned with a dark complexion and looked as if he was pregnant. Whatever he carried in his stomach made him look that way. He could pass for a woman that was pregnant with ten babies. Even his eyes and his legs were swollen too. He began to move slowly, his swollen feet throbbing on the ground. His movement would have been incredibly swift had it not been for all the weight that he had gained. He appeared to be calm and composed. It was quite evident from his face that he was on a mission—he looked focused, with his sights set on something, which appeared to be a task that needed urgent accomplishment. But, the voices that used to besiege him were not about to rest now. They had all been vigilant and patient, awaiting his return. They arrived back in droves, having a determination as strong as a rock of the igneous type; their numbers as numerous as bees in their hives, more determined than ever to press on. The stage for their final battle had now been set.

"Kwame, move on!"

"No...No! Kwame, have you lost your mind? What are you doing?"

"I'm about to do my job," Kwame responded fast as he moved.

"Do not do that job!"

"Who else will do it if I don't?" Kwame queried.

"Leave him alone! Move on, Kwame!"

"No! No! You must stop now!"

"I will not," Kwame replied, "This is my destiny. I can't shy away from it."

"His destiny must be accomplished now! Leave him alone!"

"No! Don't do it, Kwame! Don't do it!"

"Leave him alone!"

"You must not do it!"

"I love my destiny so much," Kwame said, "It must be fulfilled."

"No! What has got into you?"

"My true destiny, I am sorry."

"We thought you were on our side!"

"Sorry, that was before. I love my true destiny."

"Kwame, you must not let us down...No!"

"Sorry, I have to."

"No! You can't!"

"I must!"

"No! No! No!"

"Yes!"

"Kwame, this must be a joke!"

"Is that what you call it?"

"That is what it is! Please turn back now!"

"No!"

"Your destiny is to take sides with evil. Why did you forget that so fast?"

"I have to hang on to my true destiny."

"Great, Kwame! That is it! Hang on to it tight."

"You must stop, Kwame. Stop and turn back!"

"I can't! I love my destiny!"

"Leave him alone, you evil makers. He knows what his true destiny is. Don't even dream of stopping him now."

"Shut up! We must!"

"His destiny is to wage war against evil forces. Don't even dare to stop him!"

"We must stop him! He must not do that!"

"He is well on his way towards achieving it. What can you all do?"

"No...No...Kwame must be stopped! Kwame, you are on a dangerous path now. Don't do it!"

"I have no choice. This destiny must be fulfilled this day," Kwame said in response.

"No, Kwame! You must turn away from this path now."

"You can't stop me!"

"Kwame, stop!"

"No..." Kwame screamed, remaining focused and moving ahead, "I must denounce the voices of evil in my head."

"You traitor!"

"Call me what you like!"

"We shall skin you alive!"

"That would actually be fine!"

"Kwame, you simply cannot do this!"

"Leave me alone!"

"We won't until you stop! Kwame, please stop this!"

"I am on a mission that I can't turn away from. Can't you see that?"

"Kwame, you are a big disappointment!"

"Leave me alone now!"

"You have to stop now!"

"Leave me alone!"

"You must stop now!"

"Leave me alone. You are just wasting your time...You can't stop me from my destiny..."

"Kwame, stop!"

"Leave him alone...Let him go on and fulfill his destiny..."

"Shut up! You liars have crushed our mission! Kwame must stop now!"

"He will never stop..."

"Shut up!"

"You shut up! You have all been fools to think that evil will prevail."

"It is not over!"

"It is!"

"Oh no, it is far from being over!"

"It is better for you all to give up now and die. Evil will not prevail!"

"You are wrong! Evil is destined to prevail."

"Never!"

"It will prevail!"

"Never!"

Kwame trudged on in spite of the war waging inside his head. Voices growling hard for him to abandon his mission snorted, shrieked, snarled, squeaked, howled, and wailed in their last effort to persuade him to back off. All of them had foolishly failed to realize that he was no longer at their command. Kwame reached a spot in the forest and stopped walking. The spot was a rich store of long and decomposed plant debris. The soil in the spot was rich in humus and appeared dark in color.

Voices inside Kwame's head, which were striving to make him change his mind, had now begun to think that their progress was within sight. "Good boy...Good boy..." they cheered, "It is time to turn back now...You must turn back!" They all continued wailing, but to no avail—Kwame did not listen to them. His time had actually come. He began to feel his stomach churn. The churning spread fast all over the swollen parts of his body. The contents of all the swollen parts of his body began to migrate to his stomach. The voices inside Kwame's head ceased, having taken solace in silence. Kwame had now become a total stranger to them. His stomach was now fully distended. It appeared humongous and strange. The churning inside his stomach soon grew in intensity as all the contents were being pushed away towards Kwame's gullet—its destination being the spot that was rich in humus. Kwame's mouth yanked open as volumes of saliva came gushing out like water from a rock. It carried lots of seed with it, seeds of different shapes, sizes, and colors that were never seen before on earth. The seeds were so many in number that it took quite a while before Kwame finished vomiting. Kwame looked up after having vomited so much, a strong sense of accomplishment standing on his face alongside a smile that suggested nothing other than triumph. Then a voice called out from the sky, a very loud one, and said, "Plan accomplished!"

Kwame began to lose his hands at once. And, this was quickly followed by his legs. All parts of his body began to fold up, giving rise to the fleshy ball from which he had emerged. The ball arose in the direction of the sky, from where rain started pouring into the earth, accompanied by gusts of wind and rumblings of thunder. The ball had vanished by the time the wind and rain had stopped. Only another voice emerged from the sky. "Well done, my faithful messenger," it said.

NEW DAWN OF RELIEF AND DISAPPOINTMENT

The seeds that had been vomited out began to sprout fast immediately after the voice from the sky had uttered the last word. They were vomited in Shonga, but their growth rate was so fast that it took them less than ten minutes to mature and become full-grown trees laden with leaves. The tress began to produce fruits, whose seeds began to get disseminated by the wind from Shonga to all parts of the earth where they fell, where they began to sprout and spread again.

The V1B6F3 now had a nemesis—stubborn ones that would not surrender, having the innate capacity to thrive against all odds. Plants that could resist the ravaging effects of the V1B6F3 had now filled the earth and were multiplying fast. The hope of survival for the rattled, hungry, and extinction-threatened humanity arose and broke forth like sunrise of a youthful morning. For the few animals that had managed to stay alive, it was the arrival of prosperity. Green shoots were now springing up here and there. It was like a dream to them. They could not believe it. The very skinny herbivorous animals were thrilled at the sight of this unexpected greenery. They moved their haggard-looking bodies to where the grasses were. But, they were not in a hurry to begin chewing. They first made investigative sniffs at the grass blades to make sure that their eyes were not deceiving them. They only began to chew when they were convinced beyond all doubts that prosperity had once again smiled at them and had brought back their cherished grass. The carnivorous animals were glad to see their herbivorous preys had found food. They knew quite well that the grass-eaters having enough fresh grass meant that there would be plenty of fresh and succulent flesh for them to feed off. Jazi's web of interdependence now had restoration within its sights. World leaders began to have smiles visiting their faces once more. It was all magic to them. A magical turnaround of which they had not the slightest clue as to what had brought it. They were simply glad, not knowing whom to heap the credit on. The plant pathologists were now thrilled that something had somehow come along to do a job that they could not. "Something miraculously warded off starvation from the entire humanity." This was the remarks of many world leaders. "Many thanks to this wonder," they said, expressing their deepest appreciation and gratitude.

However, for Murktar, Abdoullah, and Farouk, this miraculous happening, which had somehow turned things around, did not herald a time to laugh at all. Laughter had become a huge luxury to them now. It never existed in the list of what could come upon their faces now—faces that were moody portraits of disappointment—which also hung around in their minds like a boxer's punching bag. All this while, they had labeled their mission a huge success. They had tagged their trademark pathogen as invincible, dubbed it the greatest, until now. Its pen name had been 'indefatigable' before now. That something had somehow found a way to stand its ground against it was a complete shock to them. What could this something be? This is the question that hovered in the minds of Murktar, Abdoullah, and Farouk. They had done all things right. They had perfected everything. They would bet their lives that they did, all well and good. But, they refused to reckon with one thing—That thing which sneaks in at will. They did not tell each other the truth before they began to celebrate. They did not tell each other the plain truth. They had assumed that the element of surprise would no longer be around in this world. And, that is what sneaked in, like it always does, like a string of unending saga. Who could stop it?

Disappointment in these men gave rise to sadness, which in turn yielded anger. This anger was very dangerous. It drove Farouk to pick up his Star nine-millimeter short gun, and pump bullets into Murktar's head within seconds. He did the same to Abdoullah, who welcomed the move, before turning the gun to his forehead and putting the period to the last chapter of his book called life. A small pool of blood began to form at a spot in the laboratory, where blood from their lifeless bodies had gathered. It was quite gory a sight!

Farouk, the youngest of the three, was forty years old. Murktar was forty-five, and Abdoullah, forty-two. All of them were tall, and they had black hair. Their faces carried bushy beards, all fifteen inches long.

The Rendevouz

Murktar loved surfing the internet—it was his favorite pastime. Many of his professional colleagues loved to go bowling or swimming whenever the demands of work allowed that, but Murktar would not. He would, instead, log on to the Yahoo Messenger chat facility to have some fun. He would chat with anyone who cared to. His chat mates often included flirtatious wives, young men, and single mothers. He would sometimes meet and chat with gay men and lesbians as well. One day, he met someone online whose bits of response tickled his fancy. This had happened well after he had spent a large portion of his time with others in the chat room. He had only a couple of minutes left before this person initiated a chat.

Hi

Hello

How are you?

I am fine. What about you?

I am fine too. Male or female?

Male. My name is Farouk.

I'm Murktar.

Where do you live?

In the United States of America.

I am in America too.

I live in Trenton, New Jersey.

I am in Philadelphia, Pennsylvania.

What do you do?

What?

I mean what you do? Your occupation.

Oh! Is that what you mean?

Yes.

I am a scientist.

Really?

Yes.

I am a scientist as well.

Oh...That's interesting.

And how is life treating you?

Not bad at all. All is well.

That is good to hear.

What about you? How are you getting along?

I am fine, and all is well.

Great!

I really have to go now.

What's the matter?

Demands of work.

That is true. I understand completely. I am also a very busy man. I feel you will be very interesting to chat with. That is what my mind is telling me right now. Can we chat again? When do you think chance will permit us to meet again?

I am not sure right now...I can say that you seem quite interesting from the little chat that we just had.

Thank you. Tomorrow? How about tomorrow?

I have a feeling that you are not the type who makes chatting very boring.

Thank you.

Tomorrow...Okay! I think tomorrow would be just fine.

Time?

Around this time.

That is fine.

Have a nice day, Farouk.

All the best, Murktar!

Murktar had enough time to go on chatting, he had just lied to Farouk since he was not sure if he was the right person to tell what he had in mind. This thing had been on his mind for months. He really wanted to share it with someone. But who? He was not sure there was anyone he could trust with it. He had a feeling that Farouk wanted to get along with him. But, he was unsure whether he would accept what he had in mind. His previous attempts had ended up in failure. A particular one flashed through his mind.

What makes you think that I will agree to that dirty plan of yours?

Why not? Think about it?

Go to hell with your plans! I will never be a part of it.

Please reconsider your stand.

I will never partake in that. Now go to hell! Go and die with that plan of yours. Go and die with that mission of yours. Go to hell!

Bye...

Coming on board with you is like engaging with wild cats engaged in a battle of claws. I don't want a romance with death.

Wait a minute

There is nothing to fear

I don't have the nerve. Bye...

Murktar did not sleep very long that night. He had only managed to get thirty minutes worth of sleep, after which he got up, further distancing sleep from his eyes. He turned on the lantern beside his bed, sauntered a bit away from his bed, and began thinking of how to see if someone else would sign up for a mission that had been in his mind for a while. He also had a dream during his brief sleep, one that brought huge inspiration to him. He saw Osama bin Laden in his dream, working tirelessly to perfect his mission of comprehensive expulsion of all infidels from the Arab world. He also observed Osama's direct involvement in the fight to foil the invasion of Afghanistan by the now defunct Soviet Union through the recruitment of fighters and his huge expenditure in the areas of logistics and weapons purchase. Murktar saw Osama voicing his disagreement to the Saudi royal family on their planned acceptance of American offer of setting up a military base on Saudi soil—calling it a plot by America to desecrate Islamic values that the sacred land of Saudi Arabia had long been known for. Murktar was quite vocal as he summed up his impression of Osama bin Laden. He thought that Osama was great and fearless. He admired Osama's courage so much that Osama's words to him in the dream found their way into his mind, his mind became comforted by those thoughts.

"Let no man who keeps delaying what he can do ever regard himself as a real man. He is as good as dead. He is utterly useless in the wake of American and Israeli impunity and injustice against our Arab motherland. His place will forever be amongst the spineless and the timid, and he neither fits in as a man nor a

woman."

Osama had told this to Murktar before walking away into a mountainous and rugged rocky terrain that was full of hidden caves with his army of staunchly dedicated young fighters, who would rather stand to fight and die than flee like chickens—men who would do anything to uphold his ideologies with the last trickle of blood flowing in their veins. He stood tall in Murktar's dream, a thick aura of confidence exuding from the great bravery he epitomized. Osama wore a white long gown and a pair of brown sandals and had a watch on his left wrist— he was a man that had a good sense of time. He loved to be aware of time at every moment—something that was vital in his operations. His very long beard was a bushy magnificence—he appeared quite handsome carrying it. He had his AK-47 hanging down his left shoulder. His left hand held some communication equipment, whose true identity was unclear to Murktar. It was either his cell phone or another gadget.

Murktar was a man who was more driven by the quest to accomplish something than be driven by the quest for more material acquisition. Even though he could very well afford to, his did not furnish his bedroom expensively. It just had a red rug on the floor, his wooden bed, a little table that carried his bedside lantern. There was also a wooden cupboard that contained his personal effects, and his wooden table stood at the left of the cupboard. A laptop was placed on top of the table and there were sheets of paper lying unarranged, making the table appear very untidy. Another thing that would quickly capture one's attention in Murktar's bedroom was his personal library. A well-polished mahogany wood, from which shelves were made, stood behind his bed by a green wall that had some Arabic inscriptions on it. These shelves were stuffed with books of varying sizes ranging from the very old to brand new. Hardbacks, soft backs, having the brown color of dust asserting itself as the true color of some of these covers. A few strings of cobweb hung here and there. Few spiders here and there were busy spinning their webs as naturally as it came to them because they did not care in the very least about what bothered Murktar. His room had no chandelier, and he never cared. Murktar was nothing but a consumed go-getter.

"That Farouk of a guy sounded lively," Murktar began talking as if there was someone with him, "He left the impression that he would love to get along with me. He sounded intelligent too. Oh...I hope my mind is not deceiving me here. That guy sounded like someone that would love to come on board. But, you never know. My mother kept telling me one thing, and that was that people are not always what they seem to be. Oh...No...But, who can I talk with? Who can I share this with? I need people. And not just any people. I need a sound team. A dedicated team. A team hell-bent on achieving excellence. I can't carry on alone. I guess this risk is one that I must take. I can't make any progress without it. That is as clear as crystal. This is a risk I must take. Not taking this risk would mean that I am abandoning this goal. No...the goal must not be abandoned. It must be achieved. I have to take this risk. Yes, I have to. I have to. I have no other choice. God is great! God is great! God is great!"

Murktar soon turned his attention to his laptop. He logged into his Yahoo mail account. He had to wait for a while for the site to load. He found that he had received an electronic mail from Professor Umar from Tehran. He was delighted to inform Murktar that his five-hundred-million dollars financial assistance had gone a long way to keep the legitimate Palestinian resistance against Israel alive and well. He also informed Murktar that part of the money was well spent in helping the cause of another formidable resistance outfit in Lebanon, which was against Israeli aggression. Umar's final words were " *We will always appreciate any more you can give towards this noble cause. We love you.* "

Murktar only smiled as a sense of joy flashed through his heart, which was gone after few moments had passed. He later walked back to his bed, sat down on it, turned off the lights, and laid his head on a pillow. His mind was as busy as a bee, as industrious as ants, rolling over many different thoughts, ideas, and worries that kept on knocking at its door and barging in at will, until the emerging light from the approaching morning began to chase away the fading night.

Murktar and Farouk got on with their chat as had been agreed upon the previous day. They were now getting to know more about each other. They shared their age in addition to sharing a few details about each other's background and profession. One thing was very important to Murktar—He saw the possibility of having a common conviction with Farouk. It placed his mind at rest, giving rise to a feeling that he would succeed, which made him very glad. A little smile on his face was a proof of this gladness.

"This is a good day," he said to himself quite softly, almost whispering, "God is great!"

He had been lost for sometime in his thoughts and joy, while Farouk waited for him to reply.

"My brother. Are you still there?" typed Farouk.

Sure, my brother.

I thought you abandoned me.

Why would I do that?

I thought as much.

I can never do that to you.

That's good to hear.

God is great!

God is great!

I was thinking...

Thinking about what?

I don't know how you will take this thing. I very much want to tell it to somebody.

What would that be?

Do you think you can handle it? Will you appreciate it?

What is that? What is that thing you are finding hard to share with a brother?

Well, a lot of people I have shared it with in the past have all despised it.

Murktar?

Yes, Farouk.

I can't tell you if I will welcome it without knowing what it is. Spill it, brother. I am the type of man that likes to help a brother who has a problem.

You are right, Farouk. I have a problem because I have not been able to get people to appreciate it so far.

What then is it?

It is anger, my brother. I want to know if you will appreciate why I am angry. I am very angry right now.

Anger? Murktar, you are a very funny human being. We all get angry. It is part of being human.

I know, Farouk. My anger is special and very justified. I wonder if what is making me angry is making you angry as well.

Share it with me.

Have you ever been so angry that you felt like hitting back?

Murktar, stop beating around the bush. Tell me what it is.

Okay. I will tell you since you have indicated your strong willingness to hear it.

Spill it! Spit it out like you are vomiting.

Okay. Here I go then...

Farouk poured some liquid into two glasses later in the day. It was in the next evening to be exact. He rose while putting back the lid on the bottle of brandy and went back to the drinks cabinet in his spacious living room. He returned after keeping back the bottle. Then he sat down again, and handed one of the glasses to the man with him, who took it gently with loads of thanks a smile on his face gave. Farouk took a sip, and his visitor did the same. Farouk's residence was quite unlike that of Murktar in the sense that he loved and appreciated exquisite furnishing. His living room was tastefully furnished with nice green sofas, violet curtains with green stripes running horizontally, and other interior fittings that made it look cozy. Farouk was a man who loved flirting with American women. He found it hard to have enough of them. It was Anita, a renowned interior decorator who was one of the many American ladies he loved to hang out with, that handled his home. And, he had to pay a whopping amount for her services. Farouk didn't allow romance to get into his business dealings with Anita. He believed that Anita was good at her trade, one of the very best in fact, and deserved to be paid well for the incredible job that she did. Farouk was a man who had an insatiable taste for attractive women on top of their game. It was no surprise at all to see him around big Hollywood stars like Alice Swanson, a blonde with a list of twenty critically acclaimed and box office hit movies in her all-impressive resume. Some of them were women whose names were already etched on Hollywood Boulevard, and therefore in the Hollywood hall of fame—women like Olivia Bard whose screen accomplishments had correctly placed in the class of Halle Berry, Drew Barrymore, Jennifer Aniston, Jeniffer Lawrence and the Canadian big name Baywatch star, Pamela Anderson. There was also a time when he would sometimes be spotted in the company of Shirley Woods, the famous, sexy American adult film star whose movies were always instant bestsellers. Shirley's sizzling touch, coupled with her alluring exploits in front of the camera had left a number of producers and directors scrambling to savor a bit of her, tossing away all professional ethics, just to have their own share of the juicy stuff that she always did on the set. Some male directors had gone ahead to send her movie ideas which had them as co-stars, instead of other men.

Farouk had a long list of women. His vacation time was spent accompanying some of these women to fashion shows in Milan, New York, Paris, and London.

Sometimes, he walked the red carpet with them in movie premiers, the Oscars and the Golden Globes. Though the length of his beard somehow made him look out of place, he never cared one bit to chop it off. The women never cared too. So, why should he? It was his belief that the women thought that he looked very handsome carrying his bushy beard. The thing he had in his mind was true all along. American women don't mind what you look like as long as you are a man capable of making the dollars flow.

***

"You won't believe what I discovered yesterday," Farouk said to his visitor after completely draining the contents of his glass. The question aroused his visitor's interest, and he wanted to know what exactly he had found out. The growing curiosity took hold of him.

"What would that be?" Abdoullah replied.

Farouk and Abdoullah were good friends. Abdoullah was a little taciturn, being much more absorbed into his work than Farouk. He did not have a public life that linked him to Hollywood like Farouk. The only limelight that he enjoyed was purely academic. The two had met over the internet, and thereafter, began to meet with each other in person whenever they could. The chat room was not the magic that really nourished their friendship. They continued to chat like many other users of that facility. Chatting with each other became an exciting pastime, leading them to discover more about each other. They later arrived at an exciting discovery that they both had the motivation to forge a common mission. It was then that their friendship reached a place where they ought to have ditched the internet chat rooms for a more intimate and purposeful one.

"Abdoullah, you won't believe this. This discovery is so compelling and so exciting that I can't believe it actually happened."

"I am lost. Tell me what you are talking about."

"Don't you understand?"

"How do you expect me to know when you have said nothing that makes sense to me?"

"Begin to rejoice, Abdoullah. Begin to rejoice, I said. Begin to rejoice."

"What?"

"What we have been looking for has been found."

"Are you serious?" a spark of excitement drove Abdoullah to speak, "Tell me the truth."

"Do I look like a man who is joking right now?"

"Are you really serious?"

"This is not one of the many hotels in Las Vegas where I go when I want to crack jokes. Does this place look to you like venues for the Oscars and Golden Globe awards?"

"Not at all. I know that very well."

"This is not the runways of Milan, London, or Paris where jokes are cracked while skinny female models strut their tempting bodies in front of a number of willing eyes."

"That is very correct."

"This is my home, Abdoullah. I talk serious business at home."

"So, this man shares in our anger?"

"Absolutely."

"He is just like us?"

"Absolutely."

"Who is he?"

"He is one of us! Same motivation. Same vision. Same mission. Same passion. Same target."

"What then are we waiting for? Let's get started!"

"You know what, Abdoullah?"

"What?"

"I love that urgency that you just showed."

"You know me. I don't love to waste a second once there is any work to be done."

"I have already told him about you."

"We now have a team that we have been searching for."

"That is right."

Murktar, Farouk, and Abdoullah began to meet secretly. They turned out to be birds of the same feather who were so excited at the prospect of being united at long last. But, to proceed in this manner, they needed to say goodbye to the usual life that they had all been used to. The cosmopolitan setting, which used to be the location for all their endeavors, would now be buried for a rustic one that was well suited to their ensuing mission. All the finery and charm of the fast-growing American cities would have to be left behind for a place that would offer some inconveniences, but which would be perfect and covert enough to not bring their mission to light. It would be a place that civilization had yet to locate—A safe heaven. And, no place was most qualified for their operation than Shonga. That would go on to be the location of Murktar, Farouk, and Abdoullah's laboratory, which later became the birthplace of the V1B6F3 pathogen—a hybrid of lethal strains of viruses, bacteria, and fungi.

THE MAN ABDOULLAH

ONE

Abdoullah was born to a poor long-bearded Afghan carpenter father and a Russian mother, who was a teacher in a girl's school in Kabul. This school had been burned down before. It then got rebuilt from the pile of rubble it was, only after Kabul slipped from the grip of the Taliban that had token over Afghanistan. The family only managed to get away. It was quite a task on the part of Abdoullah's parents to get him to attend school. They had to sell all of their livestock, and borrowed a heavy sum to make up his fees. They did not mind facing a barrage of embarrassment and disgrace from their creditors, who never failed to come whenever the payments due unto them were defaulted. Abdoullah's parents would sometimes beg these creditors to reschedule their debt, but to no avail. This often led them to borrow from one creditor to settle the debts of another. As a result, they had themselves neck-deep in debt even before they knew it.

Once, as a child, Abdoullah had been observing his father, Saeed, in his workshop. There was a sign at the workshop's entrance that had the words "CARPENTER'S PARADISE" inscribed on it. The workshop was not very spacious. It consisted of a wooden table that had rough edges. There were nails of different length and other carpentry tools scattered all over it. The floor was full of chopped-off pieces of wood, sawdust, chiseled-out barks of trees, and a few nails that had fallen off the table. It was mid-afternoon. Abdoullah had not gone to school that day since he had been sent away the previous day for not having paid his fees. His father was doing whatever much carpenters could do—driving nails into wood. He was putting finishing touches to a chair that he had been working on. Saeed suddenly stopped working and looked up, shaking his head in disgust. Then he slowly murmured, "Carpentry! I believe this must be a cursed profession...cursed profession of wood, nails, and hammer." The flesh in his forehead creased into a maze of wrinkles. "It invites itching poverty to your very door step rather than sweep it away. What do you gain? Bruised fingers. Swollen legs. Sweating it out to create a product, and, at the end of the day, it remains with you for almost forever before a buyer slips a token amount into your hands for all your hard labor. To anyone that cares to know, this is my twentieth year in this business." Saeed appraised the setting of his workshop with glances that he threw around and said, "My workshop is a grand prix venue for rats and cockroaches, and an amusement park for lizards. It becomes a swimming pool for ducks whenever the rains arrive for its roof has giant holes." He quietly went back to work on the chair until an accident occurred—He hit his thumb with the hammer. A groan saturated with pain escaped his mouth, followed by a grimace.

"What *is* this?" he said, his tone quite sarcastic, while his face carried a frown, "This is an accident that occurs at an alarming rate in this business." Saeed was angry, and his anger had deepened by now. "Yet no one reports it," he went ahead, "Let one accident happen on the road from a roadside bomb, and a day of national mourning will be declared with flags flying at half mast. Oh! A carpenter. Don't you think your reward comes only when you die?" He stopped, looked around as he thought fast, "No!" he let out in a fury, "I reject that! This is not my fate, and, henceforth, I cease to be a carpenter!"

He then became a bit calm to reflect on his rather rash decision. After having reflected for a while, he continued, "But then, if I cease to be one, how will I explain it to hunger when he visits?" Saeed quickly ran his right hand round his stomach and yawned in such a manner that his mouth was stretched out completely. "I can feel him here already. I have to make the best of my brain. Now or never."

Saeed mounted the table with his mind made up. "To anyone whom it interests to watch me," he began to announce as if he was a stage actor whose audience could not do without his engaging delivery of scintillating performance, "I want to believe you all know what it means to be a renowned carpenter. The training, the talent, and the touch—I have them all. But, I have now been stifled by poverty to mount this table. This table is the temple of my carpentry labor, and this is my sacrilege for the profession."

"What are you doing?" Abdullah, who had been watching his father all along, asked in dismay. Surprised to hear a voice, Saeed turned to the direction in which it had come, and saw it was Abdullah that had spoken. Saeed gave his son a quick 'what are you doing here?' kind of look.

"You are a child," he said to Andoullah. "You are too young to understand. You will never understand how I long to not fail you. It is my responsibility to see that you keep going to school. However, circumstances are planning very hard to make me fail you. I am very sad...Go back home, Abdoullah."

Abdoullah was only five, and he obeyed his father at once. Abdoullah was the only male child of Saeed who loved going to school. He always came out top in his class. Saeed's other children, the male ones, were not interested in going to school at all. Cultivating opium and joining the Taliban were their only ambitions. Abdoullah's parents could see that Abdoullah was a brilliant child, and they believed that out of their twelve children, he would be the one to make them proud one day. Aafia was Saeed's only daughter. She was going to become a suicide bomber at the age of ten, but was rescued from her captors who took her from Afghanistan and prepared her for a deadly mission in Lahore, Pakistan. This was against her will, even though her father had given his consent.

"Those militants would have killed me if I didn't encourage my daughter to go," Saeed had later revealed.

"Those men who took me away from my family told me that I would get to go to paradise fast if I did it," said Aafia to a Pakistani army chief, whose men rescued her as they embarked on a major offensive against a militant stronghold just around the Swat valley region.

Saeed relaxed after responding to Abdoullah's question. He lay down on the table, and sleep got the better of him quickly, transporting him to a dream world.

TWO

Saeed began to call on Aafia in the beginning of his dream. "Where are you? Aafia! Aafia!" he shouted at the top of his voice, "Let me have the lunch that I have been really looking forward to seeing."

Aafia, a girl of twenty, a little taller than her father, came carrying a covered plastic plate, a plastic spoon, and a plastic cup of water. She quietly kept all that she had carried close to the spot on the workshop table where her father sat. "Here is your lunch, father," she said. A spark of delight flashed on Saeed's face at once.

"Thank you so much, my daughter. May you never be a useless carpenter like your father." Aafia responded by stamping her left foot on the ground, making a frown on her face. This was her way of expressing displeasure over her father's comment.

"But I have told you, father, to always believe that all will be well one day," she retorted in protest. Saeed only laughed at his daughter.

"You have been saying that for the past five years. And, we have been pushed five years deeper into the pit of poverty...Young people and their young brains...They always think that escaping the claws of hardship is as natural as the moon's appearance in the sky. You can go now, Aafia. Let me eat."

Saeed looked down at the plate of food beside him and was stunned. Aafia had already been on her way out. "Come back!" Saeed screamed, "What is this?" His gaze strongly fixed on the plate.

Aafia stopped, turned, and replied. "Lunch." She had replied in a polite manner, wondering why her father had screamed.

"This is lunch, Aafia? Did you look at it? And, it took you such a long time to prepare *this*? Two grains of rice and beans each?"

"Father, that is your share."

"Oh! What a weight these grains added to the plate." grumbled Saeed.

"But, father, you have always taught me to manage even half a grain."

"You are right, Aafia. I said so. But right now, these grains will only make hunger a refugee in the territory of my stomach. Are you sure you checked the rice sack well?"

"Yes, I did."

"And there is nothing left?"

Aafia nodded in the affirmative.

"What about the beans sack?"

"There's nothing there as well."

"Did you tell your mother about this ugly development?"

"I did not."

"Why?"

"She can't make any difference."

"That is ridiculous. She is a teacher, and I, a carpenter. Who earns more?"

"You. You have a steady job. Hers is not so steady."

"Aafia, don't make me believe that you are leaning towards your mother. Are you supporting her?"

"Supporting her? No, Father! I am only saying the truth that I know."

"And, what is that truth?"

"Her job fades away anytime the Taliban return to Kabul."

"Oh...That is the dreaded thing that makes our condition worse. But, she can get help from Moscow."

"Father, do you remember that you told me my mother married you out of love, against her people's will?"

"Now I remember...Oh! See how fast I forget? She will never get any help from Moscow or even Saint Petersburg where her uncle comes from."

"Can I go now?"

"A meal of two grains for a man of my age is an interesting piece of news. What is your opinion, my daughter?"

"Father, people will wonder how it is possible and whether you really are a man...I'm sure that they will start speculating about the size of your stomach as well."

"*Even a child will barely survive on that. This piece of news will send a multitude to pursue the news vendors,*" Saeed began to think. He motioned Aafia to come closer, and she did.

"What are you thinking?" she asked.

"You can go now, Aafia," said Saeed. He then began to think more. She only took three steps when Saeed suddenly called Aafia. She stopped, turned, and grumbled.

"It is afternoon, father. I have a lot to do inside. The only room we live in is filthy with cobwebs, cockroaches, and rats. They are no longer strangers here."

Saeed dismissed Aafia's complaint with a contemptuous wave of his right arm, a gesture that had no regard for what Aafia had just said, "Let them thrive, breed, and let me think. They have found a suitable home in the room of a former carpenter. That, of course, keeps them away from the long list of endangered species. I am sure you have not heard that before." Aafia was thrilled to hear her father speak in a manner in which he never did.

"Father, you sounded so special." This made Saeed roar in laughter.

"You see...I was on my way to becoming a biologist and environmentalist before that ambition met with a ghastly fate and vanished on a platter of poverty."

"Oh...Father...It is such a pity."

"Don't pity me. Go back to our breaking news of two grains for lunch!" Saeed thought harder, "Can you write, my daughter? Can you?"

"Maybe."

"Let me know. Can you write?"

"Maybe."

"What do you mean by that? Or is that your way of saying no?"

"Blame the Taliban. Not only them. Blame yourself too."

"You are blaming me for?" Saeed's countenance reflected his sadness.

"You are not able to send me to school even now."

"Don't worry. There must be a way out of this, Aafia. We have to do this story ourselves."

Saeed suddenly brightened up with optimism, his eyes a bit aglow. "Aafia, we can make it!" he quickly said, "Reach out for sheets of paper and a pen." Aafia could not make any sense of what Saeed had been saying.

"What for?" she questioned, the disgust evident in her tone.

"Don't ask questions. Just obey! Your father is brimming with ideas now. Quick! Pen and paper!"

"The ones that you bought me when the world had not yet been in existence? I doubt if I will see one."

"Just search! Search frantically. Ask your brothers!"

"My brothers? That would be as useless as trying to sell razors to the Taliban."

"Aafia...Just search...Be fast! Hunger is hitting us fast! Let us fight back!"

Aafia left quickly, leaving Saeed to saunter in deep thought, his thumb on his lips. He then began to think aloud after a while. "I guess I have to force out the required skills. What will the caption be? A man on grains of rice and beans? No. That is not good enough." He leaned on his workshop table. "Let me see..." he continued to think aloud. "Survival on two grains of rice and beans each. Well...that sounds nice. But, is it the best? The best is what I need. However, I will have to stop here. I think the second caption is fine. Where is my daughter?" He called Aafia at the top of his voice. "Aafia!" He screamed as he got off the table.

"There is none," said Aafia when she got back.

"What?"

"No pen! No paper!"

"*How then do I write this brilliant caption down? Oh no...*" Saeed began to think. "But...wait a second!" he suddenly said, "This reminds me...Even if I write my story here, I can't print it or circulate it. That is the very naked truth."

"Father, what do you intend on doing?"

"Use your head, Aafia. Everything should not be left to your father alone. I have limitations, just like every other human. Think, Aafia! Rack your brain for a solution!"

A frown appeared on Aafia's face. She looked down as if the answers that were being sought were on the floor. "I am doing that..." she responded. However, she started complaining after a short while, "My head is becoming heavy now, and nothing seems to be coming..."

"Try, my daughter."

Aafia looked up as she was urged on. She thought hard a bit. "Nothing, Father," she announced.

"Harder, my daughter. Harder! Invention is not a day's job. Think harder!"

"Nothing is coming from my head," Aafia announced as she stopped taxing her head. She showed her capitulation by sitting on the workshop table, much to Saeed's displeasure. And, Saeed wasted no time in expressing it.

"That is why I call you porous sometimes. Now, you have smeared my face with disgrace." Saeed held his head, looking dejected. Defeat had by now begun to eat into his mind. He slowly sat on the table, next to Aafia, in a way that told just one thing—dejection. A brief moment of silence elapsed before his mouth opened to allow some words to come. "Oh...what are all these sorrows that I keep reaping in search of a way and direction...?" he wailed.

"I have it!" Aafia suddenly screamed, jumping down the table and looking excited.

"What is it now?" asked Saeed, unimpressed, turning to Aafia and asking with a look of dejection that had dawned on his face. His tone sounded like one that did not have much life in it.

"A solution, father!"

"One that manifests in you like madness?"

"Bend your back," Aafia requested.

"That is very disrespectful of you, Aafia. I have never said that to my father even though he wasted his precious youthful days getting addicted to only eating, visiting the toilet, and sleeping."

"I have an idea. I have just told you that," Aafia urged.

"No! I never said such a thing to my father...No...Not even when he became so bent that his back almost ran parallel to the sky."

"I have to climb on your back."

"What!" Saeed screamed, "Watch your mouth, Aafia, for this is our beloved Afghanistan! No romance has ever been known to exist between a father and a daughter."

Saeed screamed as Aafia pulled him down from the workshop table and began to try and get on his back. Saeed's protest continued.

"This is an attempted murder, Aafia!"

Aafia ignored him and had made some progress now. Saeed's physical resistance continued, but was not enough to keep Aafia at bay. His verbal protest continued when he realized this. "Are you out of your mind? Oh! Oh! My back! Be careful! My back! Ouch...! Those bones there might just give up completely. Bones already weak from years of excruciating labor...Aafia! You are so stubborn! Don't break things there! My back! I give up! I surrender!" Saeed carried Aafia on his back with quite a bit of difficulty. Since Aafia was obstinate about climbing on his back, and had done so inspite of Saeed's protests, Saeed decided to go along with the show. He then commenced to hop from one end of his workshop to another, a grimace on his face, chanting with Aafia.

Hop to a solution
Hop to a miracle
Hop to a panacea
Hop to your expectations

Aafia got tired of chanting that after a while, and Saeed's voice was the only one that was audible now. But, he was not chanting either, only talking.

"I do not understand your ways anymore. You overwhelm me with the games that you play. How long will you keep away from me the solution that I seek? Please do not come up with mountains when I seek the sky, or make the desert my home when I am thirsty. Now for life, tell me the solution right now. To all who care to know, my eyes are now red with frustration."

"Father, are you not talking too much for a person who complained of hunger a few minutes back?"

Saeed responded as he continued hopping. "This is your idea, Aafia. I can't remember when I ever told you that I desire to be a world class athlete at an age when it is so dangerous for the proper functioning of my heart. Hunger cannot imprison me. Don't you know that a prisoner is not only the person behind bars of iron and steel? He who casts his freedom of expression to the wind is more of a prisoner than anyone else."

A male photographer wandered into Saeed's workshop and yelled at what his eyes saw.

"Behold! A human Kangaroo..." Excitement drove him to action at the speed of light. He began to take shots. "This is the most amazing discovery of my life. Am I not lucky?"

"You have not heard anything yet," Saeed responded, while Aafia got down from his back.

"No! Do not stop now," the photographer almost screamed in protest, withdrawing his camera from his eyes. "This will make a fine story." Saeed and Aafia threw glances at each other and then at the photographer.

"Story?" they said simultaneously.

"Yes. I am a renowned photographer who earns a living on extraordinary things. I get paid for publishing pictures and writing stories about them."

"Then you are..." said Saeed, almost in wonder, "the miracle." Saeed began to scream out of huge excitement. "You are the miracle! Come closer, my distinguished visitor." He signaled Aafia to leave with a wave of his left hand. "You can go now," he added, "You can go now and wage your much-desired war against our household pests." Aafia left at once. Saeed then brought back his attention to the photographer who was staring at the rags that he wore.

"Renowned photographer...Please do not mind my appearance. It is in the brain that the power of a man resides and not in his clothes. Have you ever seen a man living on grains of rice and beans?"

The photographer stammered as he tried to find words to respond.

"I-I-...Err...do not quite understand...your question."

"I can show you a man who feeds on two grains of rice and beans for lunch."

"That is most extraordinary! Where is the man?"

"I am the one," Saeed announced proudly, "The man known as Saeed."

The photographer frantically began to take shots of Saeed. "Can I see the lunch as well?" he demanded quickly.

"Why not?" said Saeed, pointing towards his workshop table, "Over there on my table." The Photographer scrambled to the table and began taking shots of the unusual meal.

"This is incredible. Absolutely incredible!" he began to say out of surprise and shock, which the sight of the meal had brought to his heart. "This story will sell." With these words, Saeed's interest got piqued at once.

"What did you just say?"

"This story is big money!"

"Did I hear you say money?" A spurt of enthusiasm spurred Saeed.

"Sure! This is what you have around you. Use it to get what you want. In this case, it is money. I am offering you a thousand dollars."

"A thousand what!"

Saeed returned to reality, constantly saying "a thousand what!" Rubbing his eyes with the back of his left palm, he finally uttered, "That is big money! When are you going to pay it? You must pay right now! I need the money badly!"

It was then that he realized that he was no longer in his dream world. As he began to look around, he was met with the sight of his all too familiar workshop. There was no visitor around, let alone a photographer. Saeed only wished that the dream had continued. "So, it was all a dream? But...Why did it have to stop at the point where my cash reward was near? This is stupid." Saeed quickly began to think of something which he could take away from the dream. He was convinced that there must have been something of that sort. He wrecked his mind to recall the dream. Parts of it had faded off his memory. His mind was just putting together the only bits and pieces that it could extract. Suddenly, one thing that the photographer had said to him flashed in his mind. " *This is what you have around you. Use it to get what you want.*" Saeed held on to this thought and began to look around to see if there was any other thing around, apart from his carpentry tools which he would never like to use again, that he could use. And, it happened. It happened much later. He discovered to his great delight something that held a lot of promise of raising him enough money that carpentry would never. It was because of this that Abdoullah was able to go back to school. He had never been sent away from school from then on, owing to his father becoming a good farmer who excelled in tending a crop very well. The crop was not rice or tobacco, but the Taliban's darling crop—Opium.

THREE

Abdoullah's academic brilliance could not be held back from making it to its destiny, which was being in the limelight. It shone like a million stars in a pitch-dark sky. Afghanistan was no longer the place for him. He got a scholarship to study in the United Kingdom and had to bid goodbye to his obscure background, which stemmed from a rustic community. Abdoullah proved to be a brilliant student of microbiology. It was beyond every trickle of doubt amongst his teachers and other renowned scholars who thought themselves to be privileged to have come in contact with him and his first-degree works. There was no stopping Abdoullah anymore. The quest for a master's degree was next, which he achieved by receiving another scholarship in the United States, where he excelled in bacteriology—his area of interest. His master's degree program was a huge success because his research work yielded brilliant insights on the possibilities of some bacteria strains mutating to take up combined characteristics of viruses and fungi. This showed potentials to help crops ward off viral and fungal attacks. With this discovery, Abdoullah had fame knocking at his door. He turned into a distinct brand of some sort, and the whole world applauded him. The world's huge appreciation of his brilliance began to materialize when the awards began to tumble in like an avalanche, whose source—the sky—was not going to let up. Awards of plaques and laurels dropped in like free-falling apples rattled by some severe storm. To say that Abdoullah was not overwhelmed with such an outcome would amount to telling a blatant lie. The preliminary report of his research work was so greatly received that he got a grant which would enable him to carry on with it, encouraging Abdoullah to get on with his work. He had hoped that it would end up in a big scientifically beneficial breakthrough. The Nobel Prize was hovering at the back of his mind as an exciting prospect, and it urged him to go on against all odds.

He worked on and on until he got bitten by a bug that has become the scourge of the most tragic heroes down the annals, which history reserves for mankind. This was no bug other than ambition. A new ambition. There came a time when Abdoullah could no longer concentrate on his work. Cries of pain and anguish, wails of sorrow for the bleakness of the coming future were filtering through to his ears, from his roots, in spite of the distance. Even the stench of decaying dead bodies was harassing his nostrils on a daily basis. A fierce distraction then set in on him as a result—A distraction, whose only name was anger, came with its companion, hatred. American forces and those of the North Atlantic Treaty Organization were waging a war on terror in his beloved fatherland, which resulted in heavy civilian casualties to show for it. There was no way in which these forces were going to be able to justify the death of innocent Afghan children in their protracted confrontations with the Taliban and remnants of the vicious and notorious Al Qaeda network in Abdoullah's view. As the war went on, his hatred for America and the policies that it implemented in his country grew. Nothing else now would give him as much pleasure as hurting America and its allies as revenge.

FAROUK!
THE MAN OF FIERY TEMPER
ONE

His temper was one thing that he could not keep in check very easily. Finding a needle in a hay stack was a much easier task for him than keeping his fiery temper in check. He had even taken anger management classes to check this ferocious side of him. But, when it got going, it went on like a hurricane—swift and simmering, and it would almost always leave something bad behind, whenever it struck. One of his father's eyes had been the knife's target. But, it just narrowly missed it. Little Farouk was always fond of running and embracing his father whenever he returned home. He would then ask his father for the thing which he usually brought back for him. However, Farouk had got so angry that day that he gently disengaged from his father's arms, picked up a knife, and threw it at him simply because he forgot to buy him his favorite cake. Farouk's mother's scream having a high pitch rattled the ominous atmosphere, "Do not do that again!"

"Our son has got a temper. Have you not noticed it?" Farouk's father said to his wife who was also in the kitchen, preparing dinner.

"What can I do?" Farouk's mother talked back, "I would be telling a lie if I say that I have not noticed it long before now. What can I do?"

"I am not trying to predict a bad future for our son. But, I just hope that he does not kill somebody when he grows up."

"I hope so. I think he will not...He will not."

"You think he will grow out of this?"

"Sure! He will!"

"His temper is so hot!"

"Come on, Farouk, say sorry to your father," his mother tried urging him.

"No! He did not buy me cake."

"Don't be silly! Say sorry to your father now!"

"No!"

Farouk was born to Azeez, his Palestinian father, and an American mother who was from Nashville, Tennessee. He had only a brother. It was not that his parents did not desire to have more children, but his mother had a medical condition which doctors could not fix after Maleek, his younger brother, was born. His mother's womb had already been battered badly due to many abortions that started from her very first pregnancy at the age of twelve, which occurred after her first prom night in junior high school. Though Azeez was entitled to have up to four wives, he didn't really cherish that idea. So, he stuck with Latoya, the mother of his two sons, who gave him quite a number of concerns as they were growing up. Azeez was born to a Pakistani father and an Iranian mother. People almost always used the same word to describe him, and that word was one that not many people on planet earth are called by—Billionaire. He was in the league of the Oprah Winfreys, the Donald Trumps and the Warren Buffetts of this world. People could have called Azeez a businessman, a husband, or even mentioned that he was not very tall. People could have also commented on his admirable personality and result-oriented work ethic. However, the first word regularly captioned by newspapers and magazines, beamed by television screens, and on the lists of the many who knew him was that particular word—Billionaire. Billionaire Azeez Musharaf. He had been born very rich. His grandfather was an entrepreneur of repute who made a fortune from mining in gold-rich South Africa, as well as in the copper-rich Zambia. Azeez's father improved this fortune, and Azeez succeeded in multiplying it several-fold. He, therefore, had the right financial clout to fund his sons' education in any prestigious institution of their choice.

"Embrace education and seek knowledge," he had always told his sons as they grew up, "An educated mind is one that can tap into limitless opportunities."

"I am going to become a scientist when I grow up," Farouk had told his father one day, making his father being moved with joy. He was so glad that Farouk was understanding what his true calling was, and was beginning to be poised to go in the direction that would bring him lasting joy and fulfillment.

"That is so nice of you," he said to Farouk, "That is the right thing. God is great! God is great! My son, paying for your education will never be a problem. I want you to know that."

"I want to go to the moon one day."

"That is great, my son. I like that. People who go to the space are called astronauts. A good education will get you there. Good boy..." Azeez said, patting his son on the back.

TWO

If only a man's wealth could always bring him what his heart desired! If a huge financial empire was all that it would take to give a child a great future, Azeez would have been a really contented man. The likely future that his son Maleek would come to know had never crossed his mind. He was so bitter when it actually happened. He stood in the lavatory attached to his bedroom, thinking about it.

"I cannot understand why he had to take that path," said Azeez out of pain that masked the usual tone of his voice, "What did I not do right? I made sure that he never lacked anything! Why did he choose to bring disrepute to this family's name? Oh...why didn't they bring him to me so that I could strangle him to death with my own hands? So, is this how it will all end?" Anger made him leave the lavatory. He pushed open the door, barged into the massive space that was his bedroom, and flung himself unto his bed. "Send me Maleek," he wailed, "I will kill him! I will kill him! I will kill him and throw his flesh for dogs that will care to eat!"

"Oh my god!" Latoya ran into the bedroom, very rattled, "My son will never come back!"

"Let him die there!" Azeez screamed in response, "He does not deserve to be called my son now! I would kill him if had the chance! I won't mind going to jail for doing that!"

"Oh my god! What is this? Maleek..." Latoya screamed.

"That is the future he has chosen, woman! Leave me alone to lick my wounds."

The news of Maleek's being sentenced to life imprisonment in the United States could not have been more bitter to his parents. It was a scourge on the Musharaf's family history of successful entrepreneurship, a disease that would debilitate it forever, and a poison taking away its life. Maleek had brought his family name to the attention of the world for a reason that no one expected from a young man of his background. The Continental Airlines flight 253, carrying two-hundred-and-seventy-nine passengers and eleven crew members, was approaching the John F. Kennedy International Airport in New York, when Maleek failed to execute what he was prepared for. Things somehow did not go his way. It was his bad luck that the explosives hidden in his underwear did not detonate as expected. Other passengers scrambled to his seat and were able to restrain him after a scuffle had ensued. The failure was not only that of Maleek, but for those who had trained him and sent him on that mission. They quickly claimed responsibility for the act and vowed never to back off from plotting to hurt the United States of America in any way possible.

A handsome-looking Arab man having a long bushy beard, who appeared to be in his forties, was shown on a footage played by the Al Jazeera network to the world a day after the failed plot. The man ranted his threats angrily as he spoke his native Arabic language.

"You are a hero, Maleek! We salute your courage!" he said as his speech was drawing to a close, "Take this from us, America! We will come again! God willing! You will never have rest!"

Maleek's subsequent arrest and interrogation revealed that he was sent on the deadly mission by some Al Qaeda operatives in Iraq.

"Dying for a just cause brings much honor to one who does. Paradise will be his home," Maleek had said to his parents one day after his return from a trip to Iraq. They all laughed. Azeez and Latoya had told Maleek that he was right, but they had not thought deeply. They could not feel the unpalatable coming. They did not understand where Maleek was headed. They woefully failed to realize that their son must have been making dangerous contacts. His radicalization had been on since then. Their eyes were wide open, but they were so blind that they did not see it.

Maleek's brother, Farouk, was sent off to America for his high school education. It was Azeez's decision. America was where he thought his son would get a good education that he desired for him. Farouk discovered that his career focus was changing from astronomy to microbiology. There was this strong passion to know about viruses in greater detail that just got hold of him and would not go away. He spoke about it to his father one day, and he was glad to learn that he had no problem with it. "That is good too. Get on with it," Azeez had said. So, it was no surprise that Farouk attended the highly-rated University of Virology located a thousand kilometers from Philadelphia. It was not just because his father could afford to pay for his education, he was brilliant as well. Farouk was brilliant enough to meet the high standards of the university. His brilliance began to shine for all to see, like the sun's light glows each day, from sunrise, getting brighter with the passage of time. Comments soon began to make the rounds. "God creates a student this brilliant once in fifty years," one of his lecturers had said.

"That Farouk guy is something else."

"He is just outstanding."

"Awesome!"

"Oh...He is a handsome and intelligent chap."

"I think I'm in love with him."

"I want to marry him."

"Give me a break! No way! He's my man."

"But, he has already asked me to be his girlfriend..."

"He has asked me too..."

"No! You can't be sure of what you're talking about."

"He said that to me."

"No! You're totally wrong. He will never say that to another woman in a thousand years to come. So, back off!"

"You back off!"

"Let me make it clear. No one plots to steal my man and succeeds."

"You are the one who's doing the stealing. So, you better back off!"

"You back off!"

"Now I know you better. Leave my man alone!"

Farouk did very well upon graduating and became a person who was very much in demand. His published scholarly works attracted attention to him just like the sight of honey draws bears. All those that mattered in the university practically begged him to remain in their fold. He was offered a lucrative employment as a lecturer. Five-hundred-thousand-dollars annual salary was the red carrot that was dangled in front of his face, which, however, was not red enough to keep Farouk completely away from the other ideas that he had. He opted for private practice and research while lecturing on a part time basis. This was his way of not letting down those that gave him the platform to shine in the university. He had enough funds at his disposal to pursue what his heart really desired, which was to set up a research laboratory of international standard in the United States. Getting approval from the right sources was not going to be a problem. The quest for deeper understanding of viruses became a passion that burned bright in him. His fascination with viruses knew no bounds, though he still managed to make out time to catch some fun outside the confines of his practice. This was the amazing combination in his personality. He loved living in America. To him, America was the ideal place to achieve big dreams. Farouk was very much in love with the idea of the American dream, and all it stood for. And, America's bevy of sexy blonde ladies never escaped his eyes one bit.

THREE

Change, even the slightest of it, is so unpredictable. Farouk would not have believed it had anyone told him that it would be change that would creep in someday to poison his delightful mindset about America. He would have told the person to take his story to the moon or somewhere else to the world of Harry Porter. He would most definitely have dismissed such an idea. It would have been one of those things which he loved to laugh off with his mouth wide open like that of a big yawning cat. However, it *did* happen.

In Pakistan, Farouk's uncle became a casualty in one of America's drone attacks targeted at the Taliban leadership. Mullah, his uncle, was no Taliban member, but bombs are never intelligent when it comes to sparing the good guys and taking out only the bad. No matter how much vampires love a person who is not one of them, they will always toss niceties out of the window and bite that person at the sight of their blood. Farouk knew this very well, and he had even seen it in the critically acclaimed movie, *Full Moon*, that got fans so crazy, as if other equally good movies had not even been released in Hollywood at the time. His anger against America had now been born, but it was not sufficient enough for him to think of taking any action.

The affair had become quite intense when Farouk had met and fallen in love with an American girl of twenty-five. Farouk could cut off his hands for this girl, and the girl would do the same for Farouk. Wow! How love disarms anger with its tender touch. Farouk could not find any trace of his earlier anger anymore. Love had taken over and had made him forget it like a child. The girl responsible for it was Christie—A brown-eyed girl with alluring and luscious lips and a good set of front teeth, all square and white. Christie's teeth were different from some girls' whom he had met before, whose teeth were so irregular in shape and size that they made him wonder if they were sharks. Christie was a six-feet-five-inches blonde who lived in Buffalo, New York. She came to Pennsylvania to see her boyfriend, who was one of Farouk's students. Christie came around and was confronted with a heartbreak. Mike, her boyfriend, was busy making out with another beauty in campus and barely noticed her. He just did not give a damn if Christie's life was about to collapse. The sight she witnessed was nothing less than heart-shattering. She saw Mike deep-kissing her own girlfriend, who lived next door to her in Buffalo. The girl-next-door, Shamock, twenty-two, had divorced her alcoholic husband just the previous year, and she would frolic with any man that was willing—gangsters that lived by the gun, promiscuous rock stars, crack cocaine addicts, and even the clergy, who accidentally got dragged into her voluptuous nest through flirtatious overtures of hers. Men would not get enough of her whenever she was around in the Sin City—Las Vegas—and constantly tipped her with hundred-dollar bills while savoring her well-choreographed strippers' dance steps, up close and personal. Any kind of man would do for Shamock. She was indeed a bad girl, a sex junky to the very core. Christie was well aware of this. However, little did she know that her own man would one day cherish Shamock, let alone getting intimate with her. Reality bites hard sometimes. The sun had done a perfect job of illuminating enough of the dark hidden corners. Christie was all tears and downcast as she walked past Farouk who had just finished teaching a class.

"Hey!" Farouk turned and said to Christie, "A pretty dame like you should not be crying like that."

Christie did not stop. She continued to weep and began to run away.

"What happened to you?" Farouk called out aloud, "I want to be the one to get those tears off your face if you need anyone!"

It was then that Christie stopped running, and she stood still. She became a statue the moment Farouk's last words had permeated and stirred her punctured heart back to life. Nobody had told her such a thing since she began dating and had lost a package that was intact when she was born—her virginity. She stood charmed, finding it hard to put together any words that she would respond with. Twenty seconds flashed past without her finding any words...Thirty seconds...Forty!

"Are you sure you want to do that?" her slow response arrived at last.

"Are you sure you want to talk about it?"

"About what?"

"The very thing that has kept you crying. Sharing is healing. Don't you know?"

"Get off! You don't want to do that."

"Do you mind talking about it in my office?"

"I'm not sure..."

"Call me when you make up your mind, damsel. Take my number." Christie took out her cell phone and began to punch Farouk's number as he called it out.

"Farouk is my name."

"Mine is Christie."

Christie thanked Farouk after taking his number and turned to leave. Farouk too started walking away when he suddenly heard Christie's voice again.

"Wait! I'm coming with you!"

She had stopped, turned, and was running to him now.

"Life is full of ups and downs," Farouk said immediately after Christie had narrated her ordeal amidst tears, "Clean up your eyes. No need to keep crying like a little girl when you have a whole good life ahead of you." Farouk picked up his handkerchief and dabbed off Christie's tears with it. Christie appreciated this gesture, but she did not speak of it.

Farouk's office was quite big, had neat green walls, a long blue couch, and nice wood grains on its floors. It also had a lavatory. There were small packs that contained fragrances which were hanging on the wall, and it gave the whole office a lasting sweet lemon smell. But, had it not been for the presence of the three well-polished wooden shelves stuffed with Farouk's books, there would have been no way that one could tell that his office actually belonged to a lecturer rather than a modeling agency. There were a number of pictures of pretty female American models on the walls—black, white, and Latino—All on lingerie, and all caught by Farouk's camera at various times in the act of strutting their voluptuous bodies on runways.

"Mike shouldn't have done that to me," Christie railed.

"Never mind, Christie. Relax...Let me know if you feel uncomfortable here in any way."

"I'm fine. It's okay."

"You care so much about things that are eluding you."

"What?"

"That is my own humble observation. I am sorry if that hurts you."

"No...I'm fine. Get on with it."

"You keep chasing shadows when the real things are right under your nose, longing to have you notice them."

"You're hitting on me now, aren't you?" Christie asked while admiring the pictures on the walls.

"Hitting on you?" Farouk laughed. "Why should I?"

"Because I'm sure you think I'm quite pretty."

Farouk laughed again.

"I have not said that," he replied.

"Do you need to say it before I get to know?" Christie asked. "No you don't," she added. "Nice place," Christie commented as she looked around Farouk's office.

"Thanks."

"You're a lecturer here, right?"

"Right. Part time."

"You came across to me a very busy man."

"You are right once again."

"So, busy professors hit on chicks too?"

"Funny angel who would not look around," Farouk laughed again.

"What do you want me to see?"

"So many other things that America has to offer. Nice ocean views. Beautiful landscapes which nature the master sculptor endowed her with."

"O yeah?"

"Unequalled democracy in which freedom nests freely like a bird," Farouk uttered with passion.

"Yeah...," Christie responded most sweetly, "You can say that again. You're one of those birds. When are you going to land?"

"Nice men to love. Abundant as leaves on trees. Love your father, your uncles, grandfather. Your male cousins..."

"When are you going to land, flying bird?" Christie asked and made a face on which there was a smile. She turned her attention from the pictures to Farouk, and looked him straight in the eye.

"Who is left?" Farouk asked.

"I should ask you. Who's left?" Christie giggled and was soon drawn to the pictures once more.

"Who is left? Hey...Me! Love me..."

"Flying bird...I thought you would never land..." Christie laughed.

"Here I am...What do you do for a living, Christie?"

"I'm a sales person at a Walmart store in New York. I'm on vacation right now for two weeks."

"That is very nice."

"I am a model too," said Christie.

"Your tall and sleek frame suggests volumes about that. I find it great. Fantastic."

"I model lingerie, part time, for a top New York designer. And...going by the pictures I see all around, I believe you do understand me."

"Sure! That is great. It makes me salivate."

"You're crazy...I think professors full of fun are hard to find."

"You don't mean it."

"I'm dead serious."

"That is a lie."

"They have come to be known by the R word."

"Which is?"

"Rare."

"Okay! Well...would pretty New Yorkers ever accept to have a drink with busy professors in a choice Philadelphia restaurant any evening?"

Christie turned to Farouk, flashed him a sexy smile and said, "Bad boy...I thought you would never ask...."

FOUR

The connection happened very fast, and Christie was her usual lively self before she even knew it. She was done wallowing in anguish and pain over Mike's unfaithfulness. Farouk had pressed the right buttons and struck the right spots—her heart and soul. Words that he uttered mended every broken fiber in there so fast that she was all smiles again. If there was anywhere she knew that her association with Mike would be now, it would be in no other place but in the wasteland of history. Time proved to her that she could not want more in a man. Farouk was a rich, famous, and fun-loving virologist who was loving and caring. And above all, he was a man who was never stingy with his cash. He loved to take Christie to shopping malls and buy her lovely things which women like to idolize—shoes, clothes, jewelry, lingerie, handbags, perfumes, powder, and other cosmetic products of leading brands. Farouk's idea of a shopping mall was a place where he ruled with his stream of cash—The ambience, so enthralling, the window displays, so tempting and so irresistible, where the fixtures, fittings, and decorations would ignite his senses very quickly, such as in a universe of shopping where he particularly loved to take Christie. It was a place where the music and mood always fused and transcended him to a state of mind in which he would be going for only the very best without getting bored. Christie knew that she had been a fish inside a little pond that had now found an ocean to swim. Time cruised by, and their relationship grew stronger. Farouk was thinking about marriage, something that also flashed in and out of Christie's mind.

A question nearly popped out of Farouk's mouth one summer Sunday afternoon as he and Christie were sprawled on his bed, deluged with post-coital pleasure. It was that question which women loved to have their men ask them while on their knees—Will you marry me? Farouk, however, decided to leave it for another day because he had not ascertained sufficiently that Christie would say yes. He was a man that never liked to be turned down. Such an experience would be like shoving a bitter pill down his throat.

FIVE

Christie was not aware of her own nature. She was not who she really thought she was. She had been busy all along living a life that clearly evinced that all that really mattered was Farouk. The air she breathed was Farouk, until the hidden other side of her began to manifest. It made Farouk quite angry, and he confronted her. Surprises never mind their own business and never leaves this world in peace.

"You are not telling me something, Christie!"

"What?"

"Like cracks. Can't you see?"

"Oh, don't be ridiculous, Farouk. I see nothing."

"There are so many of them now. So many of them on what we have going."

"Nothing is wrong! I hate the way you imagine things. I love you! That has never changed."

"I do not know what is going on!"

"What do you want?"

"Wait a minute! You think I am a fool?"

"You're not. What do you want? This relationship is healthy. What more can you possibly request?"

"I am not a fool, Christie. Don't think that I don't know right from the day we have met that my body has been your favorite playground until now."

"Come on...Are you trying to deny that we have great sex? You know you're wrong."

"It is no longer what it used to be, and you know it!"

"I'm still giving my all, that what I began with."

"That is not true!"

"Stop being ridiculous!"

"You are far away now!"

"How dare you accuse me? You will live to apologize for this! I assure you!"

"What are you not telling me, Christie?"

"You question my faithfulness to you? Stop stressing me up!"

"You call that stress? I feel something is wrong with you, and you call that stress?"

"Get the hell out of here with your punk-ass!" Christie said, slightly irritated.

"You get the hell out!" Farouk replied

"Fuck you!"

"Fuck you too!"

"That's the way you want to play it now, huh?"

Farouk was not going to lie down and allow the disturbing thoughts that he felt continuously, to go on thriving undiscovered. He was not a novice in affairs related to women. His instincts had never deceived him whenever women in his life had begun to go astray. Farouk could swear that Christie had begun to see another man. The thought of who it could be nearly made him pass out. He began to skip meals because of the deep-seated jealousy that was ruining his life now. Christie would still visit him, treat him nicely, kiss him with all tenderness, and share moments in bed with him. But, something kept telling Farouk that she had already strayed from their relationship.

"Who is the man?" he confronted Christie again on a day in which she came visiting.

"You imagine a lot. That's your problem."

"Who is the man?" he repeated.

"Will you shut the fuck up and enjoy what we've got?"

Farouk was going to say something, but he could not since Christie had sealed his lips with a long, wet kiss, kissing his next question away.

Farouk placed a call to Los Angeles the next day, and it was the number of one of the best available hands which he dialed. That call led all the way to Illumination. The firm with a staff of three-hundred was contained in a well-lit large space demarcated by cubicles, which were offices for each of the hired personnel. These men and women of different colors and races went about their duties most professionally, perusing and analyzing documents, sketches, and pictures. Laptops were set on tables, together with cameras of varying sophistications, relevant to their organization's operations. Several phone calls always kept barging in from people who wanted jobs done for them quickly.

"Hello! This is Illumination! How may we help you today?" came a lady's voice from the other end.

"Hello! This is Farouk Musharaf calling from Philadelphia."

"How can we be of help to you, Sir?"

"Could you please put me through to Hansen?"

"I understand he's not in his office right now. Do you have any previous appointment with him?"

"No. This is the first time I'm calling."

"I see...Hansen has been away since morning on a serious assignment."

"Won't he be back today?"

"I don't think so."

"Tomorrow I guess."

"Yes. You can leave your number with me so that Hansen can get back to you."

"That won't be necessary. I will call back tomorrow."

"He will be informed that you called."

"Thanks a lot. I look forward to becoming one of your many satisfied clients."

"You're welcome."

"Bye..."

"Alright, bye!"

SIX

Hansen Langton was not a man who was easy to get on anyone's case. Farouk managed to find rest when he finally got him to take his case up after six months had elapsed. He had chased Hansen diligently all along because what he had heard about his success rate made it all worth it. The day Farouk got his lucky break was on a Saturday afternoon, after thoughts of giving up were beginning to hang around the outer borders of his mind, preparing to wade in. This lucky call, unlike many previous ones he had made, had been through in just one dial. And, the all too familiar female voice popped up in response as Farouk revealed his identity.

"Farouk Musharaf speaking from Philadelphia."

"Hey, Mr. Musharaf, you're a lucky man. Hansen is in. One moment please, while I put you through."

"Okay."

Hansen Langton was now one of the most sought-after men in his trade. But, this enviable status that he enjoyed did not come to him easy. It was not as if he was seated on a cozy settee right inside a tastefully furnished mansion with a pleasant ambience, dreaming nice dreams, while it dropped right onto his hands. It was not a piece of cake at all. No! It was very far from that!

The name given to Hansen by his parents at birth was Craig. He was a junior high school drop-out, known for his brilliant ability to get to the root of things. No matter how silly the occurrences would appear, Craig was not the kind of kid who would overlook them. He always had the urge of discovering why something had happened before he got any rest. Craig never rested when his father's favorite rooster mysteriously disappeared. He was determined more than ever, to unearth the reason for its disappearance.

"Stop hustling over this, sonny," his father had said to him with his thick

Cuban cigar placed at the right side of his mouth, with curly smoke drifting up, "The rooster is gone! It is resting in peace now."

"No!"

"It doesn't matter what happened to it."

"No!"

"Rest your ass, boy!"

"No!"

"Wait a second! Are you going to keep looking for what took my rooster?"

"Yes."

"Please yourself, you stubborn thing."

"Yes, sir!"

Craig's parents along with Craig's three brothers and sister had all given up on his quest because he could not come up with anything for quite some time. But, they were very wrong, as wrong as believing that the sun no longer existed somewhere up and beyond the clouds in space. Craig kept on going, combing everywhere in search of any clue that would lead him to a break. However, all of it was in vain. He was lying on his bed one night, thinking about what his next step could be, when two words hit his mind—"The dog!"

"Billy? What for?" Craig had never thought that Billy, the dog in their home, would be the culprit. It had never been known to show any interest in attacking the rooster. And, they had been buddies. Why would it do that? "*No. I don't think so,*" Craig thought. He extended his search for clues beyond his home and began to think that a hungry homeless prowling dog might have run in unnoticed and pounced on the rooster. He hung on to this until his mind spoke again, directly this time. *Billy, the dog!* So, Craig decided to give it a try. He began to stalk Billy, watching its every move. It noticed that it loved going to the basement. It would do this at least five times a day. And, that was when it all suddenly became clear. The white feathers coupled with spots of congealed blood told the whole story. "Billy!" Craig said to his father upon coming out of the basement with some white feathers in his right hand. "See..." he said, drawing his father's attention to the feathers. "It took your favorite rooster somewhere into the basement and ate it." Craig felt good about himself. He was only seven.

"Satisfied, huh? Good job! Will you rest now, or you've got more things to sniff out?" his father asked.

"I want to rest."

"What do you want me to do to Billy? Smoke its ass?"

"No."

"That's great. Maybe you will join the FBI when you grow up. How about that?"

"FBI? What is FBI?"

"Those are people who love to find out what human beings as bad as Billy do. Do you want to join them?"

"I don't know..."

Craig's father, Matt Stevens, worked a day in a week in an orange farm in Florida. He sometimes earned a couple of hundred bucks a day. The more oranges he could pluck from the trees, the more he got paid. The rate was twenty cents per fruit. Matt was a high-speed car when it came to that. But, deep down his heart, he knew it was not the kind of job that would give him the needed finance to support his family as he desired. His wife, Zora, worked as a cleaner in a high school that was not far from their home. Her take-home amount per week was a hundred dollars. Matt knew that their earnings together would never be enough to keep his family going. The bills kept springing up left, right, and center. So, he picked up extra jobs wherever he could in order to better support his family, working his ass off in the process to be able to pay his rent as required, as well as send his kids to school, and take care of other bills. This ensured that he was not home at most times. He sold newspapers, various tabloids, and magazines, which created an extra stream of income from his commissions. This enabled him to save up some money with which he bought books and began selling them alongside newspapers, tabloids, and magazines. His aim was to work very hard and provide his family all that which his father was not able to provide for him and his siblings while they were growing up. They didn't have decent meals most of the time. Their father didn't care if they wore clothes or not, let alone shoes. Matt and his siblings never went to a theater to see any movie or play while growing up. Their own world as kids existed without the culture of having entertainment. The lack of funds ensured that Matt didn't attend school beyond junior high. He was very angry with his own father for not taking a loan for him to go to school.

"He should have worked his ass off to ensure that we got good education," he often said as he spoke of his father, "He didn't! He went on drinking, fucking, and paying dirty strippers in night clubs with all his earnings as an automobile mechanic. He left the entire family expenditure for Mum. It was fun not attending his funeral. I wouldn't bury his dumb ass! That jerk of a father!" Matt later figured out that it was sensible to leave the "ifs" alone and strive to take his own life to the height he wanted. *If my father had been rich? If my father had bought shares in the fortune five hundred companies. If my father had been a rich investment banker. If my father had got any financial stake in Silicon Valley. If, if, if and if.*

Matt was extremely mad at Craig when he had dropped out of school. Everyone in the house believed that he had gone crazy. Matt wanted Craig and his siblings to at least go to college. "What the hell does this kid think he's doing?" he said to himself with a tinge of sadness in his voice. This was after Zora had broken the news to him. Craig knew that his father would not want to hear that he was quitting school, so it was his Mum that he had the courage to tell. Zora broke down when her ears picked up what Craig had said.

"No!" she launched her disagreement at once. A frown came to stand on her face like a concrete wall. "This isn't good for you! Craig, why are you trying to hurt everyone in here? Do you realize what you're doing to yourself? Your future?"

"Mum, I'm fine," Craig retorted.

"No, Craig! Not when you quit school!"

"Leave me alone!"

"Your dad must hear this! You must be going nuts!"

SEVEN

Matt waited for such a time when every member of his family would be together before he confronted Craig, and what other time could that be than dinner time. Everyone's plate contained copious quantity of the sea-food meal. There was shrimp soup, which smelt so well with steam flavored with seasonings, wafting through the dining room. Everyone but Matt was busy eating. Matt simply could not eat. There was no way he could eat without first releasing the weight that kept robbing him of his appetite. Craig was about putting a piece of shrimp into his mouth, when Matt's angry eyes turned to his direction.

"What the hell are you dropping out of school for? Craig, I'm talking to you."

Matt was running out of patience, as Craig kept quiet.

"Your Dad's talking to you, Craig," Zora chipped in, "Have you gone deaf?"

"You told him..."

"Yeah...I made that clear to you!"

Matt then thundered, "What the fuck are you dropping out of school for?"

Craig got startled and dropped the piece of shrimp from his right hand. He did not have a ready answer, but he was thinking.

"I don't know."

"What!" Zora added.

"What the hell's the meaning of that?" Matt queried on, "Have you gone crazy?"

"I'm fine."

"You said you don't know. What the hell's the meaning of that?"

"I don't like the school anymore."

"That's no problem. No stress! You'll be getting into another high school. Your mum and I will take care of that immediately!"

"Dad!"

"What?"

"It's not that."

"What?"

"I don't want to go to school anymore."

"You've got to be out of your fucking mind! Say that again, and I'll smoke your ass. You will go back to school tomorrow!"

"No! I'm not going back to school!" anger drove Craig to scream at his father, "I'm sick of you all!" He stood up at once and stormed away in the direction of his room. But, that was not before he had smashed his glass of water on the floor. Matt, Zora, and Craig's siblings threw glances at each other after they had ducked to ensure that no piece of glass had hit any part of their faces. Their glances were heavy with one question. Just one question. "What the hell was wrong with Craig?"

Craig had long lost interest in attending high school, but he had not known how he would break the news to his parents before now. He felt that school was wasting his time. He felt that he ought to have been making achievements. Making quick money. Rolling along in cute cars, private planes, and yachts like many rich guys whom he loved to watch on TV. Home was no more the right place for him anymore. "Nobody wants anyone like me here," he said while lying on his bed. Impulse pinched Craig and quickly got him off his bed. He put a few of his belongings in a bag and left home that night at a time when he knew that no one would notice. He just walked away into the streets without a clear picture of where he was going or how he was going to survive on only twenty bucks that he had on him. Craig wandered that night in search of a place to lay his head. He waited for what the break of dawn would have for him. He came across a black man lying on the ground in a street he walked into. This man appeared to be in his fifties and wore a very torn and dirty tuxedo that emitted a strong and offensive odor, very pungent to the nose. This homeless man had clearly not had a bath in several weeks. His shoes had holes in them, and he covered his obviously unkempt hair with a brown cap. Craig could see that the cap's true color was not brown; the long exposure to dirt had made it so. He raised his head immediately when Craig came close enough. There was fright in his eyes.

"Back off!" he screamed at Craig, "No dime on me now. You'll be wasting your time to attempt."

"I mean no harm," replied Craig.

The man managed to pick a baseball stick that lay beside him and got to his feet. He held it up and was ready to strike Craig.

"Back off! I warn you! I will show no mercy! Don't even try!"

"I mean no harm."

"What do you want? Who the fuck are you?"

"I need a place to rest my head. My name is Craig."

"Are you sure?"

"Trust me. I can be your buddy."

The man took one long look at Craig and slowly brought down the baseball stick. In spite of the raging darkness, he could see that Craig was carrying a bag. The man was about to drop his stick, when he suddenly thought differently. He could not just easily trust the little guy who had stumbled in to disturb the otherwise perfect night. He raised the stick again in a menacing manner.

"What do you have in that bag?" he asked.

"My belongings."

"I'm sure you've got a gun in there! I swear!"

"Gun?"

"Yeah!"

"No gun. I have no gun, sir."

"Empty that bag on the ground. Quickly! Don't mess with me, boy!"

Craig did as the man ordered after a bit of hesitation. The man picked up his torch from a pile of scattered things around, which were his belongings. The light soon flashed on everything that Craig had dropped from his bag. There was no sight of metal, let alone a gun. The man threw down his stick in resignation and heaved a sigh of relief.

"I mean no harm, sir!"

Craig's comment met with a slow nod from the man. A nod which said, "Yes, I believe you now."

"Sorry, I had to treat you bad! Some bad boys have been coming to steal all my money. I don't know why the hell those bad boys won't let a homeless beggar have some rest. So, I had to buy a stick to crack their fucking skulls!"

"They won't come again."

"Who told you that? You better go away, sonny! This is a bad zone. Full of bad boys! Not good for clean guys like you. Go home! You can't make it here! It's too rough!"

"I've got no home."

"What the hell happened to you, sonny?"

"Home's hell now."

"O yes...I know it now. I know that damn thing you did, boy! You quit school. That's it, boy."

"Yeah!"

"You think is a smart move?"

"Yeah."

"Look at me, boy! Take a good look at me, boy. Do I look like a mad man?"

"In a way..."

"You're right. I quit school many years before you were born, and *this* is the result."

"I don't care!"

"You don't?"

"I want to pass the night with you."

"Are you sure that's what you really want to do?"

"Yeah!"

"Really?"

"Yeah."

"Okay!"

EIGHT

Craig met a boy of his age the next day while hanging around. The boy, lanky-looking and black, just walked up to him arrogantly and introduced himself as Cone. He walked and talked as if he owned the whole world.

"Where do you belong?" he asked Craig afterwards. Craig did not understand exactly what Cone meant.

"Oh," he said after thinking about an answer, "I'm an American. I am Craig Stevens."

"That's bullshit you're talking. No one hangs out here just like that. We haven't seen your face before. We run this hood. We want to know your business here!"

"I have no family..."

"Look, you bitch ass! I'm in no mood to mess around with a dumb ass like you. Leave this hood right now before we get your sick ass smoked!" Cone said, pulling out a short gun from his waist. He grabbed Craig's neck and shoved his gun unto it. "Tell me who the fuck you work for, or you die!"

Fear grabbed Craig at once. He could literarily see the shadows of death dangling around him. "I swear!" He managed to say.

"What?"

"I work for no one! I swear! I'm just a homeless person!"

"Better not be lying. If I find a bit of lie, I will have your neck butchered, you son of a bitch!"

"I swear. I swear to God!"

"Now get your ass away from here," Cone said as he released his grip on Craig's neck, and returned his gun to his waist, "We don't need chickens like you here!"

"Cone, I want to be with you," Craig said, to Cone's surprise.

"You're kidding, right? You don't kid around here! Get the fuck off before I change my mind and get you killed!"

"I want to follow you. You and your family."

"You really mean that shit you said?"

"Yeah!"

"It's like you've got guts. It's like you've got it. What's your age anyway?"

"Fourteen."

"That's my fucking age too," Cone laughed and gave Craig a hug, "Come on, Craig. The boss has to see you."

Cone could be lively and very friendly on a good day. However, there was one thing that always made him dejected each time he remembered it. It had to do with his Jewish connection. His great-grandmother was a Jew who thrived in the era of the Second World War when there was an abundance of Nazi concentration camps. Though she stayed in the vicinity of those horrendous camps, she never stepped into any of them. Her rare beauty had made that possible. She was twenty years old then and was especially reserved to satisfy the libidos of Nazi officers who directly ran the camps. She was known to be so good at satisfying their huge sexual appetites that they had to change her name from Rabin to Sweet-nuisance. Her involvement in these illicit affairs resulted in the birth of Cone's grandmother, who never had anyone to call father. Poor her. If only her mother had been obstinate and had chosen to stick to being just one officer's fuck-buddy. However, that was not the case. She preferred to be a hole, which allowed anything that desired to get into it. Cone's great-grandmother was a Jewish whore of the nineteen thirties. And, he hated that with a passion.

From then on, Craig began to hang out with thugs who belonged to a gang whose members were in their teens, or were in their early, mid, and late twenties. Eliminator, the leader of the gang, saw Craig's commitment to learning, zeal for hard work, and liked him very much. Eliminator was not the gang leader's real name. It was only a name that his notoriety had come to earn him. He was six feet five inches tall and was a black young man with a pointed nose. His smiles were always warm, but very deceptive. They always exuded the impression that he would not hurt a fly. But, Eliminator was a fierce spider who would tear any fly to shreds. Eliminator was twenty-nine and was a man who was very generous when it came to pulling the trigger. It gave him much delight. When there were not enough incidents for him to pull a trigger, it always got him bored. His real name was Amos, and he was the product of a broken home. Amos' mum had divorced his dad when he was just three. His dad's unending adulterous escapades were the reason for the divorce. Amos's mum could not take care of him as time moved on because she too got addicted to crack cocaine. She was always going in and out of jail. It was no wonder that she was never there when Amos ended up in rough neighborhoods as a thug at the age of twelve.

Craig, in no time, learned how to use a gun. Fights would sometimes break out with rival gangs, and Craig would give a good account of himself. This did not go unnoticed in the gang, whose members lived like brothers, sharing food, beer, shelter, and every little thing that the gang had—which came from theft. The gang showed love to Craig. He began doing drugs with time, just like all the others in the gang—smoking and selling it for money in the streets and having a brush with the cops, but always managing to escape. Killing cops was not new to the gang. Anything that made itself an obstacle had to be rooted out in a ruthless manner. Bang! Bang! Bang! The gun and bullet manner.

Craig started having fun then. He referred to these moments as the sweetest of his life. "Wow!" he said to one of his gang members one day, "This is sweet! This is what my punk-ass parents wanted me to miss by keeping me in school. Oh...this is the sweetest life, sweetest fun, I swear."

"School is bullshit," said his colleague, "A place for mother fuckers! I got no time to stay in that damn shit place called school when lots of bucks are to be made in the streets here in Florida. Fuck school!" Craig could not agree more as he took a puff of his smoldering joint.

"Yeah, men, you're right, men. Fuck school and all its teachers and their monkey ass!"

"Fuck the cops! They think they can stop us from slinging dope in the streets? They gotta be kidding!"

"They must be kidding big time. This is Florida! We run it!"

"Yeah, my man! We run Florida! Any cop looking to stop us will have his ass smoked."

"Smoked real good."

The wail of siren suddenly came alive, and Craig quickly stood up from where he was to look around and assess the situation in order to determine the action that was to be taken.

"That must be them!" said Craig, "Could that be an ambulance?"

After assessing the situation, he finally said, "It's an ambulance." He sat down again and puffed his weed a little, "Some guys got killed this morning. They wouldn't turn in money they got from selling. They double-crossed their boss and got their ass roasted."

"A big price they paid for their greed. Bullets into their fucking heads!"

Another wail of siren rented the atmosphere.

"The cops?" Craig asked.

"I don't fucking know, men..." his colleague chipped in, "Any cop that wants me will get some bullets pumped into his fucking head."

"Yeah! Kill the Cops! That's what we do! We eat and breathe it!"

"That's life, men! Our life! Living by the gun and dying by the gun!"

"Yeah, men..." Craig screamed, "Call the cops when you see Craig! I won't need to talk much now. Let the cops come, and I'll let my gun do the talking! Our gang is great! That's why we are The Suckers! We suck the cops away."

NINE

The Suckers expanded their operations with time. It was necessary to meet their growing ambitions. The ten guys that made up the gang got tired of having just enough money to afford enough beer, drugs, food. Of course, they had some more to spare to pay sex workers for their services. But, owning fleets of posh cars, collections of yachts, and estates of luxury homes all over America was a huge hunger that they could not just put aside. Upping their game had become inevitable. They thought about how they could get into the drugs business big time and realized that opening a big steady supply route from Columbia, Argentina, or Mexico would need lots of input. They knew that the task would be no easy one. However, the feats of the dead but great Pablo Escobar kept them inspired. They bought a copy of a book on how the drug mogul made it to the very top of his chosen career. They read it like they never read any of their books in school and internalized every bit of it. They needed big money first. No major cartel would sell little. And, bringing in a large consignment that would satisfy the vast market that America is known to be was not going to come at a chicken fee.

The Suckers knew exactly what to do. They began to rob stores and bars in a bid to build up money. They made up to fifty-thousand dollars in each strike on their lucky days. Every member would get some money for his own upkeep at the end of each day's operation. The rest was put aside for the gang's big project. The gang was saving up money. It would have enough by two years with good luck. But, impatience was beginning to wade in. The Suckers wanted very big money in a flash. And, that meant stepping up their game further in order to haul in the big fish. "No one moves! Make a move, I blow your fucking head off! Hey! You there! Here's the bag! Gather all the money! I mean all the money. Play no pranks with me! The trigger is my best friend! It always obeys me!" Those receiving such a fierce command had no choice but to comply, in order to not get fiery-looking guns coming after their heads. It was as if the cops had been all snoring in their beds. There were no tip-offs, no phone calls. They were not aware of a thing until this ended without a shot fired. Banks had now become the target as far as The Suckers were concerned. Their first strike yielded two-million dollars. And, at this rate, they knew that their dream was now very much within range of becoming a pleasant reality. The Suckers were not about to stop now.

However, sometimes good luck decides to go to sleep and leave the stage for bad luck to play out. So, it was on one of the days that The Suckers went to rob a bank that had one brave staff that was lucky enough to run out of the banking hall into a toilet. He was fired at, but the bullets missed his head and hit a wall. He was a very lucky man indeed. It was this man who alerted the cops. He placed a nine-one-one call with his cell phone, and the cops arrived on time. The sound of the siren was what The Suckers heard and knew that a different scenario had caught up with them.

"Shit!" Eliminator screamed. "Someone's called the cops!" he said to his men, "I will kill all those mother-fucking cops. They want to try The Suckers? Let them come!"

"Yeah! Let them come and get their ass smoked," Cone screamed back.

"Time to kick some ass!" said another member, "Kick some cop ass real good."

The Suckers were not scared one bit, but they knew that a tough time lay ahead. All but Craig quickly grabbed their sacks of cash and headed for the exit. Craig had come to the bank with a bag even though Cone had got all the sacks they needed to cart away money. He had had a bad feeling about their planned robbery the previous day. He spoke to the rest of The Suckers about his ill-feelings, but none took him and his concerns seriously. They simply laughed at him and accused him of suddenly acting like a three-year-old girl. None of them even got a little inquisitive to ask him why he was taking a bag along. All of them had money in their minds. A bag was the last thing they would bother about. Craig seized a sack of money when the sound of siren announced the heavy presence of the cops. He also took the bag that he had brought with him and dashed off to the female lavatory. A heavy exchange of fire begun to ensue at the exit of the Wells Fargo Bank. Bullets were flying around from guns that were spraying them as the fray progressed. All the members of The Suckers stood their ground because they believed that no cop could scare them. Taking them on made the cops sweat. But, in the end, in the very end, the cops proved that they were real ones—Trained cops who were very good snipers. The Suckers put up a gallant fight that proved not to be enough for them to have any success. They had a taste of what they had given many cops all through their years together as a notorious gang, and that was having bullets pumped into their heads and stomachs. They were gone.

TEN

Pandemonium still reigned supreme in the bank even after the robbers were shot dead. "There's still one of them left!" voices continued to say, "You've not got them all! One went this way...To the ladies' convenience! Yes there! He went that way." Some of the cops dashed off to the female lavatory in quick response and came across an old woman who had got out of one of the lavatories. She wore a long dark-blue cotton dress that was long enough to cover up her ankles and a red blouse on top. The shoes she wore had no heels. It was a bit tattered. Her long unkempt hair was predominantly white, with dots of black hair poking out at a few places. It extended behind and rested on her back. Some of it rested on her brow in such a way that they would blur her vision. The cops did not take a second look at her. They would swear with their entire lives that she could never be their target. A red lipstick, which obviously was not well applied, was on her lips, and she wore a big black goggle that made her face not easy to see. Her steps were slow, and it was clear from the way she walked that she was suffering from a heavy bout of arthritis. The woman, who looked as if she was sixty, managed to walk out of the bank. No one bothered to look at her twice, the reigning atmosphere of fear and uncertainty being partly responsible. Why would people in a robbery scene, with one of the armed and dangerous thieves still unseen, be interested in holding back a sickly old woman with rough white hair, who obviously had long passed her prime? How wrong they were. They missed it. That woman could have been anyone. She could have been just a woman who came to the bank to cash a check or something and got strained by nature to visit the lavatory. She could have been just anyone. Perhaps even the cops' target. The cops emerged from the female lavatory with disappointment and frustration evident on their faces.

"He went there!" a traumatized staff member of the bank kept telling the cops. The cops did not say a word. There was no need to go back. They had searched very well and had found nobody. Their mind was made up on initiating a Florida-wide man-hunt for the remaining member of The Suckers as quickly as possible. The CCTV hardware in the banking hall was there to help. But, their target, Craig, had disappeared. Many eyes saw him disappearing, but all were too blind to spot him. If only the cops had stopped and arrested the old woman. Arthritis deserted her legs immediately after she managed to get out of sight. She began to walk better, but still slowly. Her pace increased in a short while, and she began to walk fast. All of a sudden, she began to run fast. She was no longer an old woman now. She was full of energy, sprinting away. "She" was Craig, doing what he did best. His bag had served its purpose. Craig carried on quickly with his next move, which was to head off to Mexico, all thanks to its lengthy porous border with America, before the man-hunt for him would become a nation-wide one. He was able to make the journey comfortably because he had four-hundred-thousand dollars on him.

Dr. Vela completed the facial procedure he had for the day and took off his gloves. He was ready to leave the hospital. His face beamed smiles and his confidence soared like an eagle. The surgery had gone very well. The twenty-eight-year-old, dark-haired man was very pleased. There was no doubt about it. He was a facial surgeon very much expected to have a successful future. He had just successfully replaced a man's face with that of another, who had died. His patient had paid him to get the face from a morgue. He would not normally agree to do such a thing, but he had to silence his protesting conscience, throwing off his professional ethics out of the window when the money was as tempting and as huge as fifty-thousand United States dollars.

"I had better sell it and make my money rather than having it buried to decay," he said to himself while considering the offer. His strong Spanish accent nearly masking the whole of English words that he spoke. "This is my golden chance. Those men at the morgue look too poor to refuse any amount that I will offer them to cooperate. This is my chance. A man must do what he has to do to earn some cash. Sugar is so sweet that no one likes to spit it out when one finds it inside his mouth. I must chew this sugar in my mouth. This is my good luck, this is what everyone prays for."

Craig took his time to fully recuperate after Dr. Vela had told him that he had healed completely. But, it got to a time that the level of cash he had left began to be a source of concern for him. He was all alone and had no relatives in Mexico. The bill for his surgery took a toll on the cash with him. The hotel bills were now eating deeper into his pocket, even though he had checked into a relatively cheap one to keep the costs down. He had to leave only after three months of his arrival. He feared becoming cashless in a foreign land—This was what he dreaded the most. But, his departure had to wait. It would not happen until his next plan had actualized. He carefully thought of what it would be so that he would be really confident that he had done a good job of it.

He finally came up with one that his gut feelings assured him would guarantee a complete departure from his past gang life. His new name later emerged, backed by proper documentation, after he had applied for and got his country's passport. He had never had one before. Hansen Langton was his new name as he headed back to the very United States, the one he sneaked away from. His new identity gave him peace of mind and the chance to sort out the new direction which he would steer his life to take. He saw that his old pictures were everywhere when he returned. He had been elevated to the post of a top fugitive. Hansen Langton could not help but laugh every time he saw his old face being beamed on television screens and shown on print publications with his old name under them. Posters flooded with his latest status were hanging everywhere.

CRAIG STEVENS
WANTED! NOTORIOUS BANK ROBBER.
BELIEVED TO BE ARMED AND DANGEROUS.
CALL 911 IF YOU HAVE ANY INFORMATION THAT COULD LEAD TO HIS ARREST.
SAY SOMETHING IF YOU SEE SOMETHING!
RANSOME AMOUNT: TEN-MILLION DOLLARS.

"They can come and arrest their asshole," Hansen Langton laughed. It was his verbal response as he came across one of the posters that he watched on the TV, while seated on his shaky bed in a shabby self-contained room which he had rented upon returning to his country. "I can see that they are very busy looking for Craig Stevens. Wow! That is huge. Ten-million dollars? Cool eight-figure sum. I guess I've got to join the hunt for Craig and grab him by his balls. Who's Craig Stevens anyway? I guess I will smoke his asshole real good when I catch him."

Hansen Langton laughed so loud that some gas seeped out of his asshole. The rotten-egg smell pervaded the entire room and struck out the fresh air that was earlier prevalent.

ELEVEN

Hansen was doing a lot of thinking now. He was thinking about the future, thinking about what to make of what was left of his life. Going back to the dark life in the streets was not an option. He was thinking about the steps to take to get back to society and begin leading a normal life. A new beginning was what mattered to him. He was getting low on cash and had to start doing something to earn some money. Then one day, an idea, which he thought was awesome, stumbled upon his mind. And, that was seeking ways in which he could begin to earn a living based on his childhood interest of throwing light to shine upon anything that is hidden. He loved the idea very much, but he knew that passion alone would not take him very far and get him to make marks. No. That would not satisfy the high level of ambition that he had now. Hansen came to one conclusion later on—He would not go places without acquiring the right skills to back up his passion for sniffing out hidden things. There was no doubt in his mind that his next step would be to enroll in a school to take classes. His ambition drove him on. He searched for the kind of school that would equip him with the skills that he required. He found one and was on his way to enrolling in a school of photography, based in Buffalo, a New York suburb, where he took up residence upon his return from Mexico. Hansen was a brilliant student. He discovered that he had had this amazing talent to capture images clearly all along, even from tricky angles. He kept on learning and honing his skills. He was very patient to learn all that he needed to even though it further drained away his already scarce resources.

Hansen left the school of photography skilled enough to do well. His shots, which carried every trace of genius, had quickly switched from being very good to being fantastic. Everyone in the school, including his colleagues had suggested overwhelmingly that he concentrated his efforts on getting good celebrity shots instead of going to the wild to capture what nature had in stock. Even though

Hansen fancied celebrities and getting good shots of them, he was not going to be a paparazzi in the way that was prevalent in the streets of Hollywood. He hated the idea of running after and hovering around celebrities. He wanted no bodyguard dismantling his equipment or giving him a knock on his face. He loved to capture celebrity images without him being seen. "Covert" was the important word in a business that Hansen was thinking of launching.

He checked the amount of cash that he still had. His mouth was agape the moment he got to know. He was alarmed when he got to know that it was as low as three-thousand dollars. But, no low-level of cash could stop Hansen now. He was, if nothing else, more than determined to launch out. He spent a thousand dollars putting up low-cost ads for his business in a few online newspapers and magazines. He also bought his first low-cost camera.

PRIVATE INVESTIGATOR FOR HIRE!!!!
FIDELITY IS HARD TO FIND IN RELATIONSHIPS IN AMERICA TODAY.
FIND OUT IF YOUR SPOUSE OR LOVER HAS BEEN CHEATING ON YOU FOR A LITTLE FEE.
YOU WON'T KNOW WHOM HE OR SHE HAS BEEN SEEING LATELY UNLESS YOU SEEK HELP
DIAL ILLUMINATION ON 2126397230 FOR HELP IN A FLASH.

One week passed after the publications had run the ad, and nothing happened. Hansen's cell phone did not even beep once. He attributed it to his bad luck and struggled to keep himself from worrying. Another week cruised by, and then another. There was still no call. Sleep began to stay clear of Hansen's eyes on most nights. He did nothing else on those nights but think. His thoughts were to decipher where he had possibly got it all wrong. He could not believe his bad luck. Not even a single person nationwide had cared to give him a call. Hansen could not keep himself from worrying any longer. What made it worse was that the money he had was fast depleting. He was on his last five-hundred dollars now. Desperation, which he had managed to ward off, had found a way in, and it was tearing him apart. Then, he came to the conclusion that his priority had to shift from thinking big to thinking of what he could do to keep getting by in the very least. Hansen was beginning to give up on his big ambition for something that would give him a chance to make money for his food and other basic bills hanging around. He left home the next morning, his destination being a nearby restaurant. He did not go there to spend money. He needed a job badly. Hansen got lucky there since the restaurant needed a guy in its dish-washing section. Anything would do as far as Hansen was concerned. He began working the next day on a paltry salary of one-hundred-and-fifty dollars a week, with a tax of fifty dollars withheld from it.

"Rich folks like you are not meant for jobs like this. What's the matter with you?" said the restaurant owner, a chef, to Hansen.

"It is the job for me, Sir," Hansen hurriedly said, trying hard to prevent desperation from sounding in his voice.

"You certainly don't look like someone who should be doing this job."

"Sir, I'm not rich. You must be thinking I'm somebody else you know about, right?"

"Sure! Are you Craig Stevens?" The restaurant owner joked. He was already laughing when Hansen responded.

"Not at all," Hansen said and laughed a little. "A bank robber? No, I can't be. I'm a law-abiding citizen of the United States. I need the job."

"You're sure you want to do it?"

"It's my job, Sir."

"You have it then. Come on! Get your ass over here. Let me take you to one of my chefs. He will show you how to go about your job once you come in, okay? As for the paperwork? Let that wait till tomorrow."

"Great!"

Hansen immersed himself in his job and was very happy to be just barely getting by. All his big ambitions had died by now. No trace of Illumination was anywhere in his thoughts anymore. He had already resigned himself to being a nobody. That was the fate that he came to accept as the definition of his life. All his energy and zeal were emptied into the only task that was bringing his bread and butter now—getting culinary utensils to be squeaky clean.

TWELVE

It was a Saturday morning in Autumn, and the clock had just struck eight-thirty when his cell phone began to ring. Hansen, who had the day off, was not interested in taking the call, the reason being that he had worked very hard the previous day and had wanted nothing to distract him from having as much rest as possible before leaving his bed. But, his phone did not understand this—neither did the person trying to get in touch. The ringtone sounded again. It broke the silence once more and struck out what was now left of tranquility in Hansen's room. Hansen was still reluctant to pick up his phone, and he placed a pillow over his head instead and went on sleeping, not knowing that his caller was not about to give up. Hansen finally got out of bed when he could no longer ignore his phone. His face had a frown on it, a part of his disturbed countenance.

"Who the hell is that?" he grumbled while heading for the table on top of which he had kept his phone. He grabbed the Nokia hardware and took it to his right ear.

"Okay, now what the fuck do you want!" he inquired in a harsh tone, the unfriendliness standing out like a rock. Hansen did not know that the caller was not someone he was supposed to have spoken to in that manner. It, however, took him only a few seconds to realize that as he heard his caller speak.

"I'm very sorry," his apology came. It was a heart-felt one. "Please I'm so sorry...I'm so sorry! Some fraudsters have been calling my number lately. I thought it was them again." Hansen soon smiled as the caller had told him that it was alright. There was nothing that the caller wanted to do as much than go straight to the point. Hansen began to listen intently as the caller spoke on. The voice was that of a female. She sounded hurt and desperate, and was practically asking Hansen to help her out of the unknown that had tortured her heart for quite a long time. By the time the caller had finished, Hansen had had his first assignment, being the founder of Illumination. And, that was how his restaurant job was swept into history. His first client had called in at last. A high profile one at that. It was a disturbed female Hollywood star, a beauty and fashion icon who was also an Academy award winner. It was her long suspicion that her man was cheating on her, and that was removing sleep from her eyes, making tears wet her pillows. She had called Hansen so that Illumination would help her prove her fears. Hansen's asking price was a hundred thousand. Fifty-thousand upfront, and the rest was to be paid upon delivering the job. He could not believe it. He could not believe that luck had finally turned around to smile at him again. This instantly made the clock of his age to begin ticking backwards. Hansen became a kid of ten that moment. He jumped onto his bed, began to scream, and kept springing up and down, continuously tossing up his pillow, until he heard a cracking sound. It was his bed that was beginning to fall apart. It was overflowing joy which made him forget that the bed had been in a bad shape. But, he just did not care. His bed finally crashed down. And, there were tears coursing down Hansen's eyes. Was it because he had no bed anymore? No! It was very far from that. They were tears brought about by flourishing bliss issuing from the very core of his heart.

Hansen carried out his first assignment so well and in such a professional manner that his star client was extremely pleased. He came up with exactly what she had been suspecting. And soon, word about Hansen and what he could do best went round. He had more clients who made sure that he became a very busy man. It was like even the wind was helping to peddle his capabilities around. His clientele base experienced more growth as time passed by. This would later translate into the fact that he could not cope with the number of jobs that were pouring in for attention—It was time for him to go for very good extra hands. He confronted this challenge by having an advertisement run in the New York Times. He got good value for the money spent on the ad, because, in the end, he was able to hire some very capable hands. The quality of jobs done for clients kept getting them satisfied and happy. This gladdened Hansen's heart, as the feedbacks that testified the quality of his work kept tumbling in. There was no man or woman happier than him now in his candid opinion.

Illumination's client base would not stop growing. A very large portion of it included big-time folks. Folks in whose lives no secrets were allowed to exist twenty-four-seven—fashion icons, renowned designers, A-list Hollywood stars, supermodels. The list would not stop growing. Even heads of corporate organizations like investment bankers having huge take-home bonuses, and oil magnates, began to catch up with Illumination's array of excellent services. America rumbled with a deep voice like a sky that was pregnant with lots of cloud for rain, when one woman who was the wife of the CEO of an oil company sought to know why her husband was always coming back late from work. She would take no more of her husband's steady reason, which was pressure—work pressure. She brought Illumination into the issue. Time passed by, and the proof came in living colors that what had always made her husband come back very late from work were doses of steamy blowjobs and tea-bagging that he was getting from his female secretary when work hours were long past.

"Work pressure, huh? Now I understand what kind of work pressure you were having to face. You devilish scallywag!" the very bitter woman hauled abuses on her husband, "Filthy philanderer! You get off my sight! And, you know what? Start getting used to knowing that I'm no longer your wife! I'm suing you for divorce right away! You and your office-whore can have some more good fucking time! Don't even bother to say you're sorry, because I'll never want to hear that fucking lie!"

"I'm sorry," said her husband, on his knees, his face like that of a wounded little boy about to cry.

"You're sorry only because you got caught! Huh?"

"I'm sorry, darling. Never will I do it again!"

"You should really see how ugly you get when you make that face and say you're sorry. Oh—they become so sorry—so so sorry—when they get caught. Dereck, it's over!"

"But I don't want it to be over!"

"Then a good way of showing it is never to fuck your secretary! It's over! I swear! Get the fuck out of my sight! It's over!"

***

Illumination had now become a virus. And, America was not just catching it, but embracing it and was most unwilling to let go off it. Folks were getting a litany of prized answers, and not sick with flu.

"Would it not be good if I get close to where much of my meal ticket comes from? I mean where I make most of my money." Hansen threw this question to himself one day while in his lavishly furnished Manhattan condo, eating his favorite cookies with a glass of milk. "I think that would be a wise move. That's where things are really happening. Nest of the good, the bad, and the ugly in the United States. Come on, we've got to get our ass in there."

From then on, it was only a matter of time before Illumination stormed L.A. with its corporate headquarters, like hurricane Katrina. But, it brought its already renowned penchant to serve, and not to uproot trees and homes, and yank away lives and livelihoods, even though the separation and divorce rates had had upward trend due to its astounding discoveries. And many kids had had to grow up not knowing the correct answer to at least one of these questions. Who is your biological father? Who is your biological mother?

THIRTEEN

Farouk's insistence on having Hansen personally involved in his own case, and not anyone else related to Illumination's equally competent staff, paid off at last. It was to cost him a cool million though. Five-hundred thousand upfront was to be paid, and the rest was to come when the job was done. He did not mind. Apart from being a rich professor, he was also the heir to his father's vast financial empire. Farouk got one of the many bank account numbers of Illumination and got his first part in the deal done. This was roughly two weeks after he had travelled to L.A. to meet with Hansen in his office.

Hansen then got his radar working, sniffing around for any scoop that would be a good lead. His search-light was as bright as ever, tracking Christie's each and every move. However, Christie was not a fool. So, there was no way she would be doing what she was doing, and not doing her utmost to ensure that her tracks were properly covered from possible peering eyes. She knew that she had to be smart. And, she was. She was damn good too. Time waited for no one, and Hansen could not have been an exception. Time moved on and left him without getting a break in six months. Impatience had by now gripped Farouk. Farouk only wanted a quick result without understanding how difficult coming up with one could sometimes prove. Hansen tried his best to make Farouk understand the need to be patient in the matter. But, Farouk would make Hansen believe that he had understood how important it was for him to be very patient, only to start expecting quick result once again. Hansen worked so hard without a break, but nothing had come up even after six more months. And, Farouk was not a man to be preached to regarding the virtues of patience anymore. That P-word was like a bitter pill going down the length of his gullet whenever Hansen mentioned it.

"Let me explain one thing that you don't seem to get in my business model, Mr. Farouk—"

"Don't give me that P thing again!" Farouk interrupted.

"I'm sorry, Mr. Farouk, we thrive on that P thing in this business. Patience. That's what we stick to when the going gets tough. My past clients knew it."

"Well, I can see that P-word has failed. Unless you are telling me that I am blind."

"It does not fail. It has never failed me. It's the rock from which our results pour out. I assure you that it's not going to start failing us in your case. Please be patient."

"Oh! That word again."

"I'm on your case, man. I'm going to hang on to it until I'm able to give you something. Is that okay?"

"Fine. But how long are we talking about here?"

"I can't tell you. All I know is that I've got to keep on digging into the matter."

"That is not acceptable, Hansen!"

"What the fuck?"

"Hansen? What do you mean?"

"One word. That's what I mean. Tired! I'm tired of this crap that you're giving me right now. First thing tomorrow morning, our accounts team will send you back your five-hundred thousand bucks, okay?"

"Wait a minute, Mr. Hansen. I did not ask for that."

"Well, that's what your attitude is saying to me right now!"

"Do not get angry, please..."

"I won't lie to you. I am very angry right now. You'll get your money back tomorrow morning. Before eight in the morning, I swear."

"Calm down! Calm down, Mr. Hansen."

"What the fuck are you trying to say? That I don't know my job? We're not talking viruses here. When it comes to that, I shut the fuck up and listen to you."

"I can't teach you your job, Mr. Hansen. I am very sorry to have got on your nerves. I see you Americans are quite hot-tempered."

"That's for you Arabs."

"I don't think so. Americans and their fucking hot temper."

"Who taught you that F-word?"

"I learnt it the day I stepped my feet on American soil."

"At the airport."

"Hey, who told you that? You are very correct."

"Mr. Farouk."

"Yes, please..."

"I'm a man that loves to go about his job most professionally."

"I heard that."

"Will you stop worrying and allow me to do my job?"

"Of course."

"That's cool. I'm on it. Go rest your ass!"

Hansen got back to his assignment with renewed vigor. It took some more time, six weeks to be exact, before an important lead surfaced. This gladdened his heart because cracking this one had proved unusually stubborn. He had finally become sure whom his target was hanging out with. New York was where they did carouse and spent some good time together outdoors on a regular basis, even holding hands and kissing. He did not see them giving each other pecks or planting quick dry kisses on each other's cheeks, but long and wet French kisses. It took him time to get the shot from a very tricky angle. He had to record their voices too in order to have a scoop of what their conversations were bordering on. Pitching his equipment at the right place for the best result became a challenge. Hansen thought quickly and found out in a jiffy that recording would not be possible without him doing one vital thing—staying close to the target. He got smart enough and walked up to the two on another day when they met again. Their rendezvous, this time, was a club—private, for members only. It was a massive area that had some spots, which teemed with jumbo-sized covers—very big umbrellas, under which people wined, dined, chatted, and generally had a jolly good time. The club had a large swimming pool. Hansen noticed that lots of young women hung out there. Some wore miniskirts, and some bikinis, showing off plenty of their voluptuous skin. The men wore pants of different colors. Most had nothing on top, leaving their chests exposed. The hairy ones were more in number. Those that were working-out had good-looking chests that could get them many female admirers. It was a show of irritating excess body fat on the chests of those who were not working-out. Some even had breasts that bulged up and would make one suspect that they contained implants.

"Hi, I'm waiting for a friend who seems hell-bent on arriving very late," Hansen began saying to the two, "Do you mind if I share your table?"

The two did not mind at all being so very engrossed in their chat. Their champagne had not been sucked more than once from the straws that were thrust into the glasses. Hansen settled down and bought himself a beer. He could now hear them properly, and the tone of their chat took no time in beginning to draw his interest. It was just so good for his assignment. The two were so busy that they did not even notice when he strapped a tiny recording device underneath the plastic table to do its job. He had got enough recorded by the time the two stood up to leave. Again, hand-in-hand that evening, strolling to wherever their hidden destination existed, which to Hansen, had to be known as fast as possible. He trailed the two, being very careful. He kept following them, but he did that slowly in order to ward off any suspicion from, most importantly, a man whose job, Hansen had noticed, was to stand around them. The person his target was hanging out with had a big mean-looking bodyguard around. One punch from this guy would get a lake of blood pouring from Hansen's nose. He knew it, and he also knew that he had no choice than to adhere strictly to being one word— careful, very careful. The two with the bodyguard entered a luxurious car and were driven away. Hansen took a cab and took off. He would not stop following the car in front of him—The Limousine, which had rolled off no assembly line but that of the auto-giant General Motors.

Even the heavens were on Hansen's side that evening. Lady luck was his mother, and she complimented his persistence and courage excellently well. The fierce-looking bodyguard had finally chosen to display the height of negligence of his duty. He was the only one who was supposed to watch the two as they went to relax inside a rented private room whose location was well out of town. It was so calm a place that the only sound that could be heard was the chirping of birds— Perfect location for those who love to do things in the clandestine. Sleep came in and caressed the bodyguard, and he went off to sleep on a journey in which he even snored. The window to the room, inside which his target slept, was left open—Just perfect for Hansen. Then came his break. He got some steamy and sizzling information through his lenses. His target was being dirty with a black fellow, who was not young but was not old either—was surely been something in between the two—must have been up to forty years old, of course. Hansen's face held a big smile as he left the suburb a fulfilled man. Chants of joy would not stop coming from his mouth all night in his hotel room. He could not wait to be in L.A. to prove to Farouk why the remaining five-hundred thousand bucks of his total fee should waste no further time before landing into Illumination's bank account.

Hansen Langton, in all his litany of accomplishments, knew that back home, his story was still that of a runaway failure. He knew that his success would not be complete without him going back to his Florida family home, where he would need to make some explanations to his loved ones, who had long consigned him to history, as one of theirs who was lost and most possibly dead. He would need to explain what had happened to Craig Stevens. He would also have to hope that his loved ones would be interested in keeping Craig Stevens permanently deleted.

"How am I going to start?" Hansen asked himself, "I long to be home after a couple of decades. Florida is calling me. Florida! Florida! Oh, sweet Florida...Oh sweet Florida of sweet oranges of bright yellow color that sweetened my mouth for years with their sweet juices. Are you frowning at me, Florida? Are you going to welcome me, the land of my birth? Why not part your lips and let me know?"

FOURTEEN

Farouk's anger doubled upon hearing her voice when she had called to inform him of her arrival. Farouk tossed his cell phone on his bed after taking the call. He sprang up with anger that was visible on his face. "She thinks I still don't know," he muttered as he picked up a small MP3 player that lay on his bed. He also picked up a brown envelope that was beside the MP3 and made straight for his living room. He started sauntering in the living room, cursing under his breath. He was barely audible, uttering something angrily in Arabic. He already knew who was at the door when he heard a knock. He went straight to the door. His fulminating anger was manifested in the way in which he walked. He opened the door and saw Christie standing. She wore a blue jeans and T-shirt on top. Her red lips looked inviting as she smiled at Farouk, who only managed to bring a brief grin to come on his face. She gave Farouk a peck on his forehead and walked in smiling, unaware of how Farouk was really feeling. Farouk shut the door and did not walk up to his visitor. He walked straight into his bedroom without even uttering a word.

"No, this is not what I expected," Christie said, "I didn't fly all the way from New York to see my man acting strange. What the hell has gone wrong?" She then walked straight to Farouk's bedroom.

Farouk was lying down on his bed when Christie walked in. The MP3 was now connected to two speakers that lay on his bed, and the envelope was in his left hand. He was staring up at the roof of the room in silence. Christie's entrance did not change this. She wondered why Farouk was behaving like that, and she had to make a move. She walked straight to Farouk, her mind busy, hustling to figure out what could have gone wrong. She placed her left hand on Farouk's left shoulder in a tender loving manner.

"Hello, sweetheart, what's the matter? What has hurt you?" she quickly asked in a tone that carried lots of care.

Christie went on to sit beside Farouk, and her lips were making their way towards Farouk's lips. But, that was the last thing that Farouk wanted now. The lips he used to adore, had turned into a huge source of irritation for him. He got up and tossed the envelope at Christie, who failed catch it. The envelope fell on the floor. Christie went for it, picked it up, and hesitated for a short while before she started reaching for its contents. Haste got the better of Farouk now. It made him reach for the MP3 and push a button. He then turned his attention on Christie. The little MP3 began making what was in it audible at exactly the same time as Christie began to look at the pictures that the envelope contained. She had them in her hands now. Her countenance changed at once as she heard voices from the MP3. She was stunned. She took a deep breath. The pictures left her hands and landed on the floor because her two hands had gone up and held her head in shock, as the voices from the MP3, especially her own voice, ached her ears.

"Kelly, I can't imagine loving anybody like I love you. They don't get it. They think they know how to give it to us. No, they don't! What do you have to say?"

"You've said it all, Christie. I've never experienced what we now have anywhere before. You give me so much pleasure."

"I would never have imagined you would be that good when I first saw you."

"It's the same for me. One look at your appearance sends one running away. I can't believe it...This is so awesome...I can't believe you're this soft and sensuous. You had me screaming....Not having enough.... Wanting more and more...of your tender touches..."

"I thought I had all I needed until I met you. How wrong I have been...You're so damn good at it. I mean putting my whole body on fire and getting the juices streaming out of my loin...No one has understood my needs more than you."

"How about having some fun again?"

"That would be cool. I can't say no to you. But...where?"

"You don't need to worry about that. I have it all perfectly worked out."

"How?"

"All we've got to do is hop into my car, and off we head to a place where we will have the world to ourselves."

"Oh...yeah...That sounds...so enticing... I can't wait to grab you now..."

"Me too...Come and give me what more you've got."

"You're welcome. Always welcome..."

***

Even If I try to deny what has come from the MP3, what of the pictures? This was Christie's thought the moment the MP3 went silent after divulging what was stored in it. Silence took over the room now. Christie could not look Farouk in the eye. She did not need a news network to announce to her that her game had gone busted. The MP3 had the voices, and the pictures said more than the words—they said it all. Pictures can't lie. They had Christie and Kelly in some of their intimate moments—making love.

It got to a time in the room when Farouk could no longer hold back tears that he had been fighting back. Three beads of it tore away from his eyes and slid down to his cheeks, after which they took off and crashed on the floor. The pictures had made his heart heavy with grief. If nothing else had been able to break his heart before now, the pictures did it perfectly because they were like a sword pushed through his heart.

"This is what I get for opening the door of my heart to love," he said at last, when his broken heart did allow him find words. "You are not the girl I used to know. You are a shadow of her. Now I know that I lost her long ago."

"We can discuss this as friends," Christie added.

"I was not taking to you!" came Farouk's response that was choked with anger.

"We can talk about this."

"Who is that woman?"

"She is just a friend. What you see was just a one-night stand."

"You still have the guts to lie? Oh...you make me sick. You think I have been blind and deaf all this while? I bet you never thought that my radar would be after you."

"I'm not lying."

"You are a liar! A big one! I found out everything when you thought that I was a fool. The woman is a New York fashion icon."

"You're correct."

"I should have known. I should have known that you girls are this sick and perverse."

"Excuse me? What do you mean?" Christie was getting angry now, her tone high, and already confrontational.

"Americans!" Said Farouk. "You American girls! Stinking Lesbians!"

"That's enough!" screamed Christie as her anger heightened. She was surely in no mood to take any more demeaning remarks from Farouk.

"Some American women are shameless! I can't believe this worthless woman-to-woman thing!"

"Show some respect for my country and for my sisters! Who the fuck do you think you are?"

"A man you ought to have cared for, and not gone about sleeping with not even men, but women."

"Wait a minute! You wanted me to care for you?"

"Yes."

"I did."

"You did not. You would not be sleeping with another woman if you cared about me. If that is not considered to be lunacy in America, I wonder what is."

"You didn't get a hundred percent of my attention because, somewhere along the line, I could see that you couldn't perform."

"What do you mean 'perform'?"

"Arab men are not good in bed, especially when they come from Palestine." Christie's aim was to hit Farouk where she thought would hurt most. And Farouk was only going to hit back.

"I never knew I was dealing with a dog whose promiscuity never ends," he said.

"You think you've been satisfying me? You think you're good because all other American girls you've dated were not bold enough to demonstrate to you how horrible you're in bed? Hello... I remain true to myself always. You weren't giving it to me like I wanted, and I sourced it from outside. Heavens only know that I got lucky."

"And a woman would do? See how rotten you sound! That stuff was created for man and woman. Not this horrible thing you have degenerated to."

"Kelly does all that you can't. She gives it to me nice and easy after her sexual spell. She gets me relaxed. Let me get this right into your thick skull. Kelly is a woman, but she's got the magic wand. Maybe you should consider taking some classes. Fifty dollars an hour will never be too much for rich guys like you who can't fuck. She's willing to teach you real good. Fuck you!"

"Some of you American girls are arrogant! I can see that your mothers had never taught you about remorse!"

"Sorry! When a man from Palestine can't fuck, he shouldn't expect an American girl to stick around his sagging dick! What else is lunacy if that isn't?"

"Shut up, you sick whore!"

"Come on! Is that all you've got?"

"Foolish whore! You make me want to vomit!"

"Shut the fuck up and listen! I didn't want to dump you outright. Your money was too cool to ignore. You really didn't expect me to hang on to you like that when you couldn't even perform, do you?"

"Get out of here! You, Whore!"

"Learn this now! What women get under the sheets matter a lot. Don't think you're the real deal just because you've got a ton of cash to throw around."

"I want this perverse American sick whore out of my home right now! Leave!"

"Shut the fuck up! I don't know why I'm wasting my time anyway. I don't have all day! Fuck you!"

"Shameless thing!"

"Is that the best you can come up with? Bring it on. Shameless Arab man who can't do shit in bed. In case you've not heard. I am now a complete fan of pussies! Thanks for listening, stupid Farouk!"

Christie started to walk out of the room, but Farouk's anger would not let him restrain himself further. He ran after her, pulled her by the sleeve of her blue T-shirt, and struck her face with his right fist. Christie bent down in pain and screamed out loud.

"Asshole Palestinian! I will get your ass locked up! I swear!"

Farouk struck her again. This time harder and on the forehead.

"Fuck you! You dirty Palestinian! Fuck you!" Christie yelled. She tried to get away from Farouk, who would not have that. Farouk grabbed Christie, struck her again on her face, and pushed her. Christie fell on the floor and was very ruffled but was not giving in to the pains that had already been inflicted on her. Her courage was aglow.

"You do not understand how a broken heart cries," Farouk screamed, "You are very lucky that I want to shed no blood."

"Go to hell! I don't care one fucking bit! Go to hell with your broken heart! Go and pick the pieces of your so-called broken heart in hell!"

As Christie sprang up, Farouk pounced on her again, struck her mouth hard, and pushed her. Christie fell on the floor like a deck of cards. She felt a lot of pain, but her courage became as strong as steel.

"You have no understanding of how your dirty relationship with that whore called Kelly has wounded my heart."

Farouk quickly grabbed Christie's left ear and squeezed it hard. The pain from that permeated every bit of Christie's nerves. She endured it to the point she could no longer take it. Then a scream escaped her mouth.

"Leave my ear alone!" Farouk did as she demanded, but not without kicking her ass with his left leg.

"Don't make me make you a lamb in the plate of a bunch of cheetahs," he warned.

"Help...Help..."

Help was quite close, but Christie did not remember.

"You both gave my heart a poisoned chalice to drink from," Farouk said, still feeling embittered.

"You have just surprised me, Farouk! I never knew...I never knew this Arab professor had anything called a heart. Do you Arabs even have hearts? This is fucking crazy! Big bullshit!"

"Do not insult Arabs! They are the best people in this world. You Americans are sick. You can never be as kind as Arabs."

"Yeah...Fuck you, asshole Palestinian! I can see that kindness. It shines like the sun all over the world right now. I see it when some of you turn yourselves into bombs without regard for the sanctity of life. You don't even spare little children. Some of you are very kind, isn't it? These human bombs respect no lives in markets and schools. They spare no wedding halls and hospitals. These bombs show no respect for even places of worship. I can see how very much some of you guys are sensible and caring like you claim. I've been blind. Thanks for opening my eyes to this remarkable kindness."

"Shut your sick American mouth! America is the cause of everything! The double standards in its foreign policies are to blame, not some of my sisters and brothers who turn themselves into bombs as their last resort."

"It's only a mad person who will believe that taking the lives of innocent people justifies his grievances against American foreign policies. That isn't going to settle anything!"

"Hey! You are going too far! Desist from saying anything bad about my people."

"Is there a word that's worse? Please, my darling...Tell me...I won't hesitate to use it."

"Shut up, you dirty lesbian! America should mind its own business, and not go about telling Arab countries how to run their affairs."

"I see...That explains why some of your brothers in Tehran, no matter how holy they claim to be, are thinking of that killer-bomb...Huh?"

"People who are fed American injustice and neo-colonialism have the right to reject and resist it!"

"With the killer-bomb? That's madness."

"Shut up! Does America not have the killer-bomb? The American madness started a long time ago."

"American madness rules the world."

"Never!"

"You guys want to get mad because America is mad? You are really sick!"

"Don't insult the very special people called Arabs! We are awesome!"

"Very special," Christie said sarcarstically. "Yeah. Very special."

"Don't make me mad! You would not like me when I am mad. I warn you, lesbian!"

"Show me your worst, sick Farouk!"

More anger surged within Farouk, making him pounce on Christie's neck and squeeze it hard. Christie could barely breathe. She struggled to get free, but all her efforts were in vain.

"I have warned you not to insult my people any further," Farouk thundered and quickly released his grip on Christie's neck, "Don't give me a good reason to commit murder." Christie started coughing from the strangulation. The squeeze that she got on her neck was so hard that it made her cough ten times. But, it was not enough to silence her.

"Go ahead! Strap some bombs to your filthy underwear and detonate us! Go ahead! That's what you love to do. I mean you, Farouk, more than anything else!"

Christie's right hand went right inside her right jeans pocket as she spoke.

"I actually wrote you a love letter," she said, "One that's sexy enough."

"What sick love? Love that you have murdered? I do not want to see it! I will burn it!"

"It's sexy, Farouk."

"Nonsense! Any sex with you is filthy. Show me no love letter! I will never be in the mood!"

"Are you sure you want no love letter?"

"Absolutely! But wait! What love letter can come from a rotten lesbian to a man?"

"Yeah...like one that's about to smoke your ass!"

"You are crazy!"

"Come on...Let me teach you a crazy way to get me wild in bed. You will never know it in a million years, will you?"

Farouk made a move to grab Christie's chest. He had a smile on his face now. His target was Christie's nipples. Christie was fast enough to make her own move. What emerged from her jeans pocket was a little can whose contents she was quick enough to spray on her attacker's face, who now wanted some fun.

"Fuck you!" Christie screamed at Farouk, who became totally disoriented. He lost the ability to find his way around. He screamed, as the pepper spray ensured that his hands were strapped to his face, making him toddle as if he was a child learning how to walk straight. This was Christie's chance. Nothing else was on her mind now than to bolt away.

A red liquid that could only be blood was dripping from the edge of her right eye. Her face, clothes, and hands were all bloody. She dialed nine-one-one as soon as she managed to leave Farouk's house. The cops soon came around. They were not blind. They saw blood—enough evidence to establish their charge. Farouk was handcuffed and eased into the back seat of their car. He was later sentenced to thirty days in jail by a law court. Farouk did not recover from the sour part of his relationship with Christie after he left jail. He felt used, insulted, and angry. He was particularly angry with the American laws that governed altercation. He saw them as being more in favor of women, which gave them the liberty to act in any way they wanted against men whom they had a relationship with. As if his ordeals from falling in love with Christie were not enough, news reached him again that another uncle of his had fallen victim to the American drone attacks in Pakistan. There was no way that Farouk could restrain himself this time from thinking of a way to inflict harm on his one enemy—'Uncle Sam'—who had hurt him far too much.

THE MAN MURKTAR

Murktar was only eight years old when he began to hear adults speaking about their deep hatred for Israel, their reason being Israel's occupation of much of Arab land. He heard more as adults spoke of things concerning Israel. This made young Murktar ask his father an unexpected question one day.

"Father, why should people with no home come and take our land?" Murktar's father did not understand where his question was headed at first.

"Which people?"

"People from Israel."

Murktar's father got to understand exactly what his question was immediately when he heard his son's response to his question. He chose not to say anything regarding that matter to his son. Murktar, in his view, was too young to start choking up his head with an issue that was wrought with much controversy around it. Even though Murktar did not get an answer then, his question resounded in his mind as he grew up.

His full name was Murktar Ahmed Az-Zawahiri. He was the fiftieth child of his father, El-Shari, and one of the only two children of his mother, Naheed, who was from Syria. Murktar's father was a poor man who never considered his status one bit as he went on impregnating all of his four wives. His understanding was, I make the babies, and their mothers will raise them. He was a man irresponsible to the core. He tried to do nothing to bring income for his large family. "Will you all get out of my sight?" he would scream at his children whenever they tried to come close to him with any of their numerous demands, "What makes you think that I am in this world to take care of your needs? Will you all disappear from here? I have made you all. It is now your responsibility to figure out how you will survive and grow. I wish not to be disturbed any further! Take my words! You need to follow my laws in this house!"

"What do you want from me?" El-Shari screamed at his wives one day they got bold enough to confront him, "Did you think that I married you so that I would take care of your children? You can leave them to starve if you won't do something! That is fine by me! Leave them to starve to death! I challenge any of you to talk back at me! Will you all get out? Get out!"

It was El-Shari's wives who had to do all sorts of jobs to raise money. This included rearing goats and sheep for sale. His wives worked hard to raise their kids, and they were also mandated to report some of the money that they made to El-Shari, who used it for his own upkeep. But one day, El-Shari decided that it was time that he broke out of the shackle of irresponsibility that had trapped him for years. It was like magic. He woke up that morning with thoughts of what he could do to earn money. Pottery was one thing that ran in his family blood. His great-grandfather was a potter. So was his grandfather. And, so was his father. El-Shari knew for sure that his own father must have passed on pottery skills to him. He scolded himself for allowing the gift to lie idle in him for years. "It is now time for me to wake up and get something done," he urged himself, "El-Shari, the son of Az-Zawahiri, you can't keep on going like this. No! This is not a path to honor. I am ashamed of myself. Women have been feeding me and taking care of all my needs, and yet I call myself a man and a husband. No! This is not right. For years now, I have not cared about respect that I lack so much amongst my peers. No! I have been stupid. This must end today. I should be the one to cater for the needs of my family. No! Enough of this ugly irresponsibility."

El-Shari gathered all the money that was left of what he had received from his wives. He counted them and smiled when he was done, for he realized that the sum would be enough for him to start a business. But, he did not do anything before he called out for his wives' attention the next day. "I think it is just right that I talk to them," he said to himself, wondering whether that would actually be a good move. "Or do I just ignore them and start off? No. That would not be a responsible move to make. The best thing to do would be to talk to them. Yes, that is it. The best thing."

The four women came and sat beside him on the ground, ready to hear what he had to say. Each of them wore a black veil that covered their faces. These veils had gaps through which one could barely see their eyes. The other parts of their faces, which could stimulate lust in a man, were hidden. Only the air would have the right answer as to how it kept making itself available for them to breathe.

What of the carbon dioxide gas that gets expelled when human beings breathe out? Surely, only El-Shari's wives, beautiful wives, were capable of teaching the world how they kept on escaping being choked to death by asphyxiation as they went about their sometimes rigorous daily chores with their veils on. They were really exceptional, their industrious nature a delight to watch.

The women had no smiles on their faces. Even if any of them had allowed a little smile to show on her face, the covering would not have allowed it to be quite visible. There were no smiles on the faces of El-Shari's wives because deep down in their hearts, they had not a single shred of doubt that they would not be told anything heart-warming. They even feared being told by El-Shari that the amount of money that was being given to him after all their labor was not enough for him. If anyone had told them that they would be told what they were eventually told, they would never have believed the person. Smiles appeared on the faces of the four women, smiles precipitated by relief, surprised at what they had heard. They could not believe that their husband had decided to say it.

"I am very happy to tell all of you today that I am no longer going to be taking from you," El-Shari had revealed, "I have realized my act of irresponsibility and have decided to stay away from it. This is the time for a new beginning from my side. I am tired of being seen as the lazy husband who only has enough strength to impregnate his wives, but one who has no strength at all to bring in any income. I have decided to get up to do something. This is what I called you for. You all can go now."

El-Shari's wives got up and left very thrilled, their mouths full of thanks and gratitude for the unexpected change that had come about in their husband, one they never envisaged would happen in El-Shari's life time.

El-Shari began to try his hands at pottery and started making objects which people appreciated and bought with time. He was glad that he had joined his wives in getting some income to their home. And, he did not want to stop there. Ambition was now beginning to tug at him to do more. El-Shari suddenly started looking for greener pastures. He found Saudi Arabia to have pastures greener than where he was. So, he left his country, Yemen, with a big ambition, which was to establish his pottery trade in a big way. He was determined to dominate the Saudi market with his products that had begun to score really well with buyers in Yemen. None of his children but Murktar was willing to move to Saudi Arabia with him. Only Murktar was close to his father in spite of the horrible shortcomings that he had in his past, which had made all his brothers and sisters be pissed off at him. Their father could go to hell for all they cared. Their perception of their father was a useless man who had made the greatest mistake of bringing them into the world. Their hatred for him knew no bounds.

El-Shari settled himself in Saudi Arabia and worked harder. His business began to flourish, and his products were loved and bought in large numbers. He soon began to receive orders from Europe, Asia, and the Americas. It was happening so fast that El-Shari was often tempted to believe that it was not real. He could not believe his own accomplishments. El-Shari successfully clawed his way up from being a man who came to Saudi Arabia having only a small amount of money, skills, and ideas, to a rich man. One could not breathe in the Saudi Kingdom without getting a whiff of the popularity of his products. His products were so much in demand worldwide that it took him just ten years to emerge a man having much financial clout. His wives and kids were not left out of this. Their status changed for the best way back in Yemen. El-Shari's wives metamorphosed from women known to rely almost absolutely on rearing small numbers of farm animals to women who drove around in flashy cars and having the luxurious things of life at their disposal. Their home used to be a ramshackle wooden structure. But, El-Shari's abundant wealth meant that they had to make a joyful switch to much better homes. Television, radio, cell phones, and other electronic products became a necessary part of their lives. They were thrilled in a very special kind of way—Thrills that they felt were special in the sense that they were short of words to describe it. They never dreamt of wealth coming to them in their entire lives, let alone having much of it. But, they had been wrong. They were wrong in actual fact for not having reckoned with change, which runs to and fro in the world of mortals and always shows up at any time of its choosing, with no one having the power to resist it permanently.

When a man turns into a business mogul, it is quite natural that his circle of friends and associates will change. El-Shari moved further up the ladder of 'who's who' in Saudi Arabia. His network of contacts soon waded into the Saudi ruling class, who found him an amiable personality. El-Shari had come across to the Saudi ruling family as an astute business man whose enviable personality spoke enormous volumes, which included, but were not limited to sagacity and honesty. In not much time, El-Shari had his own construction company and was handling three quarters of the infrastructure constructions in the oil-rich kingdom.

"I cannot explain how exactly this is happening," he told one reporter of a leading Saudi newspaper when he was asked about the secret of his success.

"Sir, you must be doing something in a very special way that you might want to share with other businessmen or young ones who are aspiring to go into business," the reporter remarked. El-Shari first grinned before his response came.

"I understand that you will never in a million years believe me. But, I honestly do nothing that other business men in this country do not do. Believe me. I work hard. I manage my organization. I motivate my staff. These are not things that are strange to many good businessmen out there."

"Could you shed a little bit of light on your background, sir?"

"All Saudis know that I am from Yemen. That is no longer news."

"Absolutely."

"I was a nobody who languished in abject poverty, whose cradle was laziness. I refused to have any ambition. I was hated. I was a despicable bunch of thrash that belonged only to the dirtiest cans."

"What was more?"

"I was disgusting, a horrible man, whose further revelation of his less than pleasant past will make you throw up."

"It was *that* horrible?"

"Yes. It was that terrible until I decided that enough was enough. Laziness and lack of ambition could not have enough of me. I had become a person that epitomized them to the very core before I woke up one day full of the desire to escape from their prison, which I had known to be home."

"Sir, rumors coming from Yemen are very rife here in Saudi Arabia. These rumors are saying that you were such a big mess and shame that the only place you brought productivity was in the area of impregnating your very fertile wives. Could you please confirm this and set the records straight?"

"Mr. Journalist, let us bounce away from personal details, okay? My wives wanted their tanks filled. That was the pressure that they mounted on me. And, I had enough volume to withstand that pressure. How many men could do so in this world without needing extra oxygen from cylinders? Go to Africa. Go to Europe. America or Asia. Such men are born once in five thousand years."

"Well, I should take it that the rumors are now as good as confirmed?"

"I have never been ashamed of that. I will not start today."

"Any comment on regarding the number of offsprings that you have?"

"Oh yes...My offsprings. Murktar has grown to be a nice young man. He is very intelligent, and he makes me proud to call him my son."

"Sir."

"Mr. Journalist, I am your prisoner today. So, go on."

"What of the other sons and daughters of yours? Any comments about them?"

"No comment!"

"Is there any chance that you would want to talk about them in the near future?"

"Mr. Journalist, you and I are under no illusion that this is not the United States of America, where people easily give out all sorts of stories to tabloids. Even confessions on how they cheat on their spouses and lovers. I know that you know exactly what I mean."

"You are implying that some secrets should remain secret?"

"Until the sun falls from the sky. Smart boy...Am I free to leave your prison now?"

"Yes, Mr. El-Shari. I am done. Thank you so much for your time. It has been wonderful having you speak with us."

"Thank you so much for your time too. It has been my pleasure."

El-Shari's wealth and influence rubbed off very well on young Murktar, who was already bitter. He was not bitter because of the amazing transformation that his father had achieved. He would have been labeled a big enigmatic youngster of course if he was. His father's wealth brought a big privilege to his hands. He was able to attend a choice school in Jeddah. But, the source of his bitterness came from what he heard. It was about an event. It was not from Yemen, his own country, but another Arab country in which he had heard that women and children were being killed. It was the invasion of Lebanon by Israel, having the support and direction of America.

Murktar's school in Jeddah was unique in the sense that it put in place a program which combined the American style of secular education and the daily Islamic teachings and worship. This was where Murktar began to learn the English language. He found it interesting and had much hunger in him to carry on learning. His first visit to the United States was when he accompanied his father on one of his many business trips. Murktar was a normal child while growing up, but no one knew that his contact with extremism had already started.

Some of his teachers noted his interest in concepts of liberation for the Muslim world from the Zionist and imperial claws of the western world. They wasted no time in getting his interest to grow and get stronger through informal teaching sessions. One of them, Al-Ghanemi, made a huge impression on the young Murktar. His frequent free speech, which carried every fiber of rare oratorical skills, was too good for Murktar to ignore. It captured and held every strand of his fancy.

Murktar turned out to be a brilliant chap in the academic arena. He moved to the United States for his first degree at the Princeton University in the state of New Jersey. His course of study was microbiology. Murktar's hunger for the liberation of the Muslim world did not die when he moved to America. He combined his studies well with his contact with Umar, an Iranian activist and a professor of particle physics. Umar was such an outspoken person that he never hid any bit of his activism towards achieving a Palestinian autonomous state. Three feet was the only chunk of height that nature thought was best for the bright mind. His long chin carried a grey beard that was six inches long. He was a huge inspiration for Murktar, who excelled in his studies and got awarded a scholarship for a master's degree. He opted to specialize in mycology because of the special interest he had developed in fungi, their very unique properties, and the huge potential that these microbes had for much industrial usefulness. Murktar became engrossed in further research in more areas of mycology as he took up a job as a lecturer. He also maintained his contact with Umar, who had become his mentor. Umar was to him, what many Hollywood, musical, and basketball figures in the NBA are to many American high school kids. Umar was his model and hero, his own Eddie Murphy, Michael Jackson, and Michael Jordan.

With time, Umar's views and activism were turning into a whirlwind, which American authorities were getting increasingly uncomfortable with. It was little surprise that he was deported to Tehran. And, this coincided with such a time when Murktar revered the man so much for the inspiration that he provided. It was only Umar who was there at hand to encourage Murktar. Umar helped him forge the will to move on when his father died. Billionaire El-Shari had been killed in Gaza during one of his visits to supply food, water, medicine and other essentials to impoverished people there. He had been killed by American bombs coming from rampaging Israeli fighter planes which attacked Gaza that had turned into a long-neglected battleground, a glaring humanitarian catastrophe with long tiger claws thrust into its neck. Those who saw his corpse said that it was a huge mess. His head was ripped off from the rest of his body, and so was his left leg. His pair of black shoes, worth a million dollars, had been tossed apart as if its worth was not even half a cent. Murktar was the only person out of all of El-Shari's sons and daughters who showed up for his funeral. He was brave enough to withstand lots of tears from streaming down his eyes as he consoled his mother, who cried a lot just like the other wives of his father did. He, however, could not restrain himself further when the remains of his father were being lowered into its final resting place—a deep hole dug for the late El-Shari Az-Zawahiri to sleep forever. It was then that Murktar cried like a little girl. His eyes were like the sky when it poured out rain. He did not cry this much because his emotions just went overboard. An invisible sword having sharp curved edges which tore through his heart was implicated. This was what his heart experienced when he remembered that not only was his father devoured by the American bombs, but some of his organs—his heart, his lungs, his liver, and his testicles—went missing.

Murktar's inheritance from his billionaire father was quite a heavy sum of money. El-Shari's reason was clear. Murktar was his only son who believed in him and stood by him when he declared his intention to shake off his inglorious past that was filled with disgusting anomalies. It was no surprise that Murktar's brothers got peanuts. When Umar learnt of Murktar's huge inheritance, which was more than ten-billion dollars in cash alone, he moved to him for assistance towards furthering the Palestinian cause. Umar nearly acquired it before American intelligence decided that he had overstayed his welcome. He, however, maintained contact with Murktar from Tehran, mostly by electronic mail. Murktar was left to lick the wound of his father's murder alone. He carried on with his life in bitterness and anger. And, from then on, America and its allies never missed out from a chance of being away from his radar of revenge mission for even a fraction of a second.

Although Abdoullah, Farouk and Murktar had died, it must never be in doubt that their stories had painted one picture, sculpted the physique of one emotion. Their dominant emotion. The ANATOMY OF THEIR FURY.